the voice we squelch

JILLIAN IBELLI

Red Penguin
BOOKS

For Victor.

one

Bang! Bang! Bang!

"Kayla, I heard something. Was that you?" Amir questioned loudly, projecting his voice from the bathroom down the hall. The shower turned off and Amir toweled off in front of the fogged mirror and cluttered vanity.

"No, it is someone at the front door. I'll answer it," Kayla responded just as loudly, a twinge of annoyance in her voice, as she much preferred to remain ensconced within the warmth of her bed. Flinging off the comforters that smelled of sleep, Kayla shifted her body upright and gathered her long tresses into a messy top knot. Dust motes and the stale scent of intimacy hung heavy in the air as early morning sun rays burst through the yellowed, dusty window blinds spraying oblong rectangles of light across the dingy grey carpet.

The deafening knocks came once again, rapid, and swift. *Bang! Bang! Bang!* Had this been a cartoon, the door would have buckled into a parenthesis and tore away from the hinges.

Ears piqued; Kayla leapt to her feet and adjusted her mismatched pajamas as she walked out of the bedroom and into the hallway. Pausing momentarily in the hallway as she passed Amir in the bathroom, they exchanged perplexed glances with one another, fully aware that neither were expecting guests.

The rapping knuckles on the other side of our door sounded again, this time accompanied by shrill male voices yelling in a Middle Eastern language. Kayla pressed her cheek against the door's plastic beige peephole and lifted the thin rectangular slide. She peered through the dusty lens to reveal a fishbowl image of two men she had never seen before.

"Amir!" The booming male voices called out. Confusion etched deep into Kayla's brow as she tentatively wrapped her fingers around the doorknob and with a turn of her wrist the knob clicked, and the front door opened.

Two middle-aged men with the pounding footsteps of storybook giants spilled into the apartment. The screeching voices thundered in intensity as they greeted a befuddled Kayla face-to-face and called out to Amir once more.

Amir froze upon hearing his native language, and after a brief stunned moment, he quickly covered his freshly showered body with a pair of faded black sweatpants that he found crumpled on the bathroom floor. He took a deep breath, tightened the drawstring on his sweatpants into a bowknot and padded into the foyer where Kayla stood with the unannounced guests.

The two men dressed traditionally in a throbe and gutra may have been a mystery to Kayla, but to Amir they were not strangers.

"What the hell is going on here? Who are these people?" Kayla questioned Amir; her eyes were frantic as she awaited his response. The men seemed to be further agitated at Kayla's presence. Their eyes narrowed into a reptilian like stare and deep scowls etched into their faces when she spoke. Surprise, shame and fear spiderwebbed across Amir's face and his mouth gaped uncomfortably into an 'O.'

The flushmount light fixture affixed to the ceiling created a dull spotlight for the show the uninvited guests were about to perform.

Methodically, Amir turned away from the two men and towards Kayla. He lifted his head grudgingly and his face morphed into the likeness of a disheartened parent who was about to tell their child that the pet hamster just died or that Santa Claus was not real.

"Kayla, listen. This is my father and uncle. I, um, have something to tell you. " Amir began, a kaleidoscope of pain was visible in his eyes. He outstretched his arms and beckoned her forward, but he was interrupted, unable to plead his case as the older of the two men wedged himself between Amir and Kayla.

The greying middle-aged man who glowered at Kayla like a mad tiger through his bronzed ruddy complexion and jaundiced eyes was Amir's father. He began to scold Amir in their native tongue, as he wagged his bony, arthritic finger at him, occasionally pointing that same accusatory finger in Kayla's direction.

The resemblance between Amir and his father was uncanny, give or take thirty years. But unlike Amir, his father did not look at Kayla with endearment. Dark, unkind eyes scrolled her up and down with disdain as he took in her visible silhouette underneath her thin pajamas.

The second man moved forward and placed a comforting hand on Amir's father's shoulder. He spoke to him in a hushed, calming tone and gestured vaguely in Kayla's direction. There was a striking family resemblance there as well.

Amir's father quickly returned his attention to the

intended source of his belligerence. Amir took his chastising with a bowed head, furrowed brow and extended bottom lip. He looked like a remorseful child who just broke Grandma's antique crystal bowl.

Amir's uncle, evidently the calmer of the two, gave Amir a knowing look and pointed with his chin towards Kayla's direction. Amir tried to speak but his throat emitted a mucous laden sob instead. His brown eyes morphed into pools of sadness rimmed in crimson. He reached for Kayla, but instincts told her to pull away.

He must have said, "I'm sorry" and "please forgive me," over a hundred times. A broken record of the same two phrases. He started in on an explanation, but Kayla could barely process his deceit laced words. Her mind only processed bits and pieces of what he said . . . in my country . . . my wife . . . finally pregnant . . . .my in-laws . . . not my choice . . . it's tradition . . . I love you.

The crushing blow of the information caused a shockwave of weakness to bludgeon the lower half of Kayla's body. She was only twenty-seven years old; 'in her prime,' society would say, but the ligaments in her knees at that moment would say otherwise.

In what felt like slow motion, Amir reached out to help steady Kayla as she slid down against the wall onto the carpeting. But Amir's uncle pulled him back, shaking his head in a solemn 'no.' Kayla's body took on a malleable form, a perfectly piped out buttercream rosette on the floor.

Amir's father asked him a question and in response he despondently pointed to the foyer coat closet. His father opened the closet door, selected Amir's black North Face coat and picked up a pair of boots that were strewn by the front door. Angrily, he threw all three items at Amir's feet. Amir's frown deepened as he slowly shrugged on the coat over his bare chest and shoved his sockless feet into his scuffed beige Timberland boots that Kayla had bought him that past Christmas.

Amir's father held fast to his forearm and dragged him to the front door, held wide open by his uncle.

"I'm so sorry, Kayla," Amir said as he craned his neck towards Kayla. He was crying, sobbing even, but it meant nothing. And then the door slammed shut.

Sometimes when a couple breaks up, they both know it will not last forever. Just a heated argument, an immature farce brought upon by lack of understanding and soon to be repaired with the glue of love and adoration. This was *not* one of those times. This was *not* one of those break-ups because Kayla was certain that she would never see Amir again.

Life with Amir had been carefree, loving, and adventurous. Kayla was happily ready to commit herself to him for the rest of her natural life, but it was over. The sun had set on their relationship.

On Sunday, February 27th, after being engaged for only one day, Kayla Montero was once again a single girl. A single girl unsure of her future.

This story could have started at the beginning, but all that ever really matters is the end.

two

The idea of having to repeat her nightmarish break-up tale repeatedly to her family and friends overwhelmed Kayla to no end. She knew she would be thrown into a situation that she could not control, having to battle a tirade of questions mixed with intense emotion. It was a downright inconceivable thought, especially since she was still processing the situation herself, desperate to make sense of everything. It was not every day that an engagement breaks off due to the impending groom having a pregnant wife in a foreign country.

Kayla viewed herself as an "Independent Woman," *Destiny's Child* lyrics stuck in her head as an ever-present reminder, but the fact remained that marriage *still* seemed to be the epitome of the 'Game of Life;' the Big Boss at the end of the video game.

Kayla could not shake the feeling of failure that weighed heavy on her shoulders. Moreover, she did not want anyone to find out the truth. Amir had carelessly strung her along; he had his cake and ate it too. Kayla's embarrassment at being brutally dumped ran deep, so in her storytelling, she shared an abridged version, a very slim glimmer of the actual truth, as she was too ashamed to admit how blind she had been.

Kayla spun a story that was as close to the truth as she could get without it being considered a total lie. Her girlfriends arrived at her house in tandem, throwing their arms around her as soon as she opened the door. Alcohol, pizza and salty pre-packaged snacks accompanied their words of encouragement. The women sat around Kayla's living room, legs tucked under themselves and eyes wide in anticipation of the gab session where she would inevitably spill the beans about the break-up.

Through misted eyes she told them that via social media one of Amir's family members had messaged her explaining that he was arranged to be married to a woman from his country. It pained Kayla to lie to her girlfriends, but the actual truth was far too difficult to say out loud. Kayla's gaped mouth friends shook their heads methodically in disgust as Kayla spun her tale. In between mouthfuls of pizza and wine, they each offered their own version of thoughtful advice.

The next item up for discussion was how Kayla would manage Manhattan rent on her own. She explained that her paternal grandfather had left her $7,000 when he passed away a year ago. That money served as Kayla's savings, her emergency fund, and she desperately did not want to break into it. But she also did not want to move as she lived four blocks away from work, walking distance. And there wasn't a chance in hell that she would go crawling back to her parents' house in Edgewater. Once Kayla left New Jersey, she had not planned on returning, besides attending holidays and the occasional Sunday meal. It was bad enough that she would have to tell her family what happened. Kayla played fortune-teller, acting out the scene in her head. She imagined her worried mother's rapid-fire questions, her disappointed father with the generic advice that serves no purpose and her sister with her lips pouted in pity and her bear hugs laced in a saccharine sweetness.

Kayla's girlfriends were half-drunk at this point and everybody seemed to buy her story, although she feared that eventually, they would discover the deceit—women always do. She felt ashamed and lying to her girls tore her insides to shreds, but Kayla could not bear to tell them the truth. Mostly because she knew she would be unable to answer the questions they had, as Kayla herself had a zillion questions that were left unanswered.

Kayla did not think it necessary to share with everyone that she cried all day *and* all night. She kept to herself that she woke up every morning puffy faced, swollen and red-eyed like she suffered from an allergy. Unfortunately, there was no Benadryl to cure this kind of suffering. *The Awakening* replaced her copies of *Bridal Guide* and *the knot*, but feminist literature did not keep the tears at bay.

For months, anxiety was Kayla's ever-present bed companion, making a full night's sleep futile. She self-medicated with marijuana, pills, and alcohol. To her dismay, she was never anesthetized. Weight began to vanish from her body, without the aid of diet or exercise. Not exactly the wedding workout she had imagined. Rounded curves became angular, and bones made an unwanted appearance, having been displaced from their sheltered bed of fat.

Typically, the scene within Kayla's mind was akin to the vivid *World of Lisa Frank;* filled with sparkles, light and love. But with her future dissolved, she was shrouded by the dark world of Edgar Allen Poe—dreary and grey like the vaults and catacombs of Amontillado, a raven forever shrieking in the distance, a bloody beating heart disturbing her mental peace. Kayla was pained so deeply because she truly felt as if she would never be anyone's Annabel Lee.

three

Eventually the darkness in Kayla's mind cleared and as the seasons changed, the intrusive thoughts began to fade. The severity of winter bid its final adieu and impatient buds await the bloom of their flowers. Father Time was masterful at his job and diligently healed Kayla's wounds. After a brief setback, happy-go-lucky Kayla Montero had returned. Knocked down and a bit bruised, but back in action.

Kayla had a temporary plan of drowning herself in her work. She held the position of General Manager of Cathedral nightclub. New York City's number one electronic dance music club; the best of its kind, the cream of the crop. She may have been unlucky in love, but she lucked out in the "dream job" department. At least one part of her vision board had been manifested.

Every Friday and Saturday night, twenty-somethings dressed to the nines lined up outside the club's front doors impatiently awaiting entrance. Bodies would shiver in the winter and sweat in the summer, but they waited their turn, nonetheless. Weather never deterred an unforgettable night at the Mecca of Manhattan clubbing.

Cathedral dominated the corner of 34th street between 11th and 12th Avenues. As made evident by its name, Cathedral was a church. Built in the mid-19th century, the abandoned gothic house of worship was given a face-life in 1978 by a previous owner, but the original design encompassing Romanesque features with medieval structures was left untouched.

The building stood tall and strong, the architectural envy of the block. The stone wall façade boasted areas of ornamental limestone overlay and wide granite columns supported pointed arches decorated with flying buttresses. The mica in the stone refracted sunlight, shining and glittering in the daytime. A beauty most party goers missed as Cathedral did not open its heavy wood doors to patrons until 10:00 p.m. sharp. Luckily, the tidal estuary that is the Hudson River sparkled in the background both day and night, its two-way brackish currents battling against one another, eventually surrendering to marry together fresh and saltwater.

Once inside the nightclub, after a pat down from the diligent security guards, guests are greeted with a massive space. The main dance floor is made of clear acrylic overlying the original flooring. Lights run horizontally underneath the hard plastic, illuminating clubber's feet. A mixture of sweat from shirtless men, designer perfume, and the musk of marijuana permeates the air. As the night progresses into morning, crumpled water bottles and dying out glow sticks will litter the floor. Once maintenance found a tooth. But it only happened once, so Kayla tried not to think about it too often. As long as it was not blood, she was happy.

An elevated DJ booth sits where the altar used to be, feeling slightly sacrilegious. Hopefully when the time of reckoning comes St. Peter will turn a blind eye. There are multiple speakers on the main floor pumping out 1,000 watts of thunderous bass. They stand tall and erect like the stone monumental figures from Easter Island. A large swing that resembles a twin bed hangs from the ceiling on a rope entwined with colorful faux flowers and vines. Scantily clad bottle girls can be seen pumping their legs, swinging the night away.

LED lights rain down a spectrum of strobing colors lighting up the dance floor and bar in short bursts. Five circular beds encased in sheer white curtains act as the downstairs VIP areas, created for people who want individualized space and attention, but still want to be in the mix of it all. There is another VIP area for those high rollers expecting a bit more privacy than on the main floor and it is about twice the price. It is also adjacent to the entertainer's "dressing" room so that is the major pull for guests.

The club's main staircase allows access to the second floor, which is an interior balcony overlooking the main dance floor. Three clear shower stalls are on display and velvet eggplant-colored couches surround them. The stalls often have plumbing issues, and the girls dislike dancing in them, but removal is too expensive, so they often stand empty like unoccupied aquariums.

Behind two heavy metal doors, down a linoleum floored corridor and off-limits to clubbers, is where Kayla's office work is conducted. Truth be told, Kayla could do all her administrative work from the comfort of her apartment, but she enjoyed having an office of her own. Down the hallway was a larger, modern, and much more ornate office that belonged to her boss, Ben Tillman. A breakroom and a bathroom were situated at the end of the hall next to the emergency exit door that was used freely.

Cathedral was a judgement free zone. There was music, alcohol, celebrities, dancing, and massive LED screens. All the amenities necessary for a good time to be had.

Most clubgoers had a preferred drug of choice. It went by a

few names: Ecstasy, molly, MDMA. Names aside, it had the same effect. A four-to-eight-hour mental vacation for people who wished to open their mind, have a good time and let loose. A little bit upper, a little bit downer. A whole lotta fun. The tiny pills came stamped with the creator's insignia, random images of happy faces, lightning bolts, superhero logos and stars to name a few. They came in hues like the Pantone color chart—lavender, mustard yellow, sapphire, pistachio, and orange. Like everything else in life, the little magic pills were to be enjoyed in moderation. If not, one could spend years chasing the feeling of that first initial high.

Cathedral as a business did as much as possible to keep the club away from the "drug den" persona that hangs onto many EDM clubs like cheap perfume. The flow of drugs into and out of the club was extremely difficult to control, damn near impossible, especially since most partygoers would start their night by eating pills right before they proceeded to line up outside the club.

Besides the amphetamine issue the club was tattooed with, there was much more to the establishment than met the eye. The club hosted special themed charity nights, and fundraising events for local foundations and causes. Any donation during these nights, no matter how big or small, was currency to gain free entry. Where else could someone gain entry to a bustling Manhattan night club with a can of corn or a Barbie doll? Charity is wonderful publicity. A win for everyone.

Dedicated to the greater good, but ultimately driven by the need for profit and revenue, Cathedral's charity events only took place on Friday nights. Saturdays were the money makers, the set list always boasted one of the world's most respected DJs.

The cover charge to dance the night away was $50.00 per person; nineteen years of age to enter, twenty-one to drink—a standard in the club circuit. The club stayed open until 8:00 a.m., not standard, but as per New York State law, the bar closed at 4:00 a.m., at which point only water, juice and Red Bull were served. Most people just ordered bottled water; avid party-goes know that it is unwise to mix uppers and downers (like alcohol) together. MDMA users are health conscious like that.

Kayla's boss, Ben Tillman, was not half bad either. She had experienced worse in the past. She remembered the married alcoholic from the café near her college campus who had tried to kiss her one afternoon after confessing to her that his wife got pregnant by someone else. And then there was the frigid bitch in the real estate office who only wore pearls and imitation Chanel tweed suits. She tirelessly complained about her mother's homecare nurse and after two weeks found fault with everything Kayla did. So when Kayla began working at Cathedral, it was a noticeable upgrade.

Cathedral began as a weekend gig while Kayla dealt with Frigid Bitch during the week. The hours soon escalated, and more responsibilities were bestowed upon her. In what felt like no time at all, she was the full-time General Manager. The hours were amazing too. She worked Friday and Saturday nights until about three a.m., often choosing to stay later and socialize with friends and artists.

Kayla's boss was pleased that he had hired her; he said so all the time. Sharing with associates and musical artists how she was a 'lifesaver,' integral to the 'running of the ship.' What he regarded most was that her competence and love for the job made *his* job easier. So much easier in fact, that he barely came into the office. Kayla was often left to 'man the ship alone,' another one of Ben's phases.

Ben Tillman was a Santa Claus shaped man, with ever present crescents of sweat beneath his underarms. He had been the owner of Cathedral for the past seven years. A baby boomer with a salt and pepper ring of hair that gave him the appeal of a medieval friar. Kayla had known him for about four years and over that time his neck had accrued two additional rolls, resembling a pack of supermarket hotdogs. To be fair, Ben's unfortunate appearance had nothing to do with his business acumen, he was always fair and honest. It was not his fault that God created him in The Shmoo's likeness. He trusted Kayla's opinion, emphatically supported her ideas, and signed her check every Friday, so that was good enough for her.

After the Amir episode what Kayla needed most was stability. Stable ground to gain her footing and allow herself to regain focus on what was important. She just needed everything to stay on course and she would be just fine.

Kayla saw Ben's name illuminate on the display screen of her vibrating cell phone. She rinsed her hands in her kitchen sink as they were covered in egg and breadcrumbs from dredging chicken cutlets for dinner. She dried her hands on a rough blue and white dish towel and reached for the phone.

"Hello?"

"Hey Kayla, how are you? Quick question, can you stop by the club around noon tomorrow?"

"Yeah, sure no problem. Did you need me to look something up for you? Because I could stop by within the hour if you need me to get something for you," she offered.

"No, no I'm fine. I don't need anything; I just want you to meet a new investor we have. He is gonna stop by tomorrow for a tour and whatnot."

"A new investor?" Kayla questioned with a slightly accusatory inflection. She was not sure what 'whatnot' meant either but decided not to ask any more questions. She clicked 'End,' on the phone after confirming that they would meet tomorrow at noon. Ben had forgotten to share the investor's name or affiliation, but it didn't really matter because while extra money was always a good thing, investors never made any structural changes, so Kayla didn't think much of it. Nothing major would change this time either. She was sure of it.

four

Cathedral's tiled bathroom smelled faintly of urine masked by commercial bleach. From the half open, frosted window, cars could be heard whizzing by hurriedly on the West Side Highway. Kayla checked her phone, it was 11:51 a.m., Ben and the new investor would arrive any minute. She could not help but feel annoyed that Ben did not even feel the need to show up a few minutes before the meeting to brief her.

Bent at the waist over a slowly dripping sink, Kayla peered closely into the wall length mirror, a few shiny gray hairs shimmered brightly through her mocha locks. A tell-tale sign that the big 3-0 lie in wait haughtily around the corner, a sinister laugh cackling eerily in the distance. Sneering, she swore aloud to herself and plucked two wiry white sprouts of hair straight from the follicle, root still attached, clinging on like a fattened larva. She made a mental note to purchase a box of dye from Walgreens and walked out of the bathroom towards her office.

Since the depressive haze from her failed relationship had finally cleared, a deeper interest in her appearance had begun to sprout. She swiped bronzer over her cheekbones to contour her round face and memorized YouTube smokey-eye make up tutorials to further accent her almond shaped eyes. She was trying her best to follow the whole look good, feel good mantra.

The groaning creak of the front doors loudly announced a guest. Kayla could hear Ben's hearty laugh making its way up the stairs towards the office hallway.

From her seated position at her desk behind her twin computer screens, she could hear footballs trudging past the grand staircase headed towards the service elevator. And thank God too, because if Ben had chosen to take the stairs, everyone would spend the first five minutes of the meeting waiting for him to catch his breath.

A minute later, she heard the rolling squeak of the elevator door opening and a bellowing "Kay!" came drifting down the hallway. It did not matter how many times she taught him how to use the intercom system, he still chose to project his voice through the halls. In response to Ben's call, Kayla picked up the folder she created with Cathedral's financials and other various documents she thought to be of interest, pushed herself backwards in her rolling computer chair, stood up and made her way down the hall to Ben's office.

Stepping lively over the threshold into Ben's office, Kayla saw him speaking with a well-dressed man younger than he. Ben was showing him framed pictures hung on the wall of celebrities that had attended the club over the years. The man nodded and pointed to a few photos himself, but Kayla got the impression that he was not all that interested and was just entertaining Ben's name dropping for the sake of the meeting.

Ben turned around from his photo tour and noticed Kayla

walking into his office. "Oh, Kay! There you are! Let me introduce you to Mr. Fiorletti. Cameron Fioletti, this is Kayla, our general manager. She is our Jill of All Trades. Don't know where I would be without this one, that's for sure!"

With an inviting smile and perfectly veneered teeth, Cameron walked towards Kayla and leaned forward with an outstretched hand to deliver a firm business-like handshake punctuated with a slight nod of the head. He took her hand in his and their palms locked in a friendly greeting. Her fingers grazed the sleeve of his suit, navy-blue fabric with barely noticeable silver pinstripes, expertly tailored and buttery soft. A suit that would probably cost Kayla about six months of rent. Easy. Black tattoo ink poked out from beneath his sport coat sleeve, running down his hand, trailing to his knuckles that were covered in Old English font letters, but she could not make out the word. The scent of his cologne enveloped Kayla's senses; hints of rosewood, crisp lemon, and spicy cardamom filled the space around him.

"Nice to meet you, I'm Cameron, but please just call me Cam. Ben has always said such wonderful things about you!"

"Aw, well I am glad to hear it! I'm Kayla, but everyone calls me Kay. It is nice to meet you as well," she responded with an overly toothy grin. Kayla turned on the charm, just like she would with anyone else wishing to invest money in the club.

Cam looked to be in his mid to late thirties. Eyes, hair, eyebrows all monochromatic and dark, like a summer nightfall with just a hint of warmth. His hair was cut closely to his head, with an occasional sliver of gray poking through, straining for attention. His skin was the color of tropical beach sand and faint lines appeared on his forehead and by the corners of his eyes. Olive undertones defined his cheekbones and jawline, which Kayla noticed was perfectly structured and a small beauty mark punctuated his right earlobe. He was classically clean cut, slight stubble on his face with the same attention seeking gray hairs. He was neither thin nor overweight, nor did his body seem like it was chiseled and defined under his suit. No Spartan abs here.

The thought then occurred to Kayla as to why Ben would want to have a meeting when the club was empty, the main floor appearing lonely and ghost-like. This could not have been Cam's first time here, she deduced. She mentally scrolled through the Rolodex of faces that she had seen in VIP in the past few months, but could not recollect ever seeing him before. Ben's voice interrupted her mental cataloging.

"OK, well let us all sit down now. I bought lunch." Ben placed a hand between Cam's shoulders and gestured towards two toffee colored leather armchairs positioned in front of his desk.

Cam pulled back one of the chairs for Kayla so that she could sit. She thanked him and smiled. As his eyes met hers, she tucked in her chin and focused on the floor, unable to hold his gaze.

Cam was about as physically attractive as Ben was thin. Well, maybe that is going a tad bit far. He was not 'face for radio' unattractive, but besides his high cheekbones and defined jawline, a *GQ* cover shoot would never be in the cards for him. Yet, there was something magnetic about him.

A crinkling sound ensued as Ben unfolded the rumpled top of the large grease-stained brown paper bag that sat on his desk. Ben peered inside like a groundhog inspecting a hole. Cam seated himself on the chair to Kayla's left and leaned back ever so slightly with his legs spread wide apart. Why was she watching him so intently? Kayla diverted her gaze back to Ben as he removed contents from the deli bag, mumbling to himself, and separating the items into three piles. The smell of pastrami and sour pickles filled the room. Three sweating Dr.

Brown's black cherry sodas were set down on the desk with a clink. Kayla rolled her chair backwards, catching Cam's attention as she rose to fetch coasters to place under their drinks before rings began to form on the reclaimed mahogany wood. The bleached rings on the office furniture made the maintenance staff crazed with agitation and Kayla never wanted to create extra work for them. Noticing her efforts, Cam nodded and thanked her as she placed a coaster in front of him. Ben was a nice guy, but cavalier about money, since he had it, so water rings on his $6,000 desk was not a big deal for him.

"So, let's talk!" Ben began as he plopped down into his desk chair. Although an inanimate object, the chair groaned in response. Ben's pudgy fingers undid the parchment paper that enveloped the pastrami sandwich like it was the buttons on the back of a woman's dress. In between bites of food that only partially made it into his mouth, Ben began the meeting by thanking Cam for taking time out of his busy schedule to meet with them. It was the way he said it, like Ben was truly humbled to be in Cam's presence. As if Cam was the Dali Lama and Ben and Kayla were mere peasants thirsting for a bit of knowledge and truth.

Cam and Kayla began to unwrap their sandwiches slowly and Ben began to talk numbers, explaining to Cam about Cathedral's income stream and how alcohol and cocktails make up over 40% of the revenue. Cam seemed interested in the numbers but did not have much to say in response, just brief head nods to illustrate that he had ingested the information. With his lack of verbal retaliation, Kayla began to wonder exactly how much money Cam would be investing in the club. Depending on the size of the investment, returns usually took around three years, but Ben had not mentioned anything about Cam's ROI, which she found odd as that is usually the first thing an investor wants to know. Kayla figured that they had spoken about the return estimate beforehand, and it was probably a moot point for her to bring up.

Chewing while he spoke, Ben began going through Cathedral's day-to-day practices and Kayla's confusion began to sprout up once again. Investors could care less about the club's maintenance schedule, or the high-tech computer system, or that the merchandise store on the main floor always sold out of size medium t-shirts first. Why was Ben sharing such random information with this man? Kayla read an article once that stated high fat diets affected cognitive function negatively and she assumed that's what was happening to Ben.

The response from Cam was lackluster, he seemed bored by Ben's spiel. His sandwich lay unwrapped, but untouched on the paper plate in front of him. Kayla was not sure if she could trust a man who was uninterested in meat *and* money. It was pastrami on rye. What was wrong with him? Whereas for her the sandwich was the only part of this meeting that she was able to comprehend. Ben continued to prattle on about the club's daily operations and Kayla decided to no longer mask her confusion. The only people that would be interested in the club's daily functions would be staff members. Or the club owner.

In an effort to deter Ben's verbal diarrhea, she questioned Cam about his business interests and endeavors. "So, Cam, what made you interested in our club? Do you invest in any other clubs?" Kayla asked casually, but with burning interest.

"Yes, I own Ruby's on West 38th and we have a sister location in Brooklyn." His response was all business, but Ben's eyes widened upon hearing his response. Was the look on his face panicked? She could not be sure.

Kayla thought for a moment, wondering if she had ever heard of his locations. "Hmmm, I don't think I've ever heard of those. What kind of music do you guys play?" she asked, intrigued.

Cam cleared his throat, shifted in his chair, and chuckled. Ben looked down and blushed. Were these faces of embarrassment? They had the guilty appearance of tween boys found hiding in the girl's locker room.

"Um, well we play all kinds of music, but, um, music is not really our main focus. We are not like *this* club." His lips were set in a coy smile, eyebrows arched evidently trying to communicate something unspoken.

"I don't . . . I don't understand." Laughing a bit nervously, her eyes shifted quickly from Cam to Ben and back to Cam again.

Cam straightened up from his previous relaxed position. "I own Gentlemen's Clubs. I have other businesses as well, but in terms of clubs, those are the type that I currently own."

He searched her face, she assumed to gauge her response, so Kayla did her best to remain composed and nonchalant.

"Oh, right. I see. That is um, that is wonderful!" she managed to croak out. She did not want to seem like a prude, but the truth was that her opinion of him changed in an instant and not for the better. Curiosity getting the best of her, she asked, "Do you have any business partners or are the clubs solely yours?"

"They're mine, but I will be selling my shares of both locations soon and looking into other ventures . . . such as this one." Cam outstretched his arms like a miniature Christ the Redeemer statue gesturing to the club. His smile was cool, and his eyes brightened as he spoke.

"Oh wow, that is great. Well, Ben and I are excited." She tried to sound as enthusiastic as possible, but was failing horribly.

"Yes! Yes, we are!" Ben echoed. "So, Kay, why don't you tell

Cam about some of our outreach initiatives." Ben gestured to the portfolio in her hand. "Go ahead Kay, tell him some things you have been working on."

Kayla spoke as directed. Standing up to open the portfolio and fanning the informational papers in front of Cam on Ben's desk, she could feel Cam's eyes on her profile, and his direct gaze made her feel uneasy.

"Here is a quick overview of some of our major events and marketing and advertising strategies," she said gesturing to the stacks of papers she just displayed on the desk. She pointed to a flyer. "We had a special event last week where we had all guests donate canned goods for victims of Hurricane Fran and in exchange, we gave them free entrance that night. We also have monthly raffles for free VIP for guests and their friends. We have been pushing social media marketing big time. We just hit 60,000 followers on Instagram," she said excitedly.

"Those all sound great! I am impressed, I really am! It sounds like you guys really know what you are doing," Cam complimented genuinely although there was a growing impatience in his voice.

"Well, I hate to eat and run, but I actually have another meeting to get to across the park. It was very nice to meet you, Kay. I look forward to seeing you again." Cam raised himself up from his chair and extended his tattooed hand towards Kayla, and then Ben.

"Ben, we will talk soon."

Cam looked at Kayla again, his gaze lingering on her for a second more than necessary and he strode out of the office.

Kayla looked in Ben's direction for some guidance, to see if he was as confused as she was by the abrupt ending to the meeting, but he seemed unfazed, sipping the last of his black cherry cola from the straw.

"Nice guy, right?"

She was in the process of formulating a response when Ben's phone rang, and he held up his index finger to her to indicate 'hold on.' She could tell that his wife was on the phone, and she took it as her cue to leave. Before she left the office, she chucked the barely looked at portfolio she had created into the wastepaper basket. She could not shake the feeling like she was being slighted. Left in the dark. Cathedral was her baby too and while she understood that she held no financial bearing, she always knew *exactly* what was going on. A sinking feeling formed in the pit of her stomach, and she prayed that there weren't any more surprises hidden around the corner.

five

Kayla's phone rang and vibrated in tandem on her nightstand. She listlessly slapped at the cheap particle board furniture until her fingers located the buzzing phone and swiped at it like a cat batting at a ball of fluffy yarn. The screen on her phone informed her that the insensitive caller was Ben, and had his signature not been inscribed at the bottom of her paycheck every week she would not have answered.

With a groggy, "Hello?" she answered the phone.

"Hey, Kay! I hope I didn't wake you!"

It was a rhetorical question. He did not care if he had awoken her from REM sleep or not, he was just being polite.

"So, I wanted to meet with you today. Is 12:30 good? I'll bring lunch."

"Um, yeah, sure that's fine. But, is everything okay, though?" she questioned, the hoarseness in her voice beginning to wane.

"Yes, of course. Everything is great! I'll see you soon," he retorted cheerfully and then hung up without waiting for a reply. She groaned aloud and yanked the sheets over her head in protest. She had been looking forward to being lazy and binge-watching *Grey's Anatomy* in flannel pajamas all day. So much for that.

Grudgingly, she trudged down the hall to the bathroom and turned on the shower faucet. Once showered and shampooed, she stood in front of her bedroom closet trying to decide what to wear. Considering this meeting was called last-minute, she assumed her Sunday best would not be required and an oversized hoodie and yoga pants would suffice.

After tying her hair in a top knot with a navy-blue scrunchie, she applied a quick swipe of mascara and dusted bronzer onto her cheekbones before chucking her keys into her handbag. She barely took a second glance at her appearance in the foyer mirror before she headed out the door. Fortunately, she only lived four blocks away, so she had a short commute.

As she strode down the street a flock of cooing pigeons scattered into the air as she approached Cathedral's back doors, her sneakers interrupting their crumb and litter breakfast. As the pigeons took flight she noticed an Aston Martin, black as an oil slick, parked across the street.

Kayla headed straight for Ben's office upon entering the club. His office door was wide open, and she was greeted by the sight of him laughing with another man. Sitting in a relaxed slouched position in the chair across from Ben's desk was Cam. An annoyed exhale exited her mouth and she wondered why Ben did not inform her that someone else would be included in their meeting. Once again, she was left in the dark.

"Hey guys," Kayla said as she entered the office with a light knock. The confusion in her voice was thick like honey and she hoped it was noticeable. She perched herself on the empty chair next to Cam and with a tight smile she nodded in his direction.

"Kay! Hey, how are you! Glad you made it! You remember Cam from Saturday, don't you?"

Of course, she remembered him. Saturday was only two days ago, but instead of responding with a sarcastic quip she managed a friendly head nod followed by, "yes, of course."

Cam straightened up in his seat and turned to face her. He was wearing another perfectly tailored suit—this one was steel grey. A silver tone watch that was likely platinum, gleamed from just outside his sleeve. He dressed like he had money and it nauseated her—but it also caused her to realize how severely underdressed she happened to be. Suddenly, feeling self-conscious she smoothed her hands over her somewhat wrinkled clothes. She wished she had chosen jeans instead, with maybe a dollop of mousse for her hair.

"It's really nice to see you again, Kay," he said with a sincere smile. She hated his flashy, 'look at me' attire, but what really bothered her was that she liked the way he said her name.

"Kay! Are you hungry?" Ben interjected. "I got hot dogs from Grey's, and look, I got you the mango juice you like. I know it is your favorite!"

She felt like a child being conned with candy. A rolling boil of frustration was bubbling up inside of her, but she pushed it down, knowing that the purpose of this meeting would soon be explained.

"Thank you, Ben," she reached over for a hot dog and didn't offer up any further conversation. She was hoping Ben would tell her what was going on, but as usual food had taken center stage in his mind. Ben offered Cam a hot dog wrapped in Grey's Papaya logo emblazoned on parchment paper, but he refused with a slight wave of hand. "Nah, I'm good," he replied. "Thanks, though."

Ben nodded while he chewed, unaware that mustard was

pooling in the corners of his mouth.

With raised eyebrows Kayla questioned the two tight-lipped men, "So, um what's going on guys?"

"Well Kay," Ben began with a full mouth, "I have some news to share with you." Thankfully, he swallowed before continuing. "Cam here has purchased all my shares of the club and, well, I guess you can say that I'm retiring!"

They both looked at Kayla awaiting a response, but all they received was her gaped mouth stare as she processed the information. Ben took another bite of his hot dog and chewed loudly as Cam smiled awkwardly.

"Oh, wow, I um . . . wow, I had no idea you were thinking about retiring. I . . . I'm sorry, I'm just . . . I am just a little surprised, that's all. I was just not expecting this." Nervous laughter escaped her mouth before she could stop it.

Kayla's face warmed and an intense heat filled her body. She wished someone would invent chairs that would swallow you up whole when placed in awkward social situations.

"I know it is a lot to take in, and I'm sorry that I didn't have a chance to discuss this with you earlier," Ben said, concern knitted into his forehead.

Her mind was a melting pot of questions, desperate for clarity. Ben laced his fingers over his belly and continued, "I know this all seems like it is coming out of left field, but the opportunity presented itself and Cam really is the best man for the job. I am very confident in his leadership abilities. This is great news, Kay, it really is." Ben beamed, his grin widening like a mischievous cartoon shark.

When she still did not respond, he continued, "I know what you are thinking, but don't worry! Cam said he will not be changing anything regarding our daily operations. My absence and his presence will not disrupt business function in any way, I assure you."

He stood up from his desk and walked over to Cam, standing behind him and placing his hands on his shoulders like a proud father would do to his son, "Cam is a seasoned businessman and Cathedral would be lucky to have him. He is retaining all the staff too of course. So, this is more of a passing of the torch so to speak." He had let go of Cam's shoulders and began walking around his soon to be vacated office.

He sat back down behind his desk with a heavy plop and shoved another mustard laden hot dog into his greedy mouth. There was something not kosher about this situation, and it was not just Ben's table manners. Kayla knew she had to say something, but there was a part of her that wished that he would choke on his hotdog. She was sure that death by Grey's Papaya was the way he would want to go anyway.

The bemusement on her face could not be contained. She knew she had no reason to be upset. It is not like she could ever afford to buy shares of the club—not in this lifetime or even the next, but it was not about that. She felt left out—Ben had never left her out of business decisions, especially ones as severe as this. She did not know what she should think, but a mixed concoction of betrayal and jealousy were sloshing around violently inside of her.

With a carefully placed hand on her arm, Cam's touch instantly built a dam on Kayla's rushing water of thoughts. Her eyes and attention trailed from his hand up his arm, taking in all his edges and the sharp lines of his jaw skewed by stubble. His touch was firm, but his hands were soft, not hard and calloused like a 'working man.' Men can only be separated into two categories, the type that can buy you a house, and the type that can build one. Evidently, Cam was not the latter.

"Listen," Cam began, an apologetic look etched deep onto his face. "I really won't be changing anything, I swear." He put his hands up as if in surrender to a gun wielding police officer. "Ben said you are great, the best even, at what you do and I believe him. I can tell you feel passionately about this club, so I am just going to stay out of your way and let you do your thing. I would never want to ruin a good thing. I promise"

"Okay, yeah sure. That sounds great. Um, congratulations! I, um . . . I look forward to working with you," Kayla finally managed to reply. Her smile was half-hearted and she was sure that her despondency was evident. She could tell that Cam was trying to make her feel better, and a small part of her appreciated the kind sentiment. As her eyes shifted downward, she noticed for the first time that he was not wearing a wedding ring. A Breitling timepiece adorned his wrist, but the fingers on his left hand were bare.

In one of his last directions to her as her superior, Ben's request was very matter of fact, "I want you to tell the staff with me in a couple of days. Send out an email blast that I want everyone to meet at 7:00 p.m. for an announcement. Tell them that is nothing to be concerned about. I don't want anyone to think that we are closing or that their jobs are in jeopardy, or anything like that. Let them know that it won't not take long, but don't let on as to what the purpose is." Ben did not even bother to look up as he chose yet another hot dog that would meet its unfortunate end in his gullet.

Kayla scrunched up her face in disgust as he took a bite of his hot dog and only portions of the pink mystery meat made their way into his mouth. She stole a glance at Cam and was unable to contain her laughter at the look of revulsion that flooded his face as he watched Ben devour his lunch. His reaction caused her to stifle a snort of laughter, which caused Cam to snicker and shake his head. Kayla was mildly comforted knowing that she was not the only one who was sickened by Ben's dining etiquette. Unsurprisingly, Ben did not notice

Kayla and Cam chuckling at him since he was balls deep in his dog.

In an effort to refocus Ben's attention away from his lunch, Kayla pressed him on the issue at hand. "I assume I should call Eric too and let him know about the transfer of ownership so he can draft a press release for you to approve before you, um, before you leave."

"Yeah, sure whatever you want," Ben answered with a dismissive wave of his hand.

Kayla turned her attention to Cam, "You will get a chance to approve the press release before it is distributed. Eric will add a quote for you and will probably want to set up a few media training sessions."

"Who is Eric?" Cam's question seemed to be directed more at Ben. He seemed surprised and vaguely annoyed that he was not aware of who Kayla spoke about. And it may have been petty, but a part of her enjoyed not being the only one on the outskirts for once.

"Oh, I'm sorry," she shook her head as if to imply 'ditzy me.' "Eric is our publicist. He works at Bernstein Public Relations. If you want, I will set up an email introduction between the two of you." Cam cut her off before she could continue.

"I'm sorry . . . media training for who? Me?" He pointed to himself for emphasis, eyebrows venturing up towards his hairline.

"Um, well yeah. Have you done interviews before?" she questioned trepidatiously. Cam looked suspiciously over at Ben, who returned his look with a side of uneasiness. Kayla's eyes darted back and forth between the two men like she was seated at the U.S. Open. She searched Ben's face for an answer, guidance, anything but received nothing. He just stared back at her and Cam blankly, his fingers laced over his planet-shaped belly. The only sound in the room was that of Ben's internal stomach gasses reporting for duty.

"Oh, um that won't be necessary, I won't be doing interviews. I don't want to." Cam's response was terse and his change in tone caught Kayla off guard, but he quickly lightened the mood.

"I get camera shy," he joked. His tone softened, but Kayla could tell that she possessed no bargaining power on the subject and Ben certainly didn't seem like he was going to support her.

"Interviews are not a necessity," Ben reassured Cam with a roll of his eyes and a dismissive wave of his hand in the air. "Kay will handle all of that. Won't you, Kay? Cam here is not about the spotlight, he just cares about logistics. A real businessman! And that is just what Cathedral needs, not just some talking head."

"Yes, of course. I, um, I agree with Ben. This is your club now, so you can do whatever you want!" Kayla laughed even though nothing she said was funny. "I will have our IT people set you up with an email address and um, yeah we can just go from there." She hoped her voice sounded cool and carefree, but if she sounded disconcerted it was because she was.

"Yes, please that would be great," Cam replied, but she could tell his interest in the conversation was waning. It seemed as if buying a club was the least important thing on his To Do list.

Undoing her scrunchie, she began to run her hand through her hair, a tell-tale sign that she was anxious. A river of chocolate tresses cascaded down the sides of her face like a veil, obscuring her peripherals and blanking out Cam from her canvas. She longed for Cousin It's ability to hide in his hair, truly an underrated superpower.

After what seemed like a minute of pause, Ben livened up

and began to speak again, directing his full attention to Kayla. "Oh, Kay, so yeah, if you can work on making next Saturday night my retirement party, that would be great."

"Wait, what? *Next* Saturday? But, that is in eleven days!"

"Kay is our resident math whiz," Ben told Cam as he teasingly wagged a finger at her. Normally, she would have laughed along, she could take a little roasting here and there, but this was insane. The entire situation was just . . .well, there is no poetic way to say it, it was just fucked up.

"I didn't know you were leaving *that* soon!" Kayla wished that she could control the inflection of confusion that coated her voice. The mood in the office shifted like a tectonic plate. As if on cue, Cam pushed back his chair, catching it slighting on the rug beneath and rose to be excused, citing another meeting to attend.

Cam shook Ben's hand, mentioned something about seeing him soon and then turned to me with the same handshake and sentiment.

"I have your card, I'll text you my number in a few minutes," he stated with a small smile. He gave Ben one last head nod before heading towards the door.

Kayla awaited the slam of the emergency exit door, ensuring that Cam had left, and turned to Ben with her hands on her hips. She swore that if she furrowed her brows anymore that day that she would need to schedule a Botox appointment.

"Okay, okay I know you are feeling pretty blindsided right now," Ben splayed his hands out in front of him like he was about to brace himself for a fall. "It just happened so quickly, and it felt like fate, you know. I am not a spring chicken anymore; age is no longer on my side. I want to live out my dream of sailing and traveling the world and well, it just *felt* right. And . . ." He stopped rambling and looked at Kayla, biting his lower lip as he took in her rigid and agitated stance. "I'm sorry, I should have started there. I truly *am* sorry I did not tell you earlier; that was wrong of me. Sophie just really needs me right now and you know we live our lives on the edge. And well, this just seemed like an opportunity I couldn't pass up. I do not want to lose any time with her."

Ben knew that by mentioning his wife, Sophie, Kayla would soften. Sophie had beaten stage 2B breast cancer and Kayla had seen the toll it had taken on Ben, let alone Sophie. She was one of the strongest women Kayla knew, and she had always looked up to her.

Heat flushed Kayla's cheeks and clavicle and she instantly felt embarrassed by her selfish thoughts. She apologized for her misguided reaction and hugged Ben tightly, with the stench of Dijon mustard filling her nostrils.

"Next Saturday sounds great for the party. I'll get right on it. It will be the most amazing retirement party anyone has ever had," she said as she squeezed his bulky shoulders lovingly. "Actually, I have an even better idea!" Kayla perked up as her creative juices began to flow. "We will make it a retirement party slash breast cancer benefit. We can ask for donations and the dress code will be pink apparel!" Ben's weak, bittersweet smile was all the thanks that she needed.

Ben was a *real* man, albeit his table manners left much to be desired, but in terms of his affections for his wife, he was truly honorable. Kayla prayed that one day she would be lucky enough to meet a man like that, someone who would *always* put her first. Fresh from nursing the emotional wounds that Amir had scarred her with, Kayla's view on love had changed. She was not only a realist, but a cynic too. She knew the fairy tale idea of love that she had held steadfast to her entire life, in actuality did not exist. In real life, Rapunzel would have died in the castle waiting for her prince.

six

Ben's announcement meeting arrived quicker than two shakes of a lamb's tail. There was not one part of Kayla that was looking forward to working under a new superior, especially one who didn't know *anything* about the industry.

Metal folding chairs with grey rubber bottoms had already been placed in neat rows by the maintenance crew by the time she had arrived at the club. All staff members except light and sound engineers were expected to attend the meeting. A few concerned staff members had reached out to Kayla inquiring about the purpose of the meeting, and it was difficult playing coy, especially since she considered many of the staff her friends. She did make it a point to pacify everyone by further assuring them that the club was not closing, Ben just had some restructuring news to share. That explanation seemed to appease everyone, as their main concern was job security.

Oblivious employees began to trickle in, the folding chairs noisily scraping against the acrylic dance floor as butts plopped into seats. Talking amongst themselves, knees bent towards one another, Kayla could tell everyone was eager to find out the purpose of the clandestine meeting. Minutes later,

THE VOICE WE SQUELCH

Ben and Cam entered together. Surprisingly, Ben was able to keep pace with Cam's stride. Kayla stood up in front of the seated staff, awaiting Cam and Ben to join her.

Cam wore a thin smile, and Kayla took in his laid-back attire. He did not don a designer suit like the last two times she was graced with his presence, instead he opted for a slim-cut charcoal sports jacket, motorcycle jeans and a pair of black leather high top sneakers that had a small silver lock on the back. She found herself intrigued, not turned off, by his attire. He looked like someone put a 2000's rapper and a couple of *Mad Men* into a stainless-steel cocktail shaker and when they poured it, out came Cam.

Waving both hands in the air like a rockstar entering a brightly lit stage, Ben beamed at his staff—or Cam's soon to be staff. Kayla could see everyone's attention secured on the new person by Ben's side. A few eyes fluttered back-and-forth between Kayla's direction and the two men. They both held a space next to her and Cam nodded a quick, 'hello' in her direction before returning his attention to his new staff. The employee chatter hushed to a silence as Ben began to speak.

"Thank you all for coming," Ben began, "this won't take long I promise." His hands were steepled in prayer position. He exhaled deeply, "I am just going to get straight to it, cut right to the main course if you will. I've decided that it's time for me to finally retire. I won't share my actual age, but it's time," he let out a forced chuckle amid the chorus of gasps. Kayla was oddly comforted to see that the staff had a very similar reaction to the news as she had just a week prior.

"My heart will always be with Cathedral and with you guys," Ben continued. "I'll always be here in spirit, but today I'd like to introduce you to Cathedral's new owner and your new employer, Cameron Fiorletti." He gestured to Cam, not that a gesture was required, as Cam was the only stranger in the room. Cam gave the group a small wave and an awkward silence settled over the group like a fog.

Kayla nudged Ben with her foot, giving him a knowing look. He nodded slightly, realizing he had to give the staff a bit more information, but upon the attention being turned to him once again, Ben's shoulders slumped forward, causing his neck and head to follow suit. He began to choke up and a thick mucus cough formed in his throat. Sensing that talking about his wife's illness to a group of people was too mentally trying for him, Kayla decided to take over. She placed her arm around his back and her other hand braced on his forearm. Kayla knew that Ben had always been good to her, and she was more than happy to act as his strength if he so needed—and she felt that he needed her at that moment.

As the confusion among the staff members grew, Kayla began to explain to everyone about Ben's decision to retire effective immediately due to the health of his wife and his desire to spend time with her. Since not everyone was aware of Sophie's condition, Kayla went into a brief description of what life had been like for Ben and his wife for the past couple of years. Slack jaws and misted eyes from the seated crowd stared back at them. Kayla looked over to Cam, who had fixed his eyes on the floor. She assumed it was his way to squelch the raw emotion in the room.

Staff members with faces like sad clowns began to rise from their seats to hug and comfort Ben, offering words and phrases of kindness and encouragement. The same people would then paste a smile on their face and direct their attention to Cam, shaking his hand and welcoming him to the club's 'family,' which in reality was just a colloquial term that held no real bearing. Kayla noticed a few female staff members lingering in front of their new boss, ogling him a bit longer than necessary, sizing him up with demure grins. Although not a head-turner, Cam reeked of young money, swag and style.

It brought a tear to Kayla's eye when she saw how supported Ben was, and it made her smile as she saw his emotion morphed from pained to jovial. The hugs lasted fifteen minutes longer and then the crowd began to disperse. Groups of staff members branched off into smaller groups as plans for the remainder of the evening were discussed.

A generic ringtone played and buzzed in Ben's khaki pants pocket. He quickly fished into his pocket for the phone and pressed the screen to the side of his face. Sophie requested that he stop by the pharmacy and pick up one of her prescriptions before he came home. As if in response to a commanded order, Ben quickly bid his goodbyes with a few handshakes before he was off, walking as quickly as his stumpy legs would allow.

Kayla suddenly felt so alone, a lone coin in a hollow ceramic piggy bank. She had the mechanics of the club down, but Ben was her go-to when she needed guidance. He had promised to only be a 'one call away;' available day or night for counsel, but she knew how that went. Kayla appreciated the imaginary veneer of support but took it for what it was—just talk to fill in the awkward void that accompanies a goodbye.

What would she do when she needed assistance? Who would she ask for advice? Who would she call? The questions whirled in her head like a blender. Anxiety, like drying cement, sat heavy in her core as she stood in the belly of the nightclub that *she* now had to run with the aid of someone she deemed a novice in terms of club management.

Without wanting to draw attention to herself as a few staff members still milled about talking and laughing with one another or with Cam, she decided to slip outside for some fresh air. Well, as 'fresh' as Manhattan air can be. A small group of employees were huddled together in conversation outside the club, so she did her best to avoid them, not wanting to engage in any more conversation.

Outside there was a chill in the air and a gust of wind blew past causing loose hairs to escape the confines of her messy bun that sat high atop her head like a make-shift crown. Several deep breaths later of polluted air, she turned on her heels and bumped right into Cam.

"Oh, hey there you are. I was looking for you," he said.

"Oh, were you? I'm sorry I didn't mean to cut out so quickly. I just, I don't know, needed a little bit of fresh air, all that emotional dumping was a bit much." A lighthearted chuckle escaped her throat which Cam returned with a tight smile.

"Yeah, that was a lot. I feel bad for him. Poor guy." He shook his head to punctuate his point, but his tone turned upbeat as he changed the topic. "So, I've got to run, but I was hoping that we could get together sometime this week so you can give me a quick overview of everything."

"Yes of course!" Kayla replied, a bit too cheerfully. "We can meet anytime, just let me know whenever you're available and I can meet you here."

He reminded her of the anthropomorphic white rabbit from *Alice's Adventures in Wonderland*, always running late for one meeting or another. She half expected him to pull out a gold pocket watch and blather on anxiously about the Red Queen.

Cam nodded and headed towards a black tinted-out SUV that Kayla had not noticed pulled up alongside them.

"Car side service, I see," she said, immediately regretting her words and lack of professionalism that spilled out of her mouth. She hoped the huge smile plastered on her face would show her quip was in good fun. Thankfully, he laughed.

Before entering the gas guzzling vehicle, he turned to her,

"I'm sorry, I never asked. Do you need a ride or anything anywhere? We're headed to Brooklyn, but we could drop you off anywhere you need to go."

"Oh, that's very sweet of you, but no thank you. I have to stay here and work for a while." *Gotta get ready for the new administration,* Kayla thought.

"Yes, of course, obviously." With a tight-lipped smile and nod of his head, he situated himself inside the leather passenger seat and shut the door. The driver of the car, who seemed to be a friend more than an employee, handed him a lit blunt, turned on his left signal and nosed into traffic. A twirl of white smoke escaped the rolled down window, absorbing itself into the atmosphere.

seven

Two days had flown by since the staff meeting took place. Kayla worked feverishly day and night on the plans for Ben's goodbye soiree. In an act of fortuitous divine intervention, the scheduled performer for Saturday evening was B-Flat, whose mother had recently achieved remission after a breast cancer diagnosis, and his manager stated that he would be more than happy to help further publicize the party.

Kayla rose to re-open the window in her office that she had closed to block out the city traffic noise during her phone call with B-Flat's manager. As she stood in front of the half open window, the smell of grilled meat wafted up into her window and tantalized her nostrils. Pleased with the outcome of the call and delighted that something was going in her favor, she decided to head outside to reward herself with a Halal food truck chicken gyro, with extra white sauce, of course.

She had just reached the emergency exit door, when she was called back to her office by the tinny sound of her cell phone ringtone. The name *Cam New Boss* emblazoned itself on her screen. Seeing his name pop up on her phone caused feelings of apprehension and excitement, but she answered as coolly as possible.

"Hello?"

"Hey Kayla, it's Cam. How are you?"

The deep, husky voice that spoke to Kayla's phone would lead one to believe that Cam was more attractive than he actually was, it was a real mind fuck.

"Oh, hey! I'm good. I'm actually in the office right now."

"Perfect. I wanted to see if you had any lunch plans for today, because I am in the area, and I thought that maybe we could go over a few things. If you aren't busy that is."

It was more of a request than a question, but she agreed and told him that meeting for lunch would be great.

She wondered if she had time to pick up a chicken gyro anyway and eat it before the actual meeting. She must have been channeling her inner Ben because that was exactly something he would have done. She missed him already.

A text made a binging noise on her phone. "I'm outside," it read so Kayla jogged down the stairs and stepped onto the drizzle speckled sidewalk.

The sky was grey and overcast with thick cotton ball clouds, raining tiny droplets onto the collar and sleeves of her beige peacoat. Awaiting a large SUV, she was surprised when the passenger window of a small black sports car rolled down to reveal a smiling Cam stretched across the seat.

She walked over to the car, apology at the ready for not recognizing him.

"I'm sorry, I should have told you which car I was driving today," he said with a light laugh.

She complimented him on the beauty of his car, finally

remembering that it was the same car parked outside of Cathedral on the day that they first met.

As she slid into the passenger seat with its butter leather upholstery, she tried to sit as daintily as possible. She felt like she should not touch anything, like his car was a museum and even apologized for the moisture beads on her sneakers, although they were barely wet.

His cologne filled the open space in the car, and her olfactory nerves heightened at the pleasant mixture of fruity notes with hints of wood. Cam was dressed more casually than usual, adorned in jeans and a hooded sweatshirt, but still put together and stylish.

Unaware of their last-minute lunch meeting, she had chosen to wear black leggings, a white spaghetti strap camisole and a black zip up hoodie. *Technically* her clothes were all designer but purchased at deep discounts from department store clearance racks. To say her outfits were past season would be putting it lightly. She hoped the pilling on the fabric was not visible and she cursed herself for always buying the cheap detergent, which was not doing her aging wardrobe any favors.

Cam raised his chin and craned his neck to check in the rear-view mirror before he pulled into traffic, narrowly avoiding a honking yellow cab. "I hope you are okay with Italian food," he said. "I know a great place not too far from here. Have you heard of Alberto's?"

She shook her head no, but smiled and responded, "I have not, but I am half Italian, so I am always up for some pasta."

He laughed at the pasta comment and slowed down at an approaching red light. His knuckles tensed on the steering wheel, and she noticed dark inked letters on his fingers that spelled out the word 'FATE.' She was not sure if his tattoo fell in the category of cool or corny, like tribal tattoos or lower back tramp stamps, but since she did not possess any body ink herself, she decided that she was in no position to judge. Although she was questioning his choice in body art, she still prayed that she did not reek of the gyro spices she had scarfed down fifteen minutes earlier. She self-consciously wiped the corners of her mouth, hoping no errant white sauce lingered.

They engaged in small talk on the ride over to the restaurant, discussing the crappy weather, traffic and if there would be parking in front of the restaurant. The parking gods heard their prayers and answered by allowing a cherry red Honda Civic with dings and dents pock marking the doors to pull out just as they arrived at the restaurant.

Once parked, Cam and Kayla exited the vehicle and walked side by side in an uncomfortable silence. The light rain ceased as they strode underneath the green scaffolding that seemed to eternally encase some buildings. Cam put his hand on the small of her back to guide her in the direction of the restaurant and his fingertips transmitted tiny jolts of electricity that radiated through her spine.

As they approached the restaurant, its front door swung open. A slight man with white hair and deep wrinkles in his jowls that looked like deflated whoopee cushions held the door open for them. They were greeted by the familiar aroma of simmering tomatoes and basil. Kayla and her grandmother had been making sauce together for as long as she could remember, and she was unable to think of a time in her life when they did not engage in the six-hour Sicilian tradition. The tradition taught her that food could fix anything, forever uniting people. As the cinematic images played in her head, she made a mental note to call her grandma and say, "Hi," as it had been a couple of days since they had last spoken.

"Good afternoon, Mr. Fiorlette," the polite maître d said in a heavy Italian accent as he bowed his head slightly. He took

Cam's hand in both of his and shook it graciously. It was evident that they knew each other as he asked Cam about how he was liking his new apartment. They followed the maître d as he led them to a booth in the back of the restaurant. He swiftly took their coats and stepped aside so that they could slide into the booth. As soon as they were seated, the next five minutes were occupied by employees, including another restaurant patron seated across from them coming up to Cam, shaking his hand and making brief small talk. Many of them smiled at Kayla or nodded in her direction after they spoke with Cam, but he never introduced her to any of their table visitors.

"Wow, you are pretty popular around here," Kayla noted as she mindlessly toyed with her fork.

"My mom was the popular one. I am just the by-product. She knew *everyone*," he responded without looking at her. He lifted his head, raised a finger in the air and two waiters rushed over, seemingly tripping over one another.

"We will start with the risotto and then the short ribs. And two glasses of Sangiovese please," Cam instructed the waiters without even glancing at the menu first. Kayla was slightly taken aback that he ordered for her, but she was a touch captivated as well. Within moments, another affable waiter placed a straw basket of seeded breadsticks and squares of herbed focaccia bread between them.

Kayla noticed his use of the past tense when speaking about his mother and the nosy part of her decided to pry. "Are you and your mom close?"

He took a sip of water from the sweating glass that the overachieving waiters had set in front of them. The ice in the glass clinked around rhythmically. "We used to be, yeah, but she died two years ago—from the same cancer that Sophie has."

"Oh, wow. I am so sorry to hear that. I really am." Kayla cursed her internal busybody.

"Thank you. I appreciate that. Anyway, I should probably start by thanking you for coming to lunch with me. I really look forward to working with you. Ben sang your praises multiple times." Another waiter arrived table side with crimson-colored wine and set a plate of cheese beside the bread bowl, explaining to them how the Grana Padano Stravecchio and Tuscan Pecorino paired beautifully with their wine. They picked at a few chunks of cheese, noting the flavor profiles and the waiter winked at Cam and he was off as swiftly as he arrived.

"So, tell me about yourself." He cocked his head to the side as he awaited her response. She self-consciously wiped the corners of her mouth with the lined napkin that lay in her lap, brushing away any focaccia crumbs or remnants of fine imported cheese.

She told him that she was born and raised in Edgewater, New Jersey, held a master's degree from NYU and had been hanging out in New York City's trendiest nightclubs as soon as she was old enough to gain entry. She interjected with different facts about the club, but he always redirected the conversation back to her—her life, her hobbies, her interests.

"And no famous DJ boyfriends?" he asked jokingly, as he plunged a piece of focaccia into the red pepper dotted olive oil, but she could tell he was fishing for information.

"Um, no. I don't date DJ's. They're serial cheaters. Too many groupies, I guess," she shrugged, but lightened her tone so that she seemed unaffected. Cam nodded slowly, aware there was more to her response. "But, I was um . . . I was engaged a few months ago actually, but it didn't work out. We're not together anymore."

"Oh, wow. I am sorry to hear that," he said, and she may

have imagined it, but she could have sworn he perked up upon hearing the news that she was no longer attached.

Cam didn't ask why the relationship dissolved, he probably didn't care, but for some reason she told him. She told him the truth. The entire raw truth that Kayla had not told *anyone*.

"The day after I got engaged, I found out that he had a pregnant wife back in his country. The way I found out was by his family showing up at our apartment to literally escort him back home. I have not seen him since."

Cam stared at her slack-jawed for a second, and then recovered. He picked up his napkin from his lap and wiped his mouth as he began to laugh. "Oh shit! That was a good one! Fuck! I thought you were serious!"

He continued to laugh until he realized that she was stone faced, mouth set in a horizontal line.

"Oh, shit. Oh, wow. You're serious. I didn't mean to laugh." Cam reached across the table to place his hand on her arm in an apologetic gesture. She could tell he was mortified, so she let him off the hook and waved off his embarrassment. To his credit it did sound insane.

"Wait, so he had a whole other wife in his country? *That is crazy!*" Cam's eyes widened at the thought.

"Yeah, I didn't know he was married obviously. His father and uncle showed up at our apartment banging on the door yelling in Arabic, and they made him tell me the truth and literally dragged him out of the apartment shirtless with just a coat. I never saw him again. He called me after and explained, but I blocked his number, and I had Cathedral's IT guy do the same for the club's number too."

Cam's bewildered look had returned, and heat flushed Kayla's face, "I'm sorry. You don't want to hear about all the stuff. I must sound like a nut. Let us, um, let us just go over some more club logistics . . ."

Cam interrupted her. "No, keep going. Tell me."

"Are you . . . are you sure?" she questioned as the heat began to fade from her cheeks.

"Yeah, I want to know," he pressed as he leaned further into the table.

"Well basically, I found out that he had a wife in Qatar, that is where he is from, *and* she's pregnant *and* the company that he works for belongs to his father-in-law. He works in the oil industry, and I thought it was weird that he never had any money, but he always told me that his dad didn't want him to be entitled, so he had to work hard until he turned thirty and then he would be promoted to second in command. And, well, I believed him. I had no idea that he was broke because he was maintaining two lives on opposite ends of the globe."

"Wait, how often was he in New York with you?" How was he able to pull it off? Cam asked incredulously as he hung onto every word of her story.

"Two weeks out of every month he was here and the other two weeks he was in Qatar. Here is the thing though, he always spoke in Arabic when he was on the phone, so he could have been talking to his wife while seated right next to me and I never would have known. But, here is the real kicker. Are you ready for this?"

Cam nodded eagerly, awaiting the next juicy morsel of information.

"His wife's family, namely her father, owns South Field Gas."

"Holy shit! I have stock in South Field."

"Yeah, well sell it," she joked. "Anyway, my fiancée's father also had an oil company. His company, while extremely profitable by anyone's standards is not South Field Gas by any means, so naturally my fiancée's father needs the marriage, correction, merger to run smoothly so that they can establish one huge crude oil conglomeration."

"Wow, that is one messed up story."

Not wanting to monopolize the conversation any further, Kayla decided to change the subject with an "enough about me," and began to inquire about his life, his hobbies, his interests, but all he said was, "I like money. And I like doing things that make money."

Feeling embarrassed and exposed, Kayla took another sip of wine and was thankful when the cavalcade of waiters arrived at the table with their dishes. The wine glasses and breadbasket were both refilled although neither were ever empty.

The short ribs fell off the bone and the risotto had a creaminess Kayla had never experienced before and she told Cam so, thanking him again for introducing her to such a wonderful spot. After eating in silence for a few minutes, Cam opened his mouth to speak but closed it before he could begin. The lunch crowd had thinned, and they were the only couple seated in their section.

"So, listen, there is actually another reason why I wanted to ask you to lunch today. I mean, don't get me wrong, I did want to get to know you better, but I also wanted to speak with you about something more specific."

"Sure, we can talk about anything. What's up?"

"Good. Good, I'm glad. So, like I said, Ben has always sung your praises. He spoke about how professional you are, as well as your ability to be discreet."

"Huh?" Kayla stopped eating and placed her fork to the side of the plate, short rib juice dripping from the tines.

"Your ability to be discreet," he repeated.

"Okay," she responded slowly. "I'm sorry. I'm not really following you. What am I to be discreet about?"

"Well, when I was speaking to Ben, he told me that you are close with many of the talent. Everybody likes you; people trust you, he told me."

"I mean, yes, I like to think of myself as trustworthy," she tapered off, unsure of where the conversation was headed.

"Well, that is refreshing to hear because I recently began dabbling in another market. One that I know is pretty popular with all your club kids and DJs."

Kayla knew he was waiting for her to respond but she didn't. After a brief pause, he continued.

"I wanted to know if you would be able to put me in contact with some of your DJ friends or VIP high rollers who might be interested."

"Are you talking about like molly? Ecstasy?"

"Yeah, whatever the kids are calling it these days."

Now she understood why he was interested to know if she had any DJ boyfriends. He is only interested in growing a drug business with high-end clientele. *Great.* Kayla's short ribs had grown cool and the risotto was beginning to form a thin film. When she didn't respond for the second time he followed up with, "you would get a cut of course."

Making sure to speak slowly so that they both understood each other clearly, Kayla thought about the proper words to choose.

"Just so that I am clear, you want me to set you up with DJs and VIPs so that you can sell them molly?"

"Yes, basically. Discreetly, of course. I am only bringing this up because Ben told me that you could help. That you make connections like this for the artists all the time, so I just figured if you were doing that anyway, then maybe you could connect them with me instead, and like I said I'll give you a cut."

He was all business. His shoulders tensed and she noticed

that he barely touched any food on his plate, and she realized that they were never there to eat lunch.

She felt betrayed and the mood reflected as such and an awkward silence filled the space between them. Cam did not let the silence hang for long though, inquiring if she had any questions and if she was interested.

Kayla swallowed hard. "I will do whatever you need. I will introduce you to all of the artists I know personally, and you can just talk to them at your leisure, about your, um, products. Would that work?"

He opened his mouth to speak but she cut him off with an upturned palm, "I don't want a cut or anything, though. I am just doing my job. Whatever you guys speak about is between you and them."

Cam seemed puzzled and studied her for a minute before speaking. "But you have to get paid. I would not feel right not compensating you."

"No, trust me it is fine. I am just introducing them to you, that's it. I am not doing anything out of the ordinary."

"Okay . . . well then maybe we can think of a different arrangement."

"Yeah, maybe. I don't know. We can talk about it when the time comes." Kayla hoped her clipped responses would put an end to the conversation.

She could not believe that Ben would offer her up for a position like this. It struck her as downright odd, and sick wife or not, she would *definitely* be confronting him about it.

A hush wedged between them, invading the airspace. She had just shared her biggest secret with a man who wanted her to be a drug liaison. She was fuming.

Without asking her if she was done with her meal, but assuming as much since her utensils never returned to the culinary masterpiece set before her, Cam put a finger up in the air and a rush of waiters arrived and removed the plates.

Cam did not ask for a check, nor did the waiters set one down on the table, he just placed two hundred or possibly three hundred dollar bills on the table and got up from his chair. The chair legs slid noisily against the laminated wood floor. Kayla followed his lead, and they made their way to the front door, snaking between the linen clad rectangular tables. The wait-staff shook Cam's hand as he left, nodding at Kayla with smiles. She returned their sweet smiles and walked towards the front door which Cam held open for her. He placed his hand on the small of her back again and she felt the same electric currents, although they were noticeably duller this time.

They walked on the sidewalk for a moment until they reached his car, still speckled with petite drops of rain. He opened the passenger car door for her, and she settled in and waited for him to come around to the driver's side. The rain had stopped, and they both made note of the hazy sun trying to peer through the clouds. When they reached the first red light Cam turned to her and rested his hand on her knee for just a second before removing it. She was taken aback by the gesture but did not flinch.

"Are you okay? You seem a bit quiet; I hope I did not offend you back there." He looked genuinely concerned and her annoyance with the situation softened.

"No, not at all," she responded, trying to sound cool and not like a stuck-up prude. "I was just a little surprised, that is all. But like I said I will introduce you to all the artists I know, and I'll help in whatever way I can."

His reasoning for buying a nightclub had finally become obvious. It was extremely disheartening that his sole purpose for buying a club was to peddle drugs to high rollers, but at least he was being honest, not hiding who he was. It was Ben that Kayla was angry with. How could he have willingly signed her up for this with not so much as a mention beforehand?

They arrived at the club in record time and Cam double parked in front of the side entrance and put on his hazards. Kayla thanked him again for lunch.

"So, I guess I'll see you Saturday for Ben's party?" she asked as she stepped out of the car and onto the now dry sidewalk.

"Well, it is *my* club now, so you will be seeing a lot of me," Cam answered with a grin. "Oh wait!" He leaned over to unlock the glove compartment, removed a pair folded Gucci sunglasses and placed them on his lap along with a Ziploc bag filled with fat, pre-rolled joints. He took a handful and outstretched his arm for Kayla to take them. "Samples. Let me know how you think they are."

Surprised, she took the fragrant gifts from him with widened eyes. *Oh great, he sells weed too. Fantastic.* She thanked him because she was not sure what else to do. It was damn near impossible to shake the 'drug den' veneer from dance nightclubs. Having an owner whose business venture was rooted in illegal substances could not possibly be good for Cathedral. Kayla wanted to kill Ben. She wanted to call him at that moment, but she knew she was too fired up and should wait until she calmed down.

Kayla stood on the sidewalk as Cam edged his car into traffic. The sounds of the New York City streets muffled in the background as she walked into the dark empty club and the metal door clanged loudly behind her. She headed up the stairs to her office, organizing her thoughts around what needed to get done for the rest of the afternoon. She plopped down into her desk chair and opened up her emails, but her mind kept drifting to her unsure future.

eight

Kayla only lived a few blocks away from Cathedral, but due to an overzealous grooming session she arrived somewhat late to the club for Ben's retirement party. Most of the staff were already in place and settled into light chatter. A few maintenance members were in the process of rolling out a long blank autograph banner that Ben could bring home with him after it had been signed by whomever was interested. As she walked through the main floor nodding her "hellos," almost everyone noted her sexy attire or causally jibed her for being fashionably late.

The decorations on the main floor were bright and cheerful because although the reason for Ben's leaving was somber, Kayla wanted his retirement party to be everything but that. She still had yet to speak to him about the conversation she had with Cam but decided that his party was not the place to do so.

Moments after she arrived, the cancer foundation team they were working with walked in carrying large tote bags and sandwich boards. The team leader, Erica, a young girl with a pinched nose and mousey brown hair, clamped her hands together and exclaimed how excited they were to be working at a nightclub event and commented on how pretty Kayla's dress was. She said she loved the color, but her eyes were fixated on Kayla's breasts.

"I am sure this beats the usual morning marathons," Kayla joked, but even as she said it, she wondered if her comment was a tad thoughtless. She excused herself from Erica and her team and told them she would be milling around all night if they had any questions. The team began to set up their various stations throughout the club with a gusto Kayla admired and wished the members of her staff could possess. Two by two, Cathedral's maintenance staff began to bring in grey banquet sized folding tables as if they were carrying royalty on a palanquin. Additional employees followed closely behind as in procession, metal folding chairs hoisted under their armpits. Kayla smiled and thanked them as they walked past, mentally noting that the last time they used those chairs was for Ben's retirement announcement—and the first time Cam was introduced to *his* new staff.

Kayla walked around the club, inspecting, and commenting on the progress. She checked the time on her phone, which she kept in a black fanny pack slung low on her waist with a thick black nylon belt and Cathedral's logo in big block white letters displayed obnoxiously on the front. Ben and Sophie would arrive around 9:00 p.m., giving the staff less than ninety minutes to complete the set up.

The evening's festivities had been scheduled hours earlier than usual as their guest of honor had no interest in late night soirees. Ben also informed them that Sophie's medication often left her lethargic and fatigued, so even eight o' clock was pushing it. Whenever Kayla thought about Sophie's situation, her heart ached for her. Sophie was the embodiment of a 'sweet as cherry pie' personality, who was unfortunately plagued with a horrible circumstance.

Kayla ascended the grand staircase to assess the pink tulle that was being wrapped around the banisters, questioning to herself if the look was too tacky. As she weighed the decision to keep or toss the tulle, Kayla noticed out of the corner of her heavily made-up eye that Ben's office door was propped open. She noticed that a few people were congregated inside the office and she immediately recognized Cam's voice among the group as the sound floated into the hallway.

Kayla raked her fingers through her hair and then up towards her temples to lift her roots and add volume to her umber tresses. Her dress was too tight, so she gave it a quick pull down to cover more thigh and another pull upwards at the sweetheart neckline to ensure that her boobs behaved, and her nipples did not play a game of hide and seek.

After she was certain she looked presentable, she ventured over to Cam's office. Her heels followed the voices and laughter that spilled out into the hall. For a split second, she panicked and froze, wondering if she should just walk away and continue with her anal-retentive inspection, but then the thought resonated with her that she actually *wanted* to see Cam. She never wanted to see Ben, not like this anyway. Kayla walked towards the open office door and saw that Cam was in her direct line of sight. Her interest in him was difficult to define. While in no way *completely* unattractive, Cam was visually unconventional—not Kayla's usual cup of tea. She did not like to use the word chubby as a means of a person's description, so Cam could be described as *well formed*. His back was broad, and his shoulders followed suit with their wide set, but his stomach softened with no nipping of the waist.

All in all, the fact was that he intrigued her, his stance always indicated control and his candor seemed to muddy the lines between arrogance and leadership. A mental conundrum he was and she found herself wanting to solve the puzzle.

Taking in his profile inch by inch she noticed that his nose seemed rounder and broader than she remembered, an unfortunate stereotypical Italian physical attribute. Kayla's father was a victim too, thankfully both her and her sister took after their mom's Tinkerbell nose. Cam's lips were full, especially his bottom lip, venturing on bulldoggish. She thought about how jealous her Restylane addicted girlfriends would be of his au natural features. He was fashionably dressed, as per usual, this evening in ripped jeans that brandished so many tears that any elderly person within sight distance would certainly comment, "Hey, sonny boy, you got a hole in your pants!" His long sleeve pitch-black crew neck t-shirt with the brand's logo running down the length of his sleeve did little to conceal the slightly rounded stomach that hid underneath. He wore the same high-top sneakers from Ben's retirement meeting, and an online search that she conducted that evening had clued her to the fact that his sneakers, Buscemi's, cost about half of her monthly rent.

Cam stood among two other men, both dressed similarly, although one was much taller and attractive than the rest. They all seemed to wear timepieces whose diamonds caught the light from the fixtures overhead. Another man, not standing within their immediate circle, stood off to the side laughing coolly into his cell phone.

Moments ago, the trio of men were seemingly immersed in deep conversation with one another, but Kayla seemed to have stolen the show, garnering their full attention. Not the biggest fan of direct eye contact, she averted her gaze until Cam's voice sliced through her budding anxiety. "Hey, Kay! It is nice to see you!"

He seemed much more upbeat than usual, a smile lighting

up on his face with an equally bright twinkle in his eye that she recognized instantaneously as tipsiness. A tipsiness eager to morph into the next stage of full on drunk.

She spied a tall bottle of The Macallano on his desk, close to half of its liquid contents already in the bellies of the men who stood in front of her.

"I'm sorry, I didn't mean to interrupt." Kayla said, alluding to the other individuals whom Cam had yet to introduce her to. She could feel everyone staring at her intently, sizing her up and forming first opinions.

"Oh, no, it's fine. It's fine." Cam responded, waving a flippant hand in the air. We were just bullshitting." He cut himself off to comment on her outfit which boasted more cleavage than Kayla remembered seeing in her bedroom mirror a couple hours prior.

"You look really nice by the way, *really nice*," his glazed over eyes roved up and down her silhouette as respectfully as possible. He was still beaming, his full lips stretched to their max, baring flawless rows of ivory white teeth.

Kayla thanked him casually, avoiding direct eye contact and attributing her fancier threads to the current event, although she had a sneaking suspicion that he was aware that was not the complete truth.

"I wanted to know if you would like to take a walk around the club with me at some point tonight and meet some of our VIP's. I just figured that this would be the perfect time for introductions because basically everyone who has supported us through the years is here to show support for Ben and Sophie."

"Yeah, sure. I'm ready. Let's go." He took a final sip of the amber contents that swirled around in his perspiring glass and set it down on a mahogany countertop covered with Ben's picture frames of celebrities and disc jockeys.

"Oh! We don't have to go now. I know you were in the middle of, um . . ." She pointed with her thumb over her shoulder indicating towards Cam's friends that stood behind her. People whose names she still did not know because Cam did not think to introduce anyone.

"No, it is no problem at all. I have been wanting for you to take me on a tour while the club was full." He took notice of her hesitation regarding the group of men who stood in the center of the office. She was still getting used to the fact that the office was no longer Ben's and she felt like she was leaving a bunch of strangers unattended.

"It's not a problem, really. They will wait for me." A small grin etched into the corner of his mouth. His friends, as if reacting to an instruction, plopped down into whatever seat was closest to them and they all proceeded to take out their phones to busy themselves until Cam returned.

Cam's long strides made their way towards the open door and Kayla's inclination was to follow him. She would come to learn, sooner rather than later, that everyone's inclination was to follow Cameron Fioletti. And she was stupid to think that she would be any different.

nine

Kayla took a boozed-up Cam on a tour of the club, stopping every minute or so to explain a fact or tidbit to him. She educated him on the fact that their house photographer would want to take photos of everything so that he should be prepared. He did not seem enthused, claiming once again to be camera shy, but reluctantly agreed to flash his pearly whites a few times.

As they snaked through the growing crowd, they both noticed Ben at the same time. He waved briefly at them and headed over to another group that was calling out to him. Sophie was not at Ben's side, but sat quietly at a large round table smiling occasionally at the two other women that were seated next to her. Sophie was fashionably styled, with a wig expertly crafted for her. But her sunken frame and pallid, papery thin skin made it obvious that she was recovering from a serious disease. Thread thin blue veins spiderwebbed beneath her translucent surface and the vision caused Kayla's heart to crumble into a million pieces. As Kayla and Cam approached Sophie, she immediately saw his facial features tighten. His outstretched smile flipped upside down, resembling a sad Norman Rockwell clown.

After Kayla said her hunched over hello to Sophie, bidding her not to stand, she wished her an amazing time on her upcoming trip. Sophie offered up a few sprouts of excitement about viewing the bioluminescent water in the Maldivian night and the cave temples in Mumbai. Kayla wondered how she would fare traveling within a cave but kept her thoughts to herself.

Cam redirected the conversation by talking about how beautiful Mumbai was and how he had a friend whose family still resided there. The three of them spoke for a few more minutes and before they said their goodbyes Cam bent down to hug Sophie and said something to her that was inaudible for Kayla as it was blurred out by the music. As Cam straightened up, Sophie took both of Cam's hands in hers and smiled at him sincerely. With a friendly wave in Kayla's direction, she turned to the other women who were seated next to her and joined in on their conversation. Not wishing to be nosy, Kayla did not ask Cam what he had said to Sophie, and nor did he offer up a response.

Kayla took in the growing crowd and inserted her earpiece that Cathedral staff used to communicate throughout the night. Within five minutes, she received an alert from the security desk that all ticketed VIPs had been accounted for. Kayla pointed towards a table of athletes that she knew Cam would be keen on meeting and headed towards them. Cam stayed closely behind her, mirroring her steps. Although he was only a few inches taller than Kayla, she could feel his presence looming overhead, shadowing her as they walked forward in tandem.

"We really have a lot of heavy hitters here today," Kayla said leaning back faintly into Cam, her voice pitched a bit higher to be heard over the music. "Let's start over here," she continued as she nodded towards a VIP section in the back corner. "We have a few Knicks players over there. Omarion Marcus and Clay Fairweather come here often. I don't know much about sports. No, sorry that is a lie. I don't know *jack shit* about sports, but they are both really chill guys and spend an obscene amount of money here every time they come, so I just pretend to know what they are talking about," Cam laughed genuinely at her comment as if it were a joke. And she laughed with him, more at his reaction than anything.

"Don't worry, your secret is safe with me. I promise not to tell," he brought his index finger to his lips and pursed them in a *shhh* motion, a Cheshire Cat like grin forming. "But just so you know the Knicks play basketball, okay, so don't mention anything about a touchdown or a hole in one or anything like that." he said, laughing heartily at his own joke.

"Ha ha, very funny. I'm not *that* clueless!" she protested with an eye roll, bumping him playfully with her shoulder. He was smiling, seemingly enjoying their comradery, at Kayla's expense, but comradery nonetheless.

"I know, I'm just fucking with you," he said with a throaty chuckle. He was sidled up alongside her and speaking closely into her ear, using his left hand to cover his mouth in hopes to beat out the music. She could feel the warmth of his whisky breath billowing down her neck as he spoke. For the briefest of moments, she thought she felt his hand creep up alongside her waist, only to drop down a moment later, his fingers grazing the roundness of her hips.

As they approached the athletes and their entourage, Kayla was greeted by the two players that she knew, engulfed by their long arms and taken into a friendly drunken embrace that rocked her to and fro. After she finished her hugs and 'hello's,' she turned to Cam to begin a more in-depth introduction with him, Clay Fairweather and Omarion Marcus. But to her surprise, he had already ventured off and was giving the players dap like they were besties.

Happy that Cam was occupied, Kayla began to go over the checklist in her phone for the event until she heard someone call her name. Manny, Cathedral's leather pants clad house photographer was raising his voice over the music to be heard. A self-proclaimed creature of the night, he had originally huffed and puffed when she had informed him that he had to be available a good three hours earlier. Manny was the ulti-mate diva, but in Kayla's opinion, was a photographic genius so she dealt with his bougie behavior.

"Oh boy, honey pie, you are going to land yourself a rich ass husband tonight with those melons hanging out." He fanned himself in mock heated exhaustion as if her sexiness was too much to take. As far as she was concerned, if a gay man thinks that you are hot then you have already won.

As Kayla ambled away, Manny pulled her back by her upper arm, leaned into her and pointed at Cam discreetly and shrugged. Manny never showed up to the retirement announcement, so while he had heard from other staff members about the change of ownership, he had yet to meet Cam in person. Kayla told him that Cam was the new owner and Manny gave him a quick once over.

"He's young and it looks like he's got," Manny rubbed his ring clad fingers together making the sign for money, insinu-ating that Cam had a good deal of it. "Too bad he's straight." Manny wrinkled his nose and shrugged. Kayla playfully slapped his arm and humorously scolded him for being a naughty boy, which prompted a laugh and an innocent exag-gerated look of 'who me?'

"Okay, hot stuff, you know the drill. I will get their atten-tion. Just go stand over there and get Mr. Money Bags to stand with you and the rest of the group." Manny was the friend that always needed reigning in. If left to his own devices, he would saunter right up to Cam and call him Money Bags straight to his face and inquire bluntly about his net worth. Kayla had seen him do it before and she was hoping that this time he would behave.

Kayla noticed that Cam was quickly becoming the center of attention in the ball players group. They had begun comparing wristwatches and were engrossed in jovial conversation. The number of diamonds and precious stones that adorned the men in front of her could have filled a pirate's treasure chest.

Manny stood by Kayla's side as they approached the group and she took note of his new python skin loafers. She complimented him on his shoes, and he just rolled his eyes, "From Óscar. He sent them from Milan since he knows I am pissed. His trip was extended by three days! Can you believe that?" He turned suddenly and looked Kayla dead in the eyes, "You know I basically own him, right?" He threw back his head and laughed like a cartoon villain. Kayla followed suit, although much less vivaciously. Oscar was Manny's partner and one of the few reasons why she believed that love still existed. Despite Manny's crass humor, they were head over heels in love. Kayla prayed for what they had, an unwavering emotional *and* physical connection. Oscar was also a big wig on the senior leadership team for Bing, hence the snakeskin shoes that graced Manny's feet. Needless to say, Manny was living the ultimate housewife life and she envied him for it. Maybe one day Kayla could meet a man who could support her so that she can express herself artistically. Kayla scoffed at the idea, causing herself to snicker out loud at the notion.

Manny left Kayla's side and began arranging the group for photos, complimenting the women as he did so. Cam managed to locate her, planting himself at her side as Manny continued to rearrange people like human chess pieces to gain his optimal shot. When finally satisfied with the positioning, he stepped back and began his countdown back from three before the repetitive shooting from his Nikon began. Before allowing his subjects to rise from their poses, he called Cam and Kayla over to stand to the right of the group and after the photo was taken Kayla asked Cam if he was enjoying meeting everyone.

"Those guys are great, so chill and down to earth. While we were talking, we found out that I know Omarion's uncle. He owns the bodega by my apartment. What a small world!" Cam was about to continue speaking, but they were interrupted by Manny directing them to sit down at the other end of the group. Cam took his orders graciously, obliging Manny (as if he had another choice) and stood to the far left of the group next to one of the player's girlfriends. Manny had instructed the poor girl to stay frozen in place because she had wanted the profile of her ornately designed heel to come out correctly in the photo, a prototype that would be featured during the upcoming Fashion Week.

As Kayla readied herself for placement for the final group of photos, she leaned her hip against the tufted black leather couch that everyone was seated on. Clay Fairweather turned to her and pulled her playfully onto his lap. His monstrous hands devoured her waist, and she could feel his fingertips digging into her midsection. He was naturally a nice guy but was evidently intoxicated and unaware of his strength. Kayla plopped onto his upper thigh, her hand barely missing the bump on his jeans that was no doubt his penis. For a relatively early event, especially a health-related fundraiser, she sure had seen quite a few inebriated individuals. Clay placed an abnormally long and toned arm around her lower back and Kayla stiffly adjusted herself. She plastered a smile onto her face, trying to sit as ramrod straight as a human spine would allow, praying that Manny would achieve his shot so that they could all disperse.

Being years away from the *#MeToo* movement, Kayla silently dealt with the red-hot feeling of discomfort that raced to her nerve endings. A feeling that was being captured in real-time on camera. Being felt up, whether the aggressor be sober or drunk as a skunk, was in no way new to her. She wished she was a novice in that department, but given her current work environment, handsy men were known to appear on an almost nightly basis. Feigning a twinkle in her eye for the photos, she continued to smile as society had conditioned her to do. As *countless* women have been conditioned to do.

Manny completed his photo taking session, thanking everyone obstreperously, especially Fashion Week shoe girl.

As the photo taking session ceased, a newly hired and eerily cheery curly haired, pixie nosed waitress by the name of Leanndra approached the group, leaning in to inquire if anyone had a drink order.

After placing orders with Leanndra, everyone began to scatter and break off into smaller groups within their VIP section. Kayla was desperate to rise from Clay's lap, but unable to due to the glue-like grip he held around her waist, and he began to babble about something. He craned his neck downwards so his alcohol laden lips would reach her ear level. The thick platinum chain that hung heavy on his neck swayed in front of her face; the four-inch diamond encrusted cross landing square on her bosom. As politely as possible, Kayla began to wriggle her way out of his grip as best as she could. The last thing she wanted to do was offend him - ever conscience of Cathedral's big spenders. Within moments, Cam appeared at her side. Glowering with deep set ridges in his forehead, he reached downwards towards Kayla, grabbed her forearm and lifted her up from Clay's lap. His force took her by surprise, but she was immediately thankful for his sudden arrival.

Cam placed a hand on the side of her waist and gently pushed her over to the side. The look on Clay's face eclipsed into shock when Cam seemingly went in for dap, but then spent a full 60 seconds speaking some very serious words into Clay's ear. Clay nodded slowly at first then much more quickly, the defined cleft in his chin bouncing up and down in agreement as Cam backed up from him and turned towards an unsure Kayla. Steering her away, he placed a protective hand on her lower back. The act seemed to comfort her, as if his hand belonged there, like the small dip at the base of her spine was made specifically for his hand and his hand only. Kayla did not ask him about what he said to Clay; she thought it best that she did not know what words that were exchanged.

"Thanks for that. They get a little handsy sometimes when they are drunk. He might have not even realized, you know. He really is the sweetest guy, usually. Occupational hazard of club life I guess." Humor used to soften the blow did not amuse Cam, as he shot Kayla an aggressive side eye that could have cut steel.

"Don't do that. Don't make excuses for him. I know what I saw, and you looked *really* uncomfortable."

"You're right, but unfortunately things like that happen a lot more than I care to admit. But all in all, thanks for helping me."

"You're welcome . . . and just so you know things like that are *not* going to be happening around here anymore, not while I am in charge, anyway."

Cam's earlier lightheartedness calcified into something more somber, and Kayla felt let down by the sudden mood swing, albeit warranted. She found herself wishing for their playful back and forth banter to return.

"Where to next?" A gentle smile strained to crack through his hardened glare, and she prayed that the rest of the evening would go off without a hitch. She thought to inquire about the men waiting in Cam's office, but he did not seem bothered about making them wait, so she figured neither should she.

They spent the next hour bouncing around the club, running into various people that were more than happy to make Cam's acquaintance. Manny appeared and reappeared randomly like camera clad Houdini. Kayla's cheeks were beginning to sting from the excessive smiling for pictures. The overly enthusiastic greetings were beginning to take a toll on her serotonin levels and she told Cam as much. Mercifully, he agreed with her, and they decided to take a ten-minute break in his office. His friends were still seated in the same places that they had previously left them in, as if frozen in time. Upon seeing Cam and Kayla enter the room, his friends looked up from their phones. Cam offered up a meaningless apology about the extended timing, but his counterparts did not seem to mind.

The well-needed break never started because Kayla's earpiece began to buzz. It was Carlos on the other end of the line. He was Cathedral's head of security. Upon answering, Kayla heard the agitation in Carlos' voice. Noticing her sullen gaze, Cam questioned Kayla as to what was happening. Kayla told him that she needed to speak with security about something and left his office to head downstairs where security was located. Before she reached the staircase, Carlos had made his way to her and was bounding his way up the stairs, two at a time.

Unbeknownst to Kayla, Cam had followed behind her after she had left his office. He asked his friends to depart via the fire door. Kayla appreciated his hands-on approach, but she was not sure how much help Cam could be when it came to club operations and issues. A major difference between Ben and Cam was that Ben knew the industry inside and out as well as everyone in it. He had clout, he had pull, and if a situation was truly unfixable, he would find a way out. He *always* did. Kayla highly doubted that Cam possessed that quality, as few individuals do. But she had to give him a chance one day and that day seemed to be staring them right in the face.

Kayla had thought that she preferred the business model of trust and delegation, but she had to admit that she *did* like having Cam by her side assisting her in dealing with the issues head on.

"What's going on?" Cam asked. He was sharing in Kayla's look of concern as Carlos, Cathedral's two-hundred-and-thirty-pound head of security and the father of four girls under the age of twelve stood directly in front of them, blocking out any other view. Carlos only reached out to Kayla when there was a major issue that he himself could not solve, so whenever he radioed in she knew to brace herself. The only thing worse than an unexpected conversation with Carlos, was the sight of Cathedral's lawyer and public relations team seated at the same table. A vision Kayla hoped would never take place as long as Cam was the boss.

Carlos beckoned with his finger over his shoulder for Kayla to follow him to one of the side stairwells. She followed closely behind him, with Cam by her side. She liked how his step always kept time with hers. When they reached the quiet stairwell, Carlos thrust his hand towards Cam, quickly introduced himself and immediately returned to the budding issue at hand.

"That asshole from a few weeks ago came back, but we

dealt with him and threw him out immediately." Carlos puffed out in between labored breaths that came from snaking through throngs of people.

"But the problem is that we only caught him, and we think some of his boys may already be here. My guys are out on the floor keeping an eye out for them. Normally, I would not bother you, but since it is such an important night for Ben and Sophie, I wanted to let you know." Carlos' arms flew up in mock surrender, frustration sewn deep into his face.

"What guy?" Cam interjected, his gaze drifting from Kayla to Carlos and then back again.

He was awaiting an answer, so she gave him a quick run-down of the current issue. If managing a nightclub has taught her anything, it is that no matter how much you plan, something will always go wrong—kind of like Murphy's Law, but with a sick beat drop added for dramatic flair.

"We have caught this guy selling molly here before and security went to remove him last time, but it ended up in a huge brawl because like ten of his boys got involved too and some girl who was just standing there got punched in the face, it was *so* horrible," Kayla sighed, shaking her head in agitation as the vivid images of that night flooded her memory. Kayla turned to face Carlos who had slumped down onto a stair and was looking to her and Cam for further direction.

"I honestly do not even know why he would want to come to this event. The tickets were $250.00 each. I mean this is a cancer fundraiser for Christ's sake! What the fuck is wrong with people?" Kayla could not contain her annoyed exasperation.

She was sure it did not need to be said out loud, but she decided to clarify for Cam anyway so that they were on the same page. "So, yeah Carlos and his team will remove the troublemakers as quietly as possible. We only like to call the cops as an absolute final, *final* option. I am sure you understand."

"I agree with you, the cops should never be the first call, it brings too much negative attention." Cam said calmly, nodding his head in agreement with her previous statement.

Cam took a few steps in front of Kayla, faced Carlos and placed a hand on his shoulder, "Listen Big Man, I need you to tell me as soon as you see anyone that shouldn't be here. Okay?" He was talking to Carlos with what seemed like a condescending tone, but she was certain that she had to be wrong. "Do you understand me?"

Carlos nodded in response, looking at Kayla briefly before returning his tired eyes to Cam. Placing his palms on either side of his hips, Carlos hoisted his massive body upwards and headed out of the stairwell, having to pivot his frame sideways to get past Cam and Kayla.

When Carlos was out of earshot, Kayla turned to Cam to affirm her support of Carlos's efforts.

"Carlos knows how to handle these situations, Cam. I trust him. He is the best there is . . . by a long shot," she offered, committed to defend Carlos. Carlos had been working at Cathedral just as long as she had, and they often looked out for one another.

"I'm sure he does a great job," Cam responded. "But, honestly, things like this need a more hands-on approach."

Kayla nodded although she was not entirely sure what she was agreeing to. Cam looked down at his watch, noting the time and that he had to get going. He asked for Carlos' direct cell phone number, and she gave it to him without question and headed downstairs. Ben was about to begin his thank you speech along with the final tally of funds raised for the evening.

Kayla was under the impression, as she believed Ben was

as well, that Cam would stay for his speech and possibly say a few words himself, but he did not. Ben did not seem to mind that Cam was not present, but Kayla did.

The night finished with speeches from Ben and Sophie, as well as the research foundation executive director who announced that the evening rounded out with an impressive amount of $119,775 raised for cancer research. A healthy mix of cheers and tears ended the event as guests poured out into the cool night, passing by the stationed off line of party goers who were patiently waiting for the special event to end so that they could *begin* their night.

Ben called Kayla's cell phone minutes later, thanking her emphatically for the event and apologizing that they had to run off without saying goodbye, but that Sophie was tired. She told him that an apology was not necessary and that they should grab lunch before he and Sophie began their voyage. She was still beyond livid with him for how he had promised Cam her discretion, but she knew it was not the time to have that discussion so she hung up the phone, feeling only partially satisfied.

Cam had only just left, yet she felt the icy chill of melancholy. But maybe it wasn't loneliness at all, but in fact, longing. A lingering sensation that Kayla had not felt in a long time—if ever.

ten

Kayla was in no way, shape or form, thinking about having a baby, but there was something about staring into an infant's face and feeling their soft fingers curl around hers that warmed her uterus.

She could not halt the smile that appeared on her face as she stared into her nephew Joseph's cool blue eyes. A blue so pure it reminded her of a spring sky. Joseph's older sister, Anaya, held on to the rails of her brother's stroller with her pudgy, dimpled hand as they stood by the apartment's front door, and Kayla strapped Joseph into the harnessed clasps of his stroller.

Anaya's newest obsession was the *Teddy's Teatime* show. It was safe to say that for the next few months, at least, *every-thing* in her five-year-old world would consist of *Teddy's Teatime*. Teddy stuffed animals, Teddy tea sets and Teddy outfits. The show was essentially about a fluffy brown teddy bear, whose name was Teddy (how original) and her friends, Ducky, Bunny and Kitty. The animatronic animals sit at a round table set with beautiful floral china cups filled with amber colored tea. A three-tiered silver stand displays tea sandwiches in three shapes, triangle, square and rectangle. Each show begins with Teddy and her friends making it a point to go over each shape multiple times, a colorful outline of each sandwich shape appears enlarged on the screen and one by one, the name of each shape is displayed in a huge font underneath the shape, all of Teddy's friends saying the shape name in unison.

The show is repetitive and annoying, not to mention that Kayla's older sister, Celeste, states that the content is a grade level below Anaya. Kayla was aware that by being childless this meant that her comments held no bearing in her sister's eyes, so she kept her mouth shut, lest her sister jump down her throat, cramming in her child development statistics along the way. But as soon as Kayla saw that *Teddy's Teatime* was hosting a pop-up shop and live action show just a few blocks away from her apartment, she knew she had to get tickets.

"We are gonna be late for Teddy!" Anaya wailed, dropping her head backwards in exaggeration, as they exited the front doors of Kayla's building. Kayla was certain that Anaya must have picked up her whining trait from her mother. Anaya was stomping down the steps angrily, her patent pink leather ballet slippers connecting loudly with the stoop stairs. A thick set of furrowed brows met with slumped forward shoulders proved that her frustration was building. Kayla had to look away from her as she did not want Anaya to see her smiling at how incredibly adorable she looked when she was mad. An attribute she did *not* get from her mother, who had the cadence of The Abominable Snowman whenever she was even the slightest bit inconvenienced.

Anaya's frustration could not be blamed as the morning was not running very smoothly. They had already tried to leave the building twice, having to return once because Joseph spit up thick foamy milk all over his coat and then a second time when he pooped the moment they stepped onto the sidewalk.

Kayla was happy to finally be walking steadily on the sidewalk towards their destination. Their steady pace slowed when Kayla felt Anaya tug at her hand.

"I hava go pee pee." Anaya looked up at Kayla with big, blinking eyes.

"Already? Didn't you *just* go before we left the house?"

"Yeah, but I gotta go again. Uh oh. I think I hava do a poop too, a *big* poop."

"Jesus! We don't have time to go back home. Let's go find you a bathroom." Kayla responded. She thought about the gooey chocolate chip muffin she served her the moment they arrived and vowed never to do that again. Thankfully, they were headed in the general direction of the club, so Kayla made a sharp turn onto the club's street and headed towards Cathedral. She fished into her purse for her key ring with the club's keys so that she would be ready as soon as they approached the doors. The look on Anaya's face reminded Kayla that time was not on their side.

"Okay, honeybee, we are going to stop at my work to do poopie okay? We are almost there; just hold it in for a couple more minutes." Their gait increased steadily to a slow jog as Kayla feared that they may have a prairie dog situation on their hands if they did not make it to the club in the next couple of minutes.

They approached the side entrance of the building, and she unlocked the wrought iron gate in the hurried manner of a drug fiend. Kayla ushered Anaya into the enclosure and with a loud bang of metal against metal, the gate slammed shut. Joseph had begun to fuss and Kayla quickly unstrapped him so they could ascend the galvanized staircase that clung to the building like English ivy.

"Come on, come on! Up the stairs, you know where to go!" Kayla could have sent Anaya to the main floor's bathrooms, but they skeeved her out. The bathrooms were sanitized with bleach every day by the club's deft maintenance staff, but Kayla knew the things that went on in there, so she *always* opted for the staff bathroom on the top floor. She swung Joseph onto her hip and followed closely behind Anaya who had begun to bound up the black steps. Every step groaned and clanked as they bound upwards and arrived at the second floor practically breathless. Kayla typed in the five-digit code on the doorknob before they were let into the building with a buzzing sound. Luckily for Anaya and her active sphincter, the bathroom was the first door on your right as soon as you entered, and she ran right in without any necessary prompting.

Anaya had been to Cathedral a dozen times. Kayla only brought her niece to the club during daytime hours, even though she constantly joked with her sister that she was going to take Anaya to a rave and Electric Daisy Carnival as soon as she was old enough. Naturally, Celeste found no humor in this, proceeding to educate her sister on the dangerous decibel levels of music at those festivals. Kayla viewed Celeste as a killjoy. To say that she and Celeste were polar opposites would be putting it lightly, but she loved her anal-retentive sister unconditionally all the same.

Joseph stopped fussing and began to drift away with Mr. Sandman as a dark pool of drool began to form on the shoulder of Kayla's moss green utility jacket. She cursed under her breath with the realization that she left her purse and the baby's diaper bag in the stroller downstairs. Both items were in the gated in corral that the cigarette smokers on the main floor used, but Kayla was certain that in their haste she did not lock the gate behind them. Cathedral never had an issue with trespassing before, but that would be the day that a homeless person strolled in and stole it all, Burberry diaper bag included. The thought of their stuff being stolen began to pick at Kayla's brain, so she gently questioned Anaya how she was doing and was answered by a plopping sound from the toilet bowl water.

A couple of minutes later a flush of the toilet indicated that she was finished and now required help pulling up her tights. Kayla struggled to crouch down and help her as she held a sleeping Joseph in her arms, his plump cheek resting hard against Kayla's shoulder. After rising to her feet, not at all gracefully, Kayla turned on the sink faucet for Anaya to wash her hands. Her thin arms dangled as far as they could into the sink but could only make it about halfway in and Kayla had to pump out the bubblegum-colored slimy soap from the dispenser into her palms for her.

With an overly aggressive lather, Anaya began washing her hands to the tune of the 'Wash your Hands Song' from *Teddy's Teatime*. After paper towel drying her little hands and dumping the crumbled brown paper towel in the wastebasket, Anaya followed closely behind Kayla as they exited the bathroom. Kayla exhaled deeply, relieved to finally head over to the *Teddy's Teatime* event and content that there should be no further disruptions.

Kayla asked Anaya to push as hard as she could to open the emergency exit push bar door so that they could head downstairs but a voice from the other end of the hall caught Kayla's attention.

With her ears and interest piqued, Kayla turned on her heels and told Anaya to hold on for a moment which prompted a groan of annoyance.

"Hello?" Kayla called down the hallway, half expecting to

hear the voice of one of the maintenance staff. She quickly realized that the sound came from Cam's office. She walked twenty feet down the hall with Anaya trailing behind her and was faced with Cam standing behind his desk, eyes cast downward towards the screen of his phone. His thumbs hoovered over the glass and pecked at the keypad. Sensing someone in his presence, Cam looked up and the sides of his mouth upturned into a smile.

"Hey, Kayla! I didn't know you were working today."

"Oh no. I'm not. I just had to make a quick stop over here for a bathroom break." She told Anaya to say hi and Anaya waved at Cam sheepishly. "This is my niece, Anaya," and then she turned to the side so Cam could see the baby's sleeping face, "and my nephew Joseph."

Cam walked over to engage Anaya, but she shrank behind her aunt's back as he approached. He inquired about the stuffed animal she was holding, and her shyness seemingly dissipated as she started in on her spiel about the wonders of *Teddy's Teatime*. Cam nodded enthusiastically in response, but Kayla could tell that he had no idea what she was talking about. Joseph began to stir, and she mentioned to Anaya that they should get going. It was what Anaya said next that shocked Kayla.

"Do you want to come with us?" Anaya asked Cam with widened eyes that twinkled.

Choosing to answer for him, Kayla interjected, "Oh no, honey, Cam is very busy. He is at work, don't you see? He does not have time to see Teddy today." Kayla smiled at Cam apologetically but was taken by surprise when he rebuffed her response.

"Well, I am not working *anymore*. Maybe I can go with you. What is this Teddy thing? Like a toy store or something?"

The *Teddy's Teatime* theme song billowed from the speakers suspended outside the building underneath the awning. A line had already formed by the time they had arrived, and they stood begrudgingly at the very end. Anaya looked up at Kayla and she could tell Anaya was about to lose her temper.

"Auntie Kay, the line is too long! Teddy is going to leave before we get inside!" The incessant whining would not stop until she got what she wanted. Kayla stole a glance at Cam who had been briefed on the walk over about what a pop-up shop for *Teddy's Teatime* would entail. Kayla had given him several outs, too many to count, but he declined every single one, insisting that he wanted to go as he smiled down at Anaya. Anaya naturally beamed in his presence.

A souped up electric blue Honda Civic tore through the street, blasting hip-hop music as it aggressively ground to a stop at a red light. Mothers who were waiting in line with them on the sidewalk could be seen giving the driver death stares as inappropriate music about strippers, money and drugs blared through all four open windows of the car.

"What an a-hole that guy is! It is like he doesn't see a huge line of women and children!" Cam seemed generally befuddled and a few moms echoed his concerns. A small chuckle escaped Kayla's lips. She had not seen Cam in this light before and it was kind of endearing.

Still seemingly agitated, a mother with twin blond girls in matching robin's egg blue dresses turned on her heels to face them and sternly concurred with Cam. Kayla also noticed that her eyes rested on his Rolex a second or two longer than necessary. The effect the lyrics had on the line of L.L. Bean clad moms was comical and when Cam saw Kayla's partially hidden smile, he returned hers with one of his own.

After a few minutes of waiting on an unmoving line, Kayla noticed Cam was starting to get as restless as Anaya and she began to worry that he was regretting his decision to join them. It was not like she did not offer him many outs. Kayla was certain that any minute he would fake a phone to call and be on his way. But he did just the opposite. He rested one hand protectively on the stroller handle and re-tucked the satin trimmed blue baby blanket around Joseph's pudgy little body. An instinctive smile broke out from the corners of Kayla's mouth, and there it stayed.

"What is taking so long! I wanna go in NOW!" Anaya's whining would just increase the longer the line remained stagnant. Crouching down so that she was level with Anaya, Kayla placed her hands on Anaya's shoulders and began to explain how patience was a virtue, but Cam interrupted her as he openly agreed with the five-year-old. He leaned into Kayla so that he could whisper in her ear. His breath felt warm against her neck and the baby hairs on her hairline stood on end, thin wispy soldiers at full attention.

"She is right you know; it has been a long time and, um, I have this tiny pet peeve—I do *not* like waiting in lines. So yeah, we aren't going to wait anymore. The baby will be in college before we get in. Follow me." He took Anaya's plump little hand in his, and walked off the line, towards the entrance. Kayla was surprised by the sudden change in plans and her hesitancy grew as she turned around to face a line tailing behind her that had nearly doubled. The line was worse than Cathedral on a good night. The hold that the children's entertainment business had on parents' wallets was no joke. Before Kayla could think of a protest, Cam and Anaya were already a foot away from the front ticket podium.

Kayla stepped off from the line and hurriedly followed Cam and Anaya while pushing Joseph in his stroller. By the time Kayla had caught up to them, Cam and Anaya were already positioned at the front door talking to a young, acne ridden employee whose polo shirt seemed a few inches too short. He wore a giant teacup name tag that read ASSISTANT MANAGER, JOHN R. and he stood next to a security guard who was the human embodiment of Mt. Everest. Kayla's first thought was that he should probably be working security at a strip club, not at a children's event.

Kayla stepped back to take in the scene unfolding before her. Cam spoke to John R. in hushed tones that came across to her as muffled and garbled. She could not hear their conversation, but the security guard glared down angrily, hovering over them like a massive vulture. Cam's hand was positioned on the podium for only a minute before he turned to Kayla, waved her over and said, "Okay, let's go in."

Befuddled, she followed after them, trying to ignore the sideways glances that were brewing by the patrons still standing in line. An irritated father in the front began to protest, justifiably so, but the manager calmed him down by stating that they were raffle ticket winners and received premium access. Pimple face may have known how to dress properly, but he was quick witted because they definitely were not raffle ticket winners.

Kayla caught up to Cam, standing a bit closer to his side than was probably necessary and questioned him about the events that had just occurred. "Um, what just happened back there?" She was smiling with intrigue, but her firmly knitted brows conveyed her confusion.

"We got inside. We were raffle winners. Didn't you hear my friend John out there?" He held fast to Anaya's hand and flashed Kayla a toothy grin, cocky and cartoonish, but she could not ignore the tiny flutter in her heart.

The burst and snap of freshly popped kernels filled the air of the lobby and as expected Anaya started to whine.

"I want popcorn! I want popcorn in a Teddy bucket!" Anaya wailed, jumping up and down like a little bunny, her long shiny hair bouncing along with her. Although Anaya was speaking to her aunt, Cam confirmed her request and headed towards the concession stand line and Anaya quickly replaced Kayla's hand with his. Kayla paused for a moment, taking note of how comfortable they looked together.

He asked Anaya if she wanted anything else and naturally, she added fluffy pink cotton candy and lemonade to the order. Cam obliged her without hesitation. The price list for the concessions was displayed on a sandwich board. Lemonade, popcorn and cotton candy were ridiculously priced at $18.00 each since they were served in Teddy collectables and Kayla almost fainted when she saw the price.

"You don't need *all* that sweetheart," Kayla interjected, but the sale had already gone through—a dinging sound emanating from the cash register told her so. Lowering herself to Anaya's level, Kayla prompted her to thank Cam. "What do we say to Cam, Anaya?"

"She already said thank you," Cam answered. Anaya stood right by his side, nodding at Kayla like a bobble head doll with an innocent grin on her face. Her tiny pink lips puckered as she took a long sip from her oversized teacup of lemonade.

The *Teddy's Teatime* theme song began to play on the speakers above their heads. *"It's Teddy's teatime, everybody grab your friends! It's Teddy's teatime, it's time for the fun to begin! Teddy, Ducky, Lamby and Dog—let's call them out one-by-one!*

The lobby quickly emptied out and they followed the moving crowd into the theater. The theater's aesthetic was that of an old school playhouse where one would expect to see a Punch and Judy puppet show. A life size version of Teddy's wood and moss-covered cottage was erected to the right of the stage and her infamous teatime table set for four was placed center stage. The whole scene, both on stage and off, was endearing and Kayla would be lying if she said she was not enjoying herself. One thought prompted another—would she be enjoying herself this much if she and the children had come by themselves as originally planned?

They found three seats as close to the front of the stage as possible. Cam held the snacks and helped Kayla balance the diaper bag as she gingerly lowered herself into the burgundy velvet upholstered seat. She desperately wished not to wake Joseph, although he would probably wake up as soon as the show began. Kayla fished in the diaper bag for Joseph's formula packets to have a bottle ready for when he inevitably woke up. Anaya was bouncing up and down excitedly in her theater seat when her barrette fell out of her hair. Cam graciously kneeled on the sticky floor and began to search for it as Joseph began to stir.

"It isn't easy. I give it to you guys—I really do!" A grey-haired grandmother seated with her daughter and grand-daughter had seen the chaotic moment and was praising Cam and Kayla. She thought they were a family. The four of them *did* look like a family. Kayla could have corrected her, but she didn't, choosing to reply with a lighthearted laugh, "I just keep telling myself it won't last forever!"

"You got that right. It does not, it flies by. Enjoy them!" Her smile was genuinely beautiful, and it struck Kayla that she was there alone without a grandpa-type by her side. Cam climbed back onto his seat victorious in retrieving the barrette which Kayla took and cleaned off with a pacifier wipe before clipping it back in Anaya's hair. Kayla learned when Anaya was born that babies have wipes for everything—butts, noses, pacifiers, hands. You name it, they got it. But it wasn't the various types of wipes that drove her fascination, she felt sparks of captivation from the man seated to her left. This man was also good with children and not married. This man who also happened to her boss and involved in a lifestyle that she knew nothing about.

eleven

Conflicting thoughts whirled around in Kayla's head like an indecisive tornado. The animatronic animals began to take stage and she did her best to quell her thoughts and focus on Anaya whose twinkling eyes were exuberating pure felicity.

As the show began, gape-mouthed Anaya relaxed into her chair, attention fixated on the moving characters on stage as upbeat instrumental music played overhead. Joseph was comfortably cradled in Kayla's arms. He had woken up relatively fuss-free and immediately began sucking away diligently on his bottle, his baby fingers wrapped around the milky barrel, and he held on for dear life.

Cam's profile was in Kayla's peripheral vision, and she noticed the perfection of his slightly upturned nose. A nose that just a few days looked snubbed and bulbous. *Huh. Interesting.*

He must have felt her glare because he leaned over and whispered into her ear. "Best play I've seen in years. The actors are a bit hairier than I usually like, but I think I'm kinda into it."

His sarcastic comment caused Kayla to laugh, but also

piqued her interest because up until that moment, she didn't think he could be funny. But maybe he was, maybe he was a melting pot of things—of really good things and she was just beginning to see him for who he really was, versus the man she had initially painted him to be. Their first interaction was bathed in a cloak of shock and dismay, and she had let it unfairly influence her idea of him. She realized that she had been wrong; she knew better than to judge people.

The show ended with the characters swaying, holding hands and inviting the audience to hold hands together in a chain and sing the 'Farewell Song' with them. The overhead theater lights brightened and two electronic doors on either side of the stage swung open.

As they exited the theater, they were greeted by a 2,000 square foot space that was covered floor to ceiling with *Teddy's Teatime* merchandise. Kayla leaned down to Anaya's level, cradling Joseph's head and neck as she did so. "Honeybee, your brother isn't going to last much longer. Let's walk around for a few minutes and you can pick out a new Teddy stuffed animal or new tea set maybe. How does that sound?"

Anaya nodded slowly and silently in agreement. She beckoned Kayla to follow her to a vendor selling 18-inch stuffed animals and plastic tea sets. Anaya and Kayla were in deep discussion about which one she wanted when the vendor called them forward.

"Which one do you want?" Kayla asked Anaya. Kayla could sense Anaya's anxiety building as she was unable to make a choice. Cam must have sensed it too because he diffused the situation by telling the vendor who happened to be a pretty girl with bronzed skin, high cheekbones, and perfectly winged eyeliner, that he would take all four characters.

All four? Yeah, sure!" The cashier hesitated for a moment before smiling wide to reveal two rows of crooked teeth. She then whipped around to pull the requested toys down from the shelf as Cam pulled out his wallet.

"No, wait! She doesn't need all four!" Kayla explained, placing her hand on Cam's forearm to stop him. "That's really sweet, but she only needs one." Kayla lowered her voice as she continued, "and, um, they are like a hundred dollars. *Each*."

"Yeah, I know kid's toys are expensive. I have a god daughter." Cam gave Kayla a tight smile, as if she was the inexperienced one in terms of child interactions. Anaya began to pull an exaggerated sad face which meant tears were sure to follow.

Cam looked down at Anaya as she slumped onto the floor. The cashier began to help another customer, apparently bored, but not surprised by their disorganized display.

"I think she wants all four." Cam gave Kayla an 'I told you so' face, called back the cashier, and asked her to ring up their original purchase. A bit of fire burning panic began to rise in Kayla's throat at the thought of Cam spending over four hundred dollars on toys. She could not fathom as to why he would spend that kind of money on a child that as of two hours ago was a complete stranger—unless he was trying to impress her, *or* he was a raging pedophile. She hoped it was not the latter, although given her luck she would not have been surprised .

Kayla thanked Cam profusely for the gifts, repeated how it was all too much and made it a point to remind Anaya what a lucky girl she was. Anaya was unable to carry all four stuffed animals, so they snaked their way through the crowds towards the stroller corral where they had originally relinquished Joseph's stroller upon arrival. Kayla tenderly placed him inside, reclining the back to the lay down position and pulled up his navy blue and white striped blanket up to his waist. Cam sidled up next to Kayla as she was bent over the stroller, tucking in a squirmy Joseph and he placed a miniature plush of

Lamby next to the baby. Joseph reached over for the new toy with his perfect little baby hand and brought the plush Lamby to his mouth.

"I didn't realize you bought something for the baby too! I really am blown away, like . . . just thank you. I mean we hijacked your afternoon, and you just came and literally made Anaya's day."

"Of course! It was my pleasure. I had fun," he responded coolly.

"You don't have to lie," Kayla laughed. "I know this isn't your typical definition of fun, but we really appreciate it!" She looked down at Anaya. "Don't we, Anaya?" Anaya nodded enthusiastically in agreement and Cam tousled her hair before glancing at Kayla again.

"Maybe next time you and I can go out by ourselves, you know, minus all the dancing bears and germy kids." Just as Cam was offering that he and Kayla spend some time alone, a toddler walked past them and vomited all over himself. "See what I mean?" Cam said, motioning towards the vomit laden boy who subsequently began to cry. At that, they headed towards the exit. Once back outside onto the sidewalk the sun caused them to squint. They walked in silence for a minute until Kayla realized that she had yet to respond to his comment.

"Oh, and um what you said before, I would really love that."

"You would really love what?" he asked.

"I would love to hang out one day at someplace that is not geared for preschoolers."

He laughed and nodded. "Yeah, okay. Great. Yeah, we will do that."

They continued to walk as Anaya prattled on about her favorite parts of the afternoon. Kayla realized that she had not checked Joseph's pamper in a while and she could also tell that Anaya was getting tired. She pulled over the stroller and bent over to change Joseph quickly while he was still in the stroller. Cam was impressed by her deftness and speed which she found cute.

After a few more minutes of strolling and small talk, they arrived at Cathedral. Cam pointed across the street to where his car was parked and then squatted down to say goodbye to Anaya, who in turn embraced him with a tight hug. He told her he would see her again soon and she nodded graciously, her doe eyes beginning to drop slightly in indication of a much-needed nap. He glanced over and patted a sleeping Joseph on the tummy as he readjusted the Lamby at his side by tucking it under the blanket.

Cam stood up straight, no longer bent over the stroller, and looked at Kayla, silent for a few seconds as he retrieved his car keys from the pocket of his jeans. They both stood in an awkward silence and Kayla realized that she didn't really want him to leave. She also had a sneaking suspicion that he felt the same way. Anaya helped end their lingering moment by proclaiming that she was ready to go home and put on her pajamas. Cam took her not so subtle request as a hint to depart.

"So, yeah, I guess I will see you at the club."

"Yeah, of course! I'll be in tomorrow and Wednesday, and on the weekend too obviously." She was speaking faster than usual and talking with her hands. She wished she could stop.

"Well, I am not too sure when I will be back, but we will catch up soon." He flashed her a grin that lit a sparkler in her tummy and headed towards his car. She stood frozen for a moment before Anaya tugged at her wrist and pulled her back to reality.

"You got all *four* of them!" Celeste exclaimed in a singsong voice. She was bent down on one knee, arms extended waiting for her precious little girl to come running into arms. Kayla loved taking care of her niece and nephew, but seeing the look on their faces when they were reunited with their mother was always her favorite part.

Celeste shot Kayla a look of confusion and shock. "You bought her all four? That is too much Kay!"

"Your aunt is going to spoil you rotten!" Celeste said to Anaya.

"It wasn't Auntie mama, it was . . . it was . . . what's his name again?" Anaya looked up at Kayla with a quizzical look on her face.

"What? *He* who?" Celeste questioned. Lucky for Kayla, the inflection in her voice was that of interest and not agitation. She knew that she was in the wrong for not calling Celeste beforehand and letting her know that someone else would be joining along in their afternoon plans.

"Oh, um, my boss. My boss bought her those."

Celeste smiled, satisfied with the explanation. "Well, well! We are going to have to write Mr. Ben a thank you letter, aren't we? Maybe draw him a pretty picture?" With a gap-toothed smile Anaya agreed emphatically.

"Why did Ben want to go to *Teddy's Teatime*?" Celeste asked, a laugh punctuating her question. But before Kayla could answer, Celeste answered herself. "Oh, wait, he has a granddaughter! Sue Ellen or something like that, right? She came and went with you guys?" Before Kayla could answer, Celeste continued with the questioning. "Oh, and his wife? How is she? She is still sick right? Poor thing."

Celeste had it all figured out, or so she thought and bent at the waist to speak to Anaya. "Did you have fun with Sue Ellen?" Celeste asked. But Kayla responded before Anaya could.

"Um, no. It wasn't Sue Ellen."

"Oh, is it Mary Ellen?" Celeste asked absent mindedly as she lifted Joseph from the stroller and stepped on its' release pedal. The stroller closed up in one foul swoop.

"No, you're right. Ben's granddaughter's name *is* Sue Ellen, but Ben *isn't* the one who came with us." Celeste stared at Kayla with inquisitive arched brows.

"It was, um, the new owner."

"Oh, yeah! That's right! You told me Ben retired. I'm sorry Kay, I can't remember what happened yesterday. They say the mommy brain dissipates after a couple of months, but I'll tell ya, it is really hanging on this time!"

Celeste told Anaya to thank her aunt and then get into the car. Mastering two-step directions was one of Anaya's current target goals and she seemed to be doing quite well.

Kayla picked Anaya up, hugged her tightly and twirled her around a couple of times before setting her down on the ground so she could hop into the backseat of Celeste's silver Mercedes GLE. Kayla occasionally teased her about her quintessential upper middle class stay-at-home mom vehicle.

Celeste turned to Kayla with a questioning look in her eye as she finished strapping Joseph into his backward facing car seat.

"So, who is this new owner? You may have told me, but you know . . ." A flippant hand wave referenced the mommy brain again.

"His name is Cameron." Kayla said, not sure what else she should add.

"How old is his daughter?" Celeste asked as she leaned up against the trunk, both children buckled in securely.

"He, um, doesn't have kids. I mean, not that I know of . . ." Kayla trailed off, pondering her own statement.

"He just ended up coming. Anaya invited him actually."

"Anaya invited him?" Celeste's tone was growing in suspicion.

"Yeah. She had to poop, so we stopped off at the club, and he was there working, and Anaya just took to him I guess and kept asking him to come. So, he did."

Celeste raised one eyebrow high like The Rock in his wrestling days and it almost made Kayla laugh.

"I was going to call you to check if it was okay, but I didn't want to interrupt your alone time."

"I see." Her response indicated that she was awaiting additional information.

"Mommy, come on!" An impatient Anaya bemoaned from the backseat.

"Here, take your tablet." Celeste produced an iPad mini from her leather Coach hobo that sat on the front passenger seat and handed it to Anaya. Kayla knew the next few minutes would be tense as Celeste dolled out screen time extremely sparingly.

"Watch *PBS Kids* or do an *ABC Mouse*. Mommy and Auntie need to have grown up talk for a few minutes."

Uh oh. Grownup talk. That was never good.

"So, tell me about this guy; this new owner with no kids."

"What do you want to know? You're mad that I didn't call you. You're right, I should have at least texted. I'm sorry."

"I'm not mad. I am just interested in knowing more about why your boss is buying your niece gifts?" She adjusted her ponytail through her grey lululemon cap and crossed her arms over her chest awaiting an answer.

"I don't know. To be nice I guess. You would have to ask him."

"Ah, interesting employee bonding tactic. And what is his name, again?"

"Cameron. Cameron Fiorletti."

She was going to Google him the second she left.

"And how old is Mr. Fiorletti?"

"Thirties, I think. Why do you want to know his age?"

"And is he married?"

"Jesus Christ, Celeste! No, he is not married." Kayla hated the defensive edge her voice took, exposing all that she was trying so hard to conceal.

"Oh, my God! Please tell me you aren't doing what I think you are doing. Your boss? Really, Kayla? Really?" Celeste blew out air in annoyance and threw her hands in the air. "You know this is *not* a good idea! Not a good idea at all!" Her head was shaking back and forth so quickly Kayla thought she would get whiplash and she told her as such, but she was not interested in the joke.

"You think this is funny? Fucking around with your employer? And what happens when it goes south? Huh? What then? Have you thought about that? What about your job? Your security? Your apartment?" She was admonishing Kayla so fast, she stopped only because she was out of breath.

"Okay, first of all, calm the fuck down and second of all I am *not* sleeping my boss. Okay? So, you can sweep all your wild accusations right out the door." Celeste glared at Kayla; her lips pursed, and her eyes narrowed into razor thin slits with laser intensity.

"Maybe you aren't right now, but you want to. That is my point."

"Why are you jumping down my throat about this? He just happened to come with us today. It was not a big deal." Kayla decided to leave out the part where he mentioned that next time they should go out alone. But it seemed like Celeste was homing in on the truth.

"Oh, come on Kay. Please spare me the generic bullshit answers. I'm not mom."

Celeste's tone softened as she stepped towards Kayla and placed her left hand, adorned with an overtly heavy rock, on her forearm. Celeste's stare made Kayla uneasy.

"It's just I don't want to see you hurt, okay? I just figured after all that happened with . . ."

She trailed off. Neither of them had mentioned Amir's name in months.

"Oh, and before I forget, could you watch the kids next Wednesday afternoon? If it's too much, I understand, I just didn't want to ask mom . . . you know with Grandma not feeling so great." A grief filled frown bloomed on her face. Celeste did not have to go into detail, they both were aware of their grandmother's fate. She had been diagnosed with coronary artery disease and had a subsequent heart attack. Watching the woman who played such an integral part in their lives slowly wither away was worse than heartbreaking, it was soul shattering.

Kayla agreed to babysit the children and Celeste drew her in for a hug.

"I'm not trying to be a bitch. I swear. I just . . ." Celeste's hands fell away, and Kayla could feel the ghost imprints on her arms. Tears began to well up in Celeste's mascara lined eyes and she paused to collect herself. "I just don't want you to end up like me, Kay. *Stuck.* I don't want you to be stuck like me. My life, my goals—they are all shot to shit now because I have other responsibilities. And maybe if I had a crystal ball, I would have chosen a different life."

Celeste's honesty stung Kayla. She was usually open about her feelings, but not to that extent. Celeste turned around to check on the kids, and Kayla craned her neck to do the same. Joseph's head lulled to the side in deep baby sleep and Anaya was fixated on her tablet, taking advantage of every second of screen time her mother allotted. Celeste's face was serene when she faced Kayla again.

"I know you are smart, just watch yourself, okay? Be smart." She pulled Kayla in for another hug before she walked towards the driver's side of her car, checking both sides of the street before she crossed, even though it was a one way.

twelve

A full week had gone by since Cam and Kayla had seen one another. When their paths finally crossed, Kayla acted calm and cavalier like she had not spent the past seven days replaying their last interaction over in her head. He would never know that her ears piqued with interest whenever she heard the side entrance door creak open, or the twang of hurt she felt when she saw he had stopped by to sign checks, but she had missed him.

On an unseasonably warm Thursday, Cam sauntered into Kayla's office wearing faded blue jeans with large stars at the hem—a signature look of a designer that Kayla knew nothing about, nor could ever afford.

"Hey, Kay! There you are. I was wondering when I would see you again. What are you doing right now?"

"Hey, what's up? I'm just working. What about you?" Kayla inquired.

"I need a change of scenery. Let's go out for a while."

Kayla didn't remember answering him, she just closed out the open programs on her computer screen, picked up her jacket from behind her chair, hooked her purse into the crook of her arm and followed him down the hallway and out the front doors.

The sounds of the city enveloped them as they stepped onto the sidewalk. The heat encased sun caused them to squint at its merciless gleaming light.

"Do you know Marions? It's a steakhouse." Cam turned to look at Kayla inquisitively.

She wanted to respond that of course she knew Marions. She didn't live under a rock, but she also enjoyed having a roof over her head, so paying rent always took precedence.

"Yes, I've heard of it, but I've never eaten there. Isn't it a bit, um, pricey?" Also, eating a steak at 12:30 in the afternoon would most definitely cause her to have the runs, but naturally she left that personal tidbit out of the conversation.

"Well yeah, it's a steakhouse," Cam paused for sarcastic effect. "They are *all* pricey. It's not a big deal though." He shrugged his shoulders to display his lack of concern.

"And, um, I am not exactly dressed properly." In a continued attempt to stall, Kayla looked down at her TJ Maxx blue ensemble and grimaced.

"What are you talking about? You look great! Come on, let's go."

She was appreciative of the compliment but was still wary. They arrived at the restaurant before she had time to concoct another excuse.

The restaurant's logo was backlit with cobalt blue and the LED lights beckoned them to approach. The glass doors that acted as walls were opened wide, black linen lined tables set with gold cutlery and silver metal chairs were lined up inside of the restaurants. The crowd gathered outside was reminiscent of a Saturday night at Cathedral and Kayla told Cam as much. He agreed with her observation and a puzzled look found its way to his face. She gathered from Cam's reaction that the restaurant was not usually that crowded.

"Hold on, let me ask this guy over here what is going on." He motioned to whom she assumed was the matière d, spoke to him briefly and returned to her with a faded smile.

"They are closed for a private event. A corporate networking thing or some shit. I don't know, but I asked if we could just sit off to the side and he said, 'no.' Can you believe that?" Cam was obviously annoyed at not getting his way.

Kayla decided to take the reins and told him to follow her. She dashed across the street like a bunny, avoiding a yellow cab that was hell bent on barreling her down. Once safely on the other sidewalk, she beckoned with a hooked finger for Cam to follow her. He hesitated for a moment, before looking both ways and proceeding to join her on the opposite side of the street.

"That cab driver almost mowed you down. You do know that right? And where are you going?" He was watching her curiously as she began to walk ahead of him.

"Right here." Kayla stood directly in front of a silver cart with a striped umbrella and a Sabrett logo sticker pasted to its side.

Cam laughed and rolled his eyes, turning on his heels to head back the way they came. He began to prattle on about another restaurant he knew of, but Kayla was hungry, and they were already standing in front of something they could eat. It only took Cam a minute to realize that she was not kidding, further evidenced by her feet that were firmly planted in line at the hot dog cart. Kayla was a firm believer that dirty water dogs were (and will forever be) the epitome of Manhattan cuisine.

"Oh, you're serious. Oh wow, okay." Reluctantly, Cam stood by Kayla's side on the line, but his head swiveled around like an owl in hopes of spotting another restaurant. "You really want to eat *here*?" His face was all scrunched up in confusion.

"Yeah, why not? Hot dogs are a perfectly good lunch. What's wrong? Are you too good for hot dogs? Aw, does the master not approve of peasant food?" Kayla teased.

"I mean, yeah, of course I do, but I wanted to take you someplace *nice*. Preferably with chairs and maybe, a plate, or I don't know cutlery, perhaps?"

"I don't *need* to go anywhere nice. I like hot dogs and I actually *prefer* this," she professed, gesturing to the atmosphere around her. The smiling middle-aged vendor called Cam and Kayla next and inquired about their order. Kayla gave him her order, one pink mystery meat dog with ketchup, one warm over-salted large pretzel and a can of Coca-Cola. Cam sighed before placing his order and reluctantly ordered two hot dogs with sauerkraut and a tiny bit of mustard and a peach Snapple. He made sure to tell the vendor that he wanted the Snapple at the bottom of the cooler because it was the coldest. His pickiness made Kayla chuckle and she paid for their food while he was still looking around for someplace better.

Kayla did her best to conceal the sheepish grin that crawled onto her face with the realization that he was trying to impress her. She also quite liked his dry, sarcastic sense of humor. She found it both adorable and unnerving. But there was still a cranial voice that was uttering, 'No, Kayla! Bad! Full stop!' The only problem was that every second she spent with Cam, the voice became fainter and fainter, until eventually she would not hear it at all. Her voice of reason, fully silenced.

With her food held awkwardly in her hand, she walked over to the planter in front of an office building and sat on its ledge. She was fully aware that she needed to have a place to sit before she would get shot a, 'well, what now' face from Cam. He nodded approvingly at her resourcefulness and followed her, seating himself closely by her side, their drinks on either side of their hips.

Kayla cleared her throat dramatically. "I am waiting for you to tell me what a good idea I had," she joked as she nudged him playfully with her shoulder.

"You are right. It was definitely quick thinking. Not exactly the height of opulence, but I'll take it." He laughed, and a tiny piece of sauerkraut escaped his lips. *Maybe he was more like Ben than she had originally thought.*

They sat on that stone planter for close to an hour, people watching and laughing at their sidewalk entertainment. They got up eventually when Kayla proclaimed that her ass hurt, and Cam concurred. As they balled up their garbage to dispose of it in a green metal garbage can on the corner of the sidewalk, they were approached by two overly cheery college students. One was a caramel skinned Spanish girl with salon worthy curls and a denim romper, and the partner by her side was a pale boy with a rounded belly, gelled hot pink hair and crescent shaped sweat stains on his t-shirt. The girl stepped forward and began to speak to Cam and Kayla.

"Hi! Excuse me, we are sorry to bother you, but we are students at the Independent Film Academy," she gestured to the building behind her, "and today we are showcasing two free short films. One of the films is eight minutes long and the other is twelve minutes long. You can choose to watch just one or both, and like I said it is free. All we ask is that you give us your honest review after." The young student seemed eager, young and hungry, and Kayla liked it.

Cam looked at Kayla and then turned back to the students.

He was beginning to tell them that they had to get back to work, but Kayla's hesitation made him change his mind.

Cam shrugged his shoulders. "Yeah, sure why not. It is only twenty minutes. Who knows? We could be watching the next Spielberg."

The students laughed at his quip and they proceeded to thank Cam and Kayla profusely. There was a pep in their step as they led them to the glass entrance doors emblazoned with an Independent Art Academy decal. Kayla had the feeling that not many people had taken them up on their free screening offer.

Cam followed closely behind Kayla, allowing her to enter the school first. They were greeted by harshly bright recessed lighting and polished blonde wood floors. A middle-aged woman sat behind a front desk. She seemed surprised to see bodies heading to the screening room. Kayla assumed she was a teacher and they both smiled at her as they passed and continued to tail the students down a long corridor. They stopped at a room tagged Theater Room 1, and the pink haired boy pushed open the heavy metal door with two tubby, hairy arms and led them into a dimly lit theater. A 120" screen hung against the wall facing about a dozen grey plush theater seats divided into two rows. The students gestured for Cam and Kayla to take the front row seats and they obliged. Kayla suddenly realized that the screening was just for Cam and herself. No one else would be in attendance. The female student turned to face them and began to speak.

"Hi, my name is Jamie Sanchez and this is Henry Billings. We are both second year film students and we just want to say thank you for taking the time to view our films. We will come back to get your honest opinions when the films have ended. We hope you enjoy them!"

The cheery twosome made their way out of the theater and

closed the door behind them. The lights darkened and the screen came to life as a numerical black and white countdown in a large grey circle appeared.

"This is weird, right?" Cam said, trying to squelch a laugh.

"That is what I was thinking. What if they murder us and then film it? Or what if they are going to play a snuff film and they just locked us in here and they are going to force us to watch it."

Cam's eyes widened and his mouth gaped into a shocked, 'O.' "Jesus Christ, I hope not." He began to laugh, but made it a point to look around and point out the exits as the movie began to play.

"The Hamster on the Skateboard" by Jamie Sanchez materialized on the screen. The opening scene was one of a cream-colored hamster on a skateboard whizzing down a street. Crowds were gathered on each side of the street cheering the hamster on as he glided down the street, picking up speed.

"What. The. Fuck." Cam's reaction was pure gold, and Kayla began to laugh so hard that she couldn't catch her breath and began to hiccup. Cam's hand covered his mouth to hold back his sniggering. In the next scene, the hamster was on stage at a comedy show and an audience of people were all clapping for him.

"You have got to be kidding me. What the hell are we watching? This is insane." Cam stage whispered.

Kayla shushed him through her hiccups and laughter, craning her neck towards the door to make sure the students hadn't slipped in during their laughing fit. As her hiccups regulated, she wiped a tear from the corner of her eye. She hadn't laughed that hard in such a long time and it felt nice.

As if sensing the mood in the room had changed Cam's face became more serious and his mouth formed a straight line. He lifted his hand, placed it ever so gently on Kayla's thigh and she froze, her breath stuck within her throat. Her eyes were drawn to his hands, his fingers, the dark wisps of hair above his knuckles and the platinum watch that decorated his wrist. She was too nervous to look up and face him, unsure if she could handle what was waiting for her, but he slowly lifted her chin with a crooked index finger until they were face to face. He did not speak; just intently held her gaze and she watched as his chest rose and fell with each breath. Three breaths later, or what seemed like forever, he leaned in to kiss her. The stubble on his chin scratched at her face, but she found that she didn't mind. His tongue parted her lips and goosebumps formed on her flesh at the taste of him. His pillow soft lips enveloped her and she pivoted towards him so she could easily return his kiss. She felt a want to bite down on his bottom lip but felt it too forward even though his fingertips had already plunged deeper into her thigh.

Kayla's mind was whirring with thoughts as he pulled his lips away from hers. She kept her lips half parted hoping he would return.

"Sorry," he apologized. "I guess hamsters get me going."

Kayla began to laugh again, but she aimed to control herself since she did not want a hiccupping jag to ensue. Apparently, the hamster film had ended, and they were smack-dab in the middle of the next film. The second film depicted a couple arguing with one another in a lush green garden, followed by the woman standing over a gravestone. In the next scene the woman was making out aggressively with another woman.

Cam, evidently not a fan of macabre art, rolled his eyes and whispered to Kayla that they needed to get out of the theater sooner, rather than later. He shot up from his seat and grabbed her by the wrist.

"Come on, follow me." He pulled her in the direction of the

exit and they were greeted by the two students who had been waiting quietly outside the door.

"I am so sorry, but I was just paged, I need to get back to the hospital. But, very fine work guys, really! We loved it when the hamster was on stage at the comedy show. Oh, and the women going at it like wolves after the cemetery scene was truly chef's kiss."

"It was an amazing metaphor for life. Great job guys, really!" Kayla added in for effect.

"Thank you so much!" The students responded excitedly in unison; hands clasped together tightly at their chests. Cam and Kayla hastily walked down the hall, apparently on their way to his imaginary surgical emergency.

Kayla could hear the students talking as we exited the front door. "See, I told you they would get the life metaphor!" The girl ribbed the pink haired boy who nodded seriously in agreement.

When they were finally outside and 'free' as Cam jokingly put it, his cell phone actually did ring and he let go of Kayla's hand to retrieve the device from his pocket. Her fingers remained crooked in muscle memory, saddened to be left alone. And then it hit her, correction *hurdled* into her, that nothing was going to turn out the way she had planned.

thirteen

The first kiss at the film school theater led to many more throughout the following weeks and there was a bit of heavy petting thrown in there for good measure. Hot dogs and pretzels became their daily lunch special and Cam's interest in fancy restaurants faded away. He went from showing up at the club sparingly to stopping by almost daily. They spoke of club matters often, but many of their conversations grew deeper and emotionally charged, as did their feelings for one another.

One afternoon, they were both on a never-ending conference call with Cathedral's overzealous interior designer Hermione Hester. They were having an in-depth conversation discussing décor ideas and designs for the club when the sounds of tiny voices, followed by pounding footfalls and screams of excitement from little lungs caught their attention.

Cam muttered a low, "Oh, shit," and headed out of Kayla's office and into the hallway.

"I am sorry, Hermione, I am going to have to cut this short. We seem to have an unexpected client that has just popped in, but all your ideas are amazing as usual. We can just greenlight everything and as long as we stay on budget, we trust all your designs." Kayla bid her farewell before she could say much else. She felt bad for rushing her off the phone, but she was much more interested in the children's voices that she had just heard. As she walked out of her office and into the hallway, she saw Cam kneeling on one leg in front of a little boy and a little girl. A man about Cam's age looked on, seemingly harried. Both children were Carter's catalog cute with big rosy cheeks.

Sensing her presence, Cam turned around to introduce her to his friend and his three children. He had mentioned Anthony to her in passing and she was excited to meet the person he referred to as his best friend.

Anthony looked like Cam, they could have been brothers, except Anthony's face was overall more attractive and he also had a trimmer waist. But he wasn't dressed nearly as well, and he was frazzled as all hell.

He extended his hand to shake Kayla's as Cam introduced them. He awkwardly hoisted an over-filled diaper bag onto his shoulder and placed a baby carrier onto the floor. Smiling wide, Kayla shook his hand and knelt down to get a closer look at the baby in the carrier, who she learned was nine weeks old.

"Sorry for all the commotion." Anthony said, motioning to the children. The children had begun to run in circles and chase one another. "Their mother isn't feeling well, so I have these little buggers today. This is Emilia, she is four and this is Emilio, he is seven. And this big guy over here is Eamon."

The older children were three years apart, and their names were as similar as their faces. All three of them had sparkling blue diamond eyes which must have been the mothers, because the fathers were green and tired.

Anthony looked down at his children proudly, but they only stood still for a minute before they were off again like they had ants in their pants. Kayla decided not to comment on how all the children's names began with, 'E,' it seemed like Anthony had heard that before.

She smiled at the kids as they ran into each other accidentally and then began to fight by scratching at each other. Anthony tried to separate them, but the baby began to stir, making cat-like noises that would probably become full on wails any moment. Kayla could tell Anthony could use some assistance and she was due to take a break anyway. She also never passed up on a chance to hang out with little humans. The children were running around like feral cats, and as she had predicted, wails from the baby commenced. Anthony began to frantically search for a bottle in the diaper bag. Kayla felt badly for him and hoped his wife would get over her ailment quickly before her husband lost his mind.

"Sorry man, it will just take a minute." Anthony gave Cam a pleading look and returned to the baby. Cam seemed like he felt bad for him as well but was unsure about how to help.

"Listen, if you guys have stuff to do, I can watch the kids." Kayla offered. Cam seemed relieved, but Anthony declined saying that his children, 'could be a lot.' *No shit, I have eyes*, Kayla thought, but chose to smile politely instead.

"I know we just met, but I am really good with kids. They always take to me." She sat cross legged on the floor in the center of the hall next to the baby carrier and took the baby out. She placed the infant in her lap as he continued to cry. She held her hand out so Anthony would give her the diaper bag and she fished out the powder formula container, a water bottle and a baby bottle. She asked Anthony if the baby drank four ounces or six ounces at a time. He returned her question with a blank stare and began to hem and haw before deciding on four ounces, which led her to believe that six ounces was most likely the correct amount, so that is what she made.

Anthony and Cam watched as baby Eamon silenced and

snuggled into Kayla, contented. Emilia and Emilio had ceased fighting although they were still running amuck. When they ran past her she loudly whispered, "Hey guys, do you want to know a secret?"

The children slowed their pace, interested in her secret. They stood in front of her as she swayed their baby brother in her arms. She grabbed a burp cloth from the diaper bag, rolled it up and used it to prop up the baby's bottle and lay it on his stomach so she could make use of her hands.

"If you guys want to know the secret, you are going to have to listen to your Daddy. I know that sometimes it can be hard to listen, but maybe we can sing the 'Calm Down Song' together. Do you know that song?" The children shook their heads with an emphatic, 'no,' and plopped down in front of Kayla, wide-eyed.

"Oh well, I am just going to have to teach you guys then, aren't I?" Kayla checked the milk level in the baby's bottle and then began.

"Okay, listen and watch me." She started to sing. *'Eyes are watching'* and she covered her eyes, *'ears are listening,"* and she covered her ears, *'body's calm'* and she hugged her chest, *'mouth is quiet,'* and she put a finger to her lips. *'This is how we listen, this is how we listen, when Daddy speaks. When Daddy's speaks.'* The children watched her in awe, and she sang the song again, knowing from Celeste that repetition is key with children. She looked up to Anthony, mouthing for him to speak, as it said in the song. It took more prompting before Anthony caught her drift, but eventually he got it and was able to take over to tell the children to stop fighting and play nicely until Daddy was done with Uncle Cam.

"Oh my God, thank you so much! That was amazing! They can be so, well you saw how they can be and wow, just wow!

You have got to teach me that song!" Anthony was practically breathless, and Kayla felt touched.

Kayla stood up with Baby Eamon, patted his back to burp him and told the children that the secret was that in her office she had a treasure trove of candy, which was true. She had a trio of tall glass apothecary jars filled with sugary goodness in various colors and flavors, more for aesthetics than anything.

She did not know how much Anthony knew about her, or about Cam *and* her, but whatever they were, she hoped that she had gained the best friend's vote of approval.

fourteen

As the weeks continued, Kayla and Cam's physical affections for one another were becoming difficult to suppress. Cam wished to move their relationship to the stage where clothing became optional, he verbalized as such whenever he had the chance, but Kayla was nowhere near that step. The lines of their relationship had yet to be clearly defined and she found the fear of being heartbroken again paralyzing—even just in thought. Given her past trauma, Cam would have to be content with making out like teenagers for just a little while longer.

One slow night at the club, they were sitting together on the couch in his office sharing sesame chicken take-out when Cam straightened up. "Oh, shit what time is it?" he asked as he looked down at his watch.

"Almost midnight, I think," Kayla responded. "Why?"

"A few of my boys are going to stop by tonight, but I almost forgot because you've been distracting me," he teased. At that moment, they both heard the emergency exit door creak open. Cam could tell from the loud voices and laughter that poured into the hallway that his friends had arrived. He got up from the couch and stuck his head out of his office, calling them to join him.

Cam's friends were well-coiffed and dressed in designer suits just like he was—the exact opposite of his best friend Anthony. Cam pointed them out to her by name. Kayla's glance lingered on his friend, Lazy, who was the tallest and most attractive of the group. Cam described him to her as his, 'right hand,' and when she later inquired as to why his name was Lazy, he explained that as a kid he had a lazy eye, but it had since been corrected.

After briefly introducing Kayla to everyone as the Manager of the club, Cam plopped down onto one of the plushy armchairs and began to drink in their compliments. They lauded him on his purchase of Cathedral and praised his investment savvy. Kayla stood and smiled awkwardly during the friendly banter, as she was not exactly included in the conversation and felt slightly out of place.

Cam did not introduce the women that were part of the group by name, but every one of them were video model hot and surgically enhanced. Jealousy panged in Kayla's stomach as she compared their beauty to hers. She had a hunch that they were strippers but knew better than to pass judgment— that was until she could *feel* judgment being passed on her.

An ice glare that could freeze hot chocolate was being shot straight in her direction. Cam laughed casually at something one of his friends said and he absentmindedly wrapped an arm around Kayla's waist. Normally, Kayla would be overjoyed if the guy she liked displayed evident PDA in front of his friends, but they had an unhappy audience member, and she was shooting daggers at them with her sepia-colored eyes.

Her name was Delilah, and Kayla was instantly struck by how beautiful she was. Now to be fair, she most likely had one of New York's most adept plastic surgeons sculpt her perfect face and body, but she was still striking nonetheless. Her balayage dyed hair cascaded down her shoulders, ending mid-back with honey blonde tips. A thin, sharp stroke of black liquid eyeliner enhanced her almond shaped eyes and diamond studs adorned her ears. Every time she moved a multitude of gold bangle bracelets that handcuffed her wrist made a slight jingle. Her hourglass figure was beyond enviable, as was the designer berry colored bandage dress that hugged her curves with absolute perfection and further complimented her sandy colored skin.

Delilah was seated on the butter leather couch along with the other women, but she did not seem to care about their conversation because she was fixated on the interactions between Cam and Kayla. After about twenty-five minutes of slanted eyes trained in her direction, Kayla decided that she needed to figure out who this woman was and why she seemed bothered by her presence.

"Can we go into my office for a minute? I have a quick question for you." Kayla whispered into Cam's ear when there was a lull in conversation with his friends. He furrowed his forehead in question but nodded in agreement and excused himself from his friends.

When they were safely ensconced in her office, she shut the door. Cam was right at her heels, keen to find out why she asked to speak to him in private. Grinning, Kayla stepped forward and placed her arms around his neck. Returning her affection and obviously forgetting that she had a question for him, he began to trace his hands over her silhouette. She found it prudent to question him about Delilah at that moment, lest he became further distracted. She placed her palms on his chest and gently pushed him away so that she could create space between them. A look of confusion knitted onto his face.

"So, what is with you and that girl Delilah?" Kayla asked, biting the bullet.

Cam's face morphed into something more serious. "What do you mean? I don't know what you are talking about," he responded with an air of defensiveness.

"That girl Delilah. You know . . . the really fucking pretty one that is currently sitting on the leather couch in your office. And let's just say that if looks could kill, you would be planning my funeral right now." Kayla put her hands on her hips for emphasis and cocked her head to the side, hoping her stance would signify that she would not tolerate another bullshit response. But he was silent.

"I want to know the truth. Is she someone . . . someone that you are involved with?"

"What do you mean by *involved*?" His nose scrunched up like he smelled dog shit. He was stalling and she did not like it. As far as she, or any woman for that matter, is concerned, stalling is synonymous with lying.

"You know *exactly* what I mean. Have you two slept together? Or are you sleeping together right now?" She was going to keep pressing until she received an answer that she deemed satisfiable.

"She used to work at that club that I used to own. But as you are aware I'm selling that club now." He took a deep breath and exhaled slowly.

"And?" Kayla prompted. "Have you two slept together?" Her hands were still on her hips, bracing herself for the answer she already knew was coming. She just needed to hear him say it.

Cam's demeanor softened and he took her in his arms in an attempt to loosen her ramrod straight posture. But he soon let go when he realized that her stony expression would not waiver.

"That's a yes, isn't it?" A shockwave of hurt coursed through her body.

Exasperated, Cam rubbed the back of his neck. "Why are we doing this right now?" He brushed a few strands of hair away from her face before he continued with his reply. "I am more concerned with me and you. Trust me, you have nothing to worry about." He let a crooked finger trail down the length of her stomach as his eyes scanned up and down.

"It has been my experience that when someone tells you not to worry, you should in fact worry. Please just tell me the truth because right now. All I am thinking about is how many times that mouth has been on your dick." Kayla's crassness shocked him, and his posture tensed. Hell, she shocked herself.

"Jesus Christ, Kayla! You really want to have this conversation? You really want to know about all the women I've been with? Really Kayla, really?" He looked taken aback, disgusted even.

"No, Cam, I am not asking about *every* woman. Do not put words in my mouth. I am asking about the woman who is currently in your office and has been shooting daggers at me with her eyes since she got here. Just her. She is the only one I am asking about."

Eventually, he exhaled loudly and procured an answer for Kayla to digest. "It wasn't anything serious, okay? I promise. We just hooked up a few times, purely out of convenience, ya know. That was it." He held up his hands as if in surrender.

"Hooked up like, kiss or hooked up like sex?"

His head lolled to the side, "Kayla, look at me. It was before you, and it meant nothing. Can we please just drop this already because I am *really* starting to lose my patience." He was no longer smiling, and the lighthearted banter had dissipated.

She noticed the quick change in his temperament, and she

hated knowing that he was agitated with her. The only thing she was interested in knowing was the truth.

"Please don't be angry with me," she lowered her voice and pouted her lips in an effort to gain his sympathy. "I'm just saying that I noticed she was staring at us the entire time, but her girlfriends weren't, so it was kind of like a red flag for me." Cam nodded, accepting her retort.

"I don't know if you can tell, but I don't really want to share you." She nibbled at his ear lobe for effect and his agitation began to deflate.

Cam relaxed his body against her detritus covered desk. "We used to, you know, *hang out* occasionally, but we don't anymore. She and I know the same people, but that's it. I am telling you the truth. I mean how could I possibly be with any other women when I am with you practically every day eating those terrible hot dogs and dry ass pretzels."

His joke eased her worries, but she also learned that his mood could shift at the drop of a hat.

"Just don't make problems where there are none. Okay?" He asked, although it wasn't really a question.

Kayla nodded slowly and the radio on her desk dinged, interrupting them before she could say anything else. The bar on the main floor needed Kayla's assistance, so if their conversation wasn't over before, it was definitely over then. Sighing deeply, she headed downstairs to the bar to put out whatever fire had cropped up. Cam gave her a quick kiss and told her he was going to take his friends into one of the VIP sections and that she should come back when she was done.

On her way downstairs, she caught a glimpse of a couple dancing. Their bodies were mashed together as they moved fluidly like merpeople in the sea. Their fingers greedily dug into each other's flesh as the beat dropped. A prophetic vision of Cam and Delilah mirroring the enmeshed couple in front of her caused a Catherine wheel of jealousy to erupt in her body. Kayla rushed over to the bar, so she could rapidly rectify the issue and get back to Cam and keep an eye on Delilah.

Kayla had not attended Bible study in over fifteen years, but she did know that it was Delilah who cut Samson's hair and took away all his power. So, she was fairly certain that Delilah was not a very favorable character in the Good Book. Kayla briefly wondered why Delilah's mother would even give her that name—had she never heard of a self-fulfilling prophecy?

Kayla liked Cam. She liked him a lot, more than she probably should have, but no matter what he said, a part of her still did not believe him. Because at the end of the day he was still a man, and men lie. Amir had taught her that much.

fifteen

Kayla walked around Cathedral's main floor, pointing to random things around her, all in various states of disrepair. She was prattling on, shaking her head disapprovingly and although Cam did not entirely understand her annoyance, he mirrored her agitation. He often just agreed with her because it made her smile and that made her eyes twinkle. He didn't know it was physically possible for an eye to twinkle, but Kayla's did.

Cam could feel there was something different about Kayla, from the first moment he saw her. She possessed a magnetic quality with a force so strong that it was impossible not to gravitate towards her. He would come to realize that it was her purity that he coveted. She was untouched by greed and malice, unlike most of the people he knew, and very much unlike himself. Cam felt like being in her presence cleansed his soul.

Kayla had ceased her complaining about the club's laundry list of issues and was staring at him intently with a wry smile. She looked like the cat who ate the canary, so he asked her what was up.

She clasped her hands together excitedly and told him that she wanted to show him something upstairs. She grabbed his hand and led him to the shower stalls, which felt like a human sized aquarium. The room kind of gave Cam the creeps, but he kept his opinion to himself. Once inside the glass encasement, Kayla turned to face him. Her eyes were wild, bright and filled with that twinkle that he so adored.

She took a deep breath and held her hands in front of her in a 'stop' motion. "Okay, so here it is. This is what I want to do. I want to turn the showers from an eye-sore into a silent disco."

Cam cocked an eyebrow. "A *what*? Isn't that like an oxymoron?" He hadn't a clue what she was talking about. His amateurish knowledge of the nightlife circuit had once again reared its ugly head.

A small chuckle escaped her mouth at his lack of knowledge. Cam could care less what she was going to say, he would approve it anyway. Her idea obviously fell within budgetary guidelines. And if not, he knew that she already had a plan in place to raise any necessary funds. She was resourceful like that. Even if the club was bankrupt, Cam would personally fund any idea Kayla had. He believed in her ideas, in her potential.

"Okay, so a silent disco is like a room in a club where everyone has a set of wireless headphones and there is an area where you can choose what kind of music you want to listen to. Let's say you are in the mood for trance, but I'm feeling more of a hardcore dubstep kind of vibe, we can go to a silent disco and still party together, but listen to what we want."

Cam stood in silence for a moment, processing what Kayla had said. He did not think the idea made much sense, but he was still a novice in the club entertainment department, and her animated energy sold him on the idea. Her velvet smooth voice and vivacious attitude could sell ice to an Eskimo.

In the brief time Cam had known Kayla, she had made an impact on him. An impact so profound that he found her to be the most intelligent woman he knew. Hell, she could probably even go toe to toe with some of the most intelligent businessmen he knew too.

"I know it is kind of difficult to visualize," she continued, "but it has been really successful at a few festivals and the atmosphere is always super chill. I think it would be amazing to have a silent disco room and this area is *perfect!*"

"I love it," Cam interjected. "It is a great idea. It really is. It's innovative and fresh. I'm with it, one hundred percent."

"I am so happy you like it! I was so nervous that you wouldn't get it and think it was silly!"

Cam decided not to tell her that she was correct. He *didn't* get the idea and he *did* think the concept was silly, but she was clapping and bouncing up and down excitedly and the last thing he wanted to do was ruin the mood.

"I guess we should start by having these shower bodies removed," Cam said, motioning towards the exposed pipes.

"Only like half of them work anyway," Kayla said with a shrug as she reached for a lime encrusted silver handle and turned on the shower. The pipe groaned and water began to trickle out. Kayla began to retreat her statement about the plumbing being faulty until the 40" rectangular rain shower head came crashing down from the ceiling. Kayla shrieked and jumped back as Cam simultaneously pulled her away from the crashing chrome metal. Water from the broken shower head began to spew down in torrents. Unable to avoid getting wet, Cam reached for the handle to turn off the water, but the handle popped clear off. Kayla too was unable to stay dry and half her body had become soaking wet.

"Oh, my God! I can't believe that happened! We have to call the plumber!" Kayla began to walk out of the shower stall, but she slipped and landed square on her bottom with a thud. She ended up directly under a stream of water, her head completely soaked and her hair plastered itself. She let out a little yelp and Cam raced over to pull her up from the tiled floor.

At the sight of Kayla appearing like a drowned rat, a fit of uncontrollable laughter bubbled up between them. They caught their breath and composed themselves as they hurried off to the only side of the room that didn't have water gushing from the ceiling.

"I cannot believe that that just happened! I'll call Louie, our plumber. He is gonna lose his shit when he sees this I bet. Let me run downstairs and get us some dry clothes from the merch shop, although I don't know what we are going to do about shoes . . ." Kayla stopped speaking mid-sentence.

Cam had stopped listening to her minutes ago. Instead he was aware that there was only a thin layer of fabric separating him from his conquest, a conquest that he had waited more than long enough for.

Kayla ran a hand through her hair, raking the wet strands away from her face. Cam watched her chest rise and fall methodically as she took slow deliberate breaths. Her fingers began to toy with the fraying hem of her denim mini skirt, and he stepped towards her until they were centimeters away from one another. They both stood unmoving as the tension built between them until it was nearly unbearable. The air was thick with pheromones, and water hailed down behind them assaulting the tile floor with fat droplets.

Kayla backed herself up against the glass wall and Cam followed. She brought her hands up to the sides of his face and tilted her head upwards to kiss him. They both felt the same electric current run through their body as her tongue entered his mouth.

Kayla's breath hitched as Cam slipped his hands under her tank top. He flattened his palms against her wet skin and raised her shirt over her head. Goosebumps rose on her skin like braille and the thin iridescent hairs on her arms stood at attention. His hand found the curve of her breasts and she reached around her back to undo the hooks of her bra. Kayla interrupted their kiss by pushing him back gently with one hand. She slipped her bra off, gathered her breasts in her arms like she was cradling a baby and then let them drop. Before she lost her courage, she undid the button on her skirt and let the heavy denim fall to the tiled floor. Kayla bit down on the side of her bottom lip as she awaited a response from Cam. She had no idea that attempting to be sexy would be so anxiety-inducing.

She thought she saw Cam's eyes widen in intrigue, but he stayed silent which made her think that maybe she had completely misread the situation. Kayla had a myriad of thoughts whirling about in her head, and every single one of them was second guessing her previous actions. A blush of embarrassment tinged the apples of her cheeks, and she cursed every early 2000's rom-com that had inspired her to be so brazen.

Kayla thought Cam's absence of speech was due to his lack of attraction for her less than perfect body. She was unaware that she had rendered him speechless and that he was his tongue paralyzed by the beauty that lay before him. Cam's silence had become too much for Kayla to bear and she crossed one arm over her breasts and the other over her stomach.

"I'm sorry I don't look like the girls you are used to." Doused in humiliation she slowly crouched down to gather her wet clothes, but Cam reached out for her before she reached the floor.

Cam hugged her body close to his with a force that he had

not intended and surprised bloomed on Kayla's face. He gripped her hair in his hand, turning her neck to the side like he was a vampire about to take a bite, but sucked gently instead until she began to giggle.

She whimpered quietly and her hand flew to her mouth as she felt foreign fingers enter her. Cam pulled away from her and she watched intently as he tugged his t-shirt over his head. He undid his belt buckle hastily and it made a tinny clanking sound as it made a connection with the tiled floor.

"Lay down," Kayla instructed quietly, but with command.

As a general rule of thumb, Cam normally despised being told what to do, but something told him that this demand would be to his benefit.

Body self-consciousness subsided, Kayla's sly grin appeared again as she laid Cam's wet t-shirt flat on the ground and patted it as an invitation for him to lie down. She climbed atop him, kissed him once on the mouth and then made her way further down until she had enveloped him in her mouth. Cam would later come to find out that her impressive fellatio skills had come from an oral sex class that she had taken with one of her gay friends and he silently thanked her instructor.

Kayla lifted her head up to look at Cam and began to crawl up towards him.

"Are you on the pill?" Cam asked. He had condoms in his car, but it was parked too far away and they were already naked, not to mention wet.

Kayla nodded slowly, weighing the decision in her head. She knew that she should make him get dressed and go to the car or the nearest bodega, but her hormones were telling her not to ruin the mood.

"Don't worry, I don't have anything. I promise." Cam took her face in his hands and began to kiss her as he laid his body on top of hers. Kayla wrapped her legs around his waist, and he didn't ask any more questions.

Kayla's lips parted and her eyelids fluttered shut as Cam gave into his natural born instincts and made love to her like a princess of a country he just conquered. Not many words were exchanged, save a few clumsy giggles. Cam was a painter and Kayla was his canvas—begging for art. If they could have, the two of them would have remained intertwined within that glass case forever.

sixteen

The day after Cam and Kayla's first amorous interaction, the plumbers removed the shower body, and Kayla began implementing a time frame for the silent disco construction. She was overjoyed that Cam had been on board with her idea, especially since she could tell he hadn't a clue what she was talking about.

There was just one teeny, *tiny* problem. She had let a man —who was not her boyfriend or husband—leave his DNA inside of her. Oh, and she also let him do it every day since, sometimes even twice. The worst part was that Kayla had read enough magazine articles to know that if a man wants to be with you, he will literally go get you. And Cam had not set out to claim her, she just gave herself up willingly without a question. She knew that they should have had the 'what are we' conversation before she let him pluck her flower and she chastised herself for not holding out just a little bit longer.

Saturday night arrived and the club was insanely packed, as it often was when DJ Moxie was scheduled to perform. Kayla still had not spoken to Cam about the status of their relationship and a nagging voice inside of her reminded her that she needed to speak with him, just to get it over with. She decided that she needed to dress the part, figuring that the hotter she looked, the more difficult it would be to turn her down. It was backwards thinking, laden in a lack of self-esteem, but at the time she did not see it that way. Kayla just wanted acceptance. She *needed* it, unaware of how much damage and trauma her relationship with Amir had truly caused.

She paired a beige ribbed dress with a matching corset, and it created the perfect hourglass shape, albeit posing a breathing challenge. When she arrived at the club Cam was already there seated on the couch in his office, legs spread far apart speaking on his cell phone. When he saw her enter his office he perked up and told the other person on the line that he had to go.

"Wow, look at you! I am going to have to keep my eye on you tonight," he half-joked. He got up from the couch and lifted her arm to give her a little twirl, admiring her corset manufactured curves. He enveloped her in his arms and gave her a quick kiss before rambling on about some business deal that he was upset about.

"I shouldn't be complaining though. None of that stuff matters now that my stress reliever is here," Cam said with a laugh. He sat back down on the couch and reached out for her, pulling her down with him. He began to kiss her neck and she knew the next words out of his mouth would be him telling her to lock the door, but that couldn't happen. She needed to say her piece.

"Okay, hold on. Stop for a minute," Kayla said, forcing out a giggle. She lightly pushed him away from her and cleared her throat to begin. "I, um, I want to talk to you about something."

"Oh, yeah? What's that?" Cam asked flatly as he exhaled slowly and leaned back into the couch.

"Okay, so um here it is. I just want to know what *this* is, like what is going on between me and you?" Kayla cast her eyes downward, unable to tolerate his gaze and hoping against all hope that this would not be their last intimate interaction.

"Well, we're having fun. I mean I am at least, aren't you?" Cam trailed his fingers up her thigh for emphasis.

"Yes, of course I'm having fun with you, but that is not what I'm talking about, and I think you know what I mean."

"Baby, listen, I know where you are going with this, but I like the way things are between us now. I'm not really into the whole boyfriend, girlfriend thing. You know that I care about you, and that is all that should matter. We don't need *labels*."

There it was. Exactly what she did not what want to hear and precisely why she had been procrastinating in having the conversation. She had thoroughly enjoyed living in her tiny pink bubble of blissful ignorance, but the poniard had been thrust and her bubble had burst into a million sad little pieces.

"I see, well I should probably get downstairs. It is starting to fill up," Kayla responded, raising herself up from the couch and doing her best to squash any visible emotion.

"Wait. What? You're leaving now?" Cam asked through knitted eyebrows.

She should have kept walking towards the door, retained whatever semblance of respect she had left, but no. Instead, she chose to whip around on her heels and tell him how she really felt.

"Do me a favor. Enlighten me. Are men like you given one generic manual on how to be a douchebag? Step 1, see a nice girl. Step 2, bed nice girl. Step 3, treat nice girl like complete shit. Is that it? Is that how it goes?" If Kayla were a cartoon character, grey smoke would have been billowing from her ears. Her glare was steely, and he advanced towards her, reaching out to grab her wrists, but she yanked them away.

"Kayla, come on. You know it is not like that. Be realistic. I have a busy life. I have a lot going on and when you put labels on things it just messes everything up. And honestly, I can't deal with screaming matches and jealousy and all that other stuff. I'm sorry, I just can't."

"Okay, I get it," Kayla replied sarcastically. "We will just continue having sex every day, but just never publicly commit to one another. Okay. Yeah, cool. That sounds great." She knew she sounded immature, but she couldn't keep her mouth shut.

"Look! You, see? We are arguing already! This is *exactly* what I am talking about. I neither want nor have time for *this*!" Cam's voice was steadily rising, and it fueled Kayla's anger even further.

She threw her hands up in the air in defeat. "You're really infuriating, you know that? And don't raise your voice at me!"

Cam couldn't resist one final jab. "I'm infuriating? Me? Are you serious? Wow. You know what? I thought you were different; I was *really* wrong about you." Kayla could tell Cam regretted the words the second they escaped his mouth. The look on his face was her confirmation.

Kayla's gaze dropped to the floor. Her anger was spent and rapidly dissipating into sadness, a stinging behind her eyes told her so, but the last thing she wanted was for Cam to see her crying.

"Hey, listen . . . I didn't mean it like that. Let's just talk about this, okay?" Cam's face softened and his tone lightened, but Kayla didn't care. He said what he said, and he obviously meant it. A lava hot panic rose in her throat, and she could feel the walls of his office closing in on her. Kayla felt like she couldn't breathe, although that was probably the corsets doing. Regardless, she needed to get out as soon as possible.

"No, it's fine. You said what you said. I have to go anyway; Moxie is going to be on soon."

"Who?" Cam asked with an air of annoyance.

"He is the DJ that is playing tonight, Cam. You would know that if you actually did anything around here. Because so far, the only thing you have put any effort into is trying to get into my pants and you succeeded with that, so congratufuck-inglations to you!" Kayla bent her waist in an exaggerated bow and slammed the office door behind her. She thought she heard Cam calling after her as she jogged down the stairs to the main floor, but she ignored him.

"Kayla, hey! What's up? How have you been?" DJ Moxie asked in his English accent. He was sitting in the Artist VIP lounge, texting on his phone and surrounded by his entourage. He stood up and looked her up and down admiring her dress and it made her blush. They embraced for a hug and a kiss on the cheek. Kayla and Moxie had an aggressive flirtation going on for some time, but then she met Amir and all her prospects turned to dust in the wind.

Moxie's real name was David, and his eyes were every shade of hazel. His mocha skin was pore less and his abs were perfectly chiseled. It should probably be said that Moxie was not the best DJ, but he had a generous female following due to his model-like features and physique, so his shows were always well attended—if not sold-out.

They exchanged small talk, and he visibly perked up when the conversation drifted to Kayla and Amir's break-up. He made it a point to mention that he would be staying at The

Standard for the next two nights. Kayla pivoted around the hotel comment by inquiring if he or any member of his team needed anything before he started his set. She expected him to say that he was all good, but he didn't.

"Oh, yes, love. There actually is something. I heard there is a new owner, and that he has the hook up. Is he here? Or can you call him for me?"

Shit. Shit. Shit.

"Yes, I think he is still here. He is in Ben's old office. Follow me." Kayla said with a forced smile.

Cam's office door was left ajar, and Kayla knocked lightly. He called out for whomever was outside of his door to come in and he seemed surprised when Kayla materialized before him. It annoyed her that a satisfied smirk arrived on his face as he seemed to think that she was returning to him, shrouded in apology and with her tail between her legs. Cam's smug expression dissolved when he saw that she had an overtly attractive six-foot celebrity DJ in tow. There were two other men in the office with Cam and she recognized one of them as his good-looking friend Lazy, and she nodded in his direction.

"Cam, this is Moxie. He wanted to talk to you." Cam shook his hand, and they began to converse amicably. Kayla could feel Cam trying to meet her eyes, but she could not bear to look at him.

Cam gestured to a seat, and Moxie reclined into the plush fabric and told Cam how much he wanted to buy. Kayla took that as her cue to exit and quietly excused herself. There was no way she could have expected what happened next.

"You don't have to leave," Moxie said to her as she attempted to slip away. "We are all mates here. Right, Kay?" Moxie joked with an overzealous laugh. Kayla returned his laugh with a manufactured chuckle, and he patted on the arm of his chair for her to sit. Moxie must not have registered the look of confusion on her face because he stretched his arm around her backside and pulled her into him so that she was perched awkwardly on the arm of the chair.

Moxie's fingers lingered on her thigh for a second as he spoke to Cam about product amount and pricing.

Kayla had been afraid to look at Cam, not wanting to see his reaction, but when she looked up it was not as bad as she had originally thought. It was worse. Much, much worse. Cam's jaw tightened as his fists clenched. Kayla watched as his eyes narrowed in on the spot where Moxie's hand had rested on her thigh. Cam's breathing slowed, and Kayla watched his chest rise and fall methodically. He reminded her of a predator about to pounce on its prey and the hairs on the back of her neck stood up.

"Everybody out." Cam's voice was low and even. Kayla didn't think anyone other than she heard him because Moxie continued speaking, unable to feel the tension that was building in the room.

"You." Cam pointed at Moxie. "Get out of my office."

This time everyone heard him. Lazy and the other man that was in Cam's office walked over to Moxie and stood on either side of him.

"I'm sorry, mate, did I say something? I . . ." Moxie rose from his seat, perplexed.

"I think it's time for you to go now, friend." Lazy gripped Moxie on his bicep and walked him to the door as Moxie weaseled his way out of Lazy's grip. He shot Cam and Kayla a dirty look and walked out of the office, presumably to complain to his agent. Lazy and the other man exited with Moxie, closing the door behind them before Kayla could walk out with them.

"Not you." Cam's voice was even and controlled, and it scared the ever-loving shit out of Kayla.

She spun around slowly, afraid to raise her head and see what lay ahead of her.

"Look at me when I am talking to you," Cam ordered. But Kayla was in no way accustomed to being ordered around and purposely ignored his request.

"Kayla, *look* at me. I am not going to ask you again."

When she could no longer ignore him, she lifted her head and his face was poised inches from hers.

"Do you think this is a joke? Huh? You don't get your way, so you let some D-list celebrity feel you up right in front of me? In front of my boys? What the fuck were you thinking?" Spit spewed from his mouth as he spoke.

"I don't know why he did that. It's not like he and I ever . . ." Kayla's voice came out weaker than she had intended, but she could not control it.

"Oh, no? Because it looks like you gave him the green light at some point."

"Why do you even care?" She shot back, pushing him away forcefully with both of her hands. "You don't even want me, so why does it matter to you who touches me?"

With a palm pressed firmly against her collar bone, Cam shoved Kayla up against the wall. Her body tensed, frightened for a moment as his hand pressed down harder on her chest. Pinned tightly up against the wall, she was left with no exit.

"Who the fuck said I don't want you?" The intensity that raged from him stunned her and she knew he could feel her heart beating through her chest. Kayla's sternum begged to give way from the pressure of his palm, which he eventually moved, but only to punch a hole through the wall out of anger and frustration. There was enough room for her to move away, but she chose not to.

She should have been scared. She should have seen the blindingly bright red flag, but she didn't. All she saw was passion, an intense desire brought on by *her*. She knew it was wrong, but she had never had an effect on anyone like that before and wanted more of it.

"Don't you ever say that again. You have no idea how badly I want you." Cam said through gritted teeth.

Cam turned away from her, muttering expletives under his breath. Kayla knew that she should have left. Hell, she should have submitted her resignation, but instead she hugged him from behind. The heat from his body melted into hers and she ran her hands up his chest before she whispered into his ear. "I don't want to fight with you. I don't want to fight with you *ever*. I just wanted it to be me and you. That's all. Me and you, and no one else."

Cam turned to face her, exhaled deeply and leaned his forehead into hers as his arms interlocked tightly around her spine. She felt safe in his embrace again and didn't realize how much she had missed him in the hour that they were mad at each other.

"I wanted to kill him when I saw him with his hands on you. Do you know that?" Cam whispered into her ear. "Kayla, I *need* you to understand who I am . . . and what I'm capable of."

"I'll never do anything to upset you again. I just need to know that you are mine," she responded, her breath hot on his neck. She had brandished her heart on her sleeve for the second time that night.

"I've been yours since the moment I saw you," he replied.

No one had ever said anything like that to her before and she let that phrase enslave her.

Kayla felt renewed by her honest conversation with Cam. Their relationship quickly kicked into high gear, exactly the way she had hoped. They had your typical dinner and a movie date nights and sleepovers. Sleepovers always took place at his state-of-the-art Brooklyn Heights condo, even though Kayla only lived a few blocks away from Cathedral. Cam said he preferred his apartment, so she didn't argue. He even cleared out a drawer in his bedroom dresser for her and gave her the whole medicine cabinet in the guest bathroom.

Cam was good to her, and she believed him when he said their arguments would never become explosive again. The only issue that gave her pause was that Cam's friends/employees had begun to hang out at the club quite regularly, which meant that Delilah kept returning like a bad habit. Thankfully, the public evidence of Cam and Kayla's relationship seemed to have tempered her fire. For now, anyway.

seventeen

The next month was exactly as it should have been—the emotional intimacy was constant; the laughter was frequent and the thirst for knowledge about one another was unable to be quenched.

Things between Cam and Kayla were at an all-time high and she was enjoying riding the crest of the wave.

After Kayla and Cam's volatile argument, they were rarely apart, and she barely stayed at her own apartment. With Kayla around, the services of Cam's long-time housekeeper who came three times a week was no longer necessary. Kayla cooked and cleaned his apartment, taking on all domestic duties. She had felt bad initially about the housekeeper losing her job, but when she spoke to her about it, the housekeeper admitted that she was happy that Cam had found a nice girl because she had begun to think that he was gay. Kayla decided it was best that she kept that conversation to herself and not share the housekeeper's comments with Cam.

Occasionally, Kayla would think back to when Cam claimed that he didn't even want to be in a relationship and now they slept in the same bed together practically every night. Kayla stayed at his apartment so often that he began to feel bad about her paying rent for an unoccupied apartment, so he took over the payments. She had protested, telling him it was too much, but he waved her protests off, stating that it wasn't a big deal, and she should save her money for herself.

Thankful to God for sending Cam to her, Kayla had even begun to pray again. She even opened up to her girlfriends and told them all about him—well, the good things, anyway.

When he finally met her friends for lunch one afternoon, he turned on the charm, and even upped the wattage some. They were won over, and practically swooned over him within the first half hour. Under cohesive agreement, they sent Kayla approving texts afterwards. With positive affirmations from her girls, there was only one step left, and that was for him to meet her family.

Unfortunately, things can only go right for so long until something goes so wrong you are forced to reevaluate *everything*.

eighteen

On an abnormally windy day, Kayla's grandmother died. She departed from this Earth around twelve noon, when the sun was the highest in the sky.

The English language has yet to create words that can properly describe the level of grief and emotion that Kayla felt during that time. There would be no point in trying; any attempt would be futile.

Cam held Kayla after her knees gave out and she collapsed on his kitchen floor upon hearing the news via telephone. Kayla's mother was the bearer of this gut-wrenching news and she was barely audible, throaty sobs taking precedence.

Cam laid next to Kayla the whole night as she sobbed into the pillow. He never really offered any words of comfort; he just stroked her hair and listened to her—and that was all she ever really needed.

"That's not a problem, right?" Cam looked at Kayla sidelong with arched eyebrows. He was uncomfortably awaiting her response as he chewed his gyro, absentmindedly flicking an errant cube of chicken from the Styrofoam take out container onto the floor.

When her expression went from tepid to something a bit darker, Cam put down his gyro, sucked some runaway tzatziki sauce off his thumb and gulped a bit too loudly for Kayla's liking. She stopped eating as well, pushing her moussaka forward and chewing on the tines of her plastic fork for a few seconds before sticking it straight up in the mashed potatoes. Cam eyed her fork cautiously.

"It's just that I haven't been to a funeral home since my mom and . . ." Cam's voice trailed off, but Kayla wasn't sure she believed his excuse.

"Nope. No problem at all." There was no way she could have delivered her response more flatly. He seemed unsure of his next move, which was very unlike him. Buckets of trepidation filled his eyes as he dared to continue speaking.

"I just figured your grandma's wake would be a weird time for me to meet your parents . . . your whole family is going to be there, and they are all going to be so sad. It's just too awkward." He rubbed Kayla's thigh in a way in which she was sure he intended to be comforting, but he missed the mark. He was *way* off.

"Okay, yeah sure. I wouldn't want you to do anything you are not comfortable with." Kayla had hoped he heard the molasses thick sarcasm that layered her words, but it seemed to have gone right over his head, as he breathed out a sigh of relief.

"I knew you would understand." He kissed the side of her head and returned to his lunch, dipping a thick hand cut fry into a glob of generic brand ketchup. He had a dollop of white sauce that looked like bird shit on his left cheek and Kayla chose to not tell him about it.

Men have a funny way of taking one step forward and a *thousand* steps back.

nineteen

Seeing how loved Kayla's grandmother had been by others warmed her to the core. Kayla could feel her grandmother's presence as she lay comfortably in her casket, a mahogany box of eternal rest until the end of time. She could also hear her judging people's outfits and taking note of who came and who did not. She was a character like that, a real spit fire. How Kayla wished she had but an ounce of her gusto, a tinge of her resilience. It was past dinner time when the second half of the wake ended. Kayla's somber family seemed slightly uplifted by the visible love bestowed upon them as friends and family paid their respects.

As the night ended, they thanked the Funeral Director and his assistant, and told them to have a good night and that they would see him tomorrow afternoon for the second and final night of the viewing. Families rarely waked their loved ones for two days anymore, but Kayla's grandmother had always believed that two days was the proper amount of viewing time, so that is what they did.

Kayla was originally set to stay at her parents' house that night, but she wanted to see Cam. He had called and texted her words of encouragement during the day, but she missed him. She wanted to feel his arms around her. She wanted the kind of comfort that only he could provide.

She told her parents that she was going to meet up with a couple of her friends and would meet them back at the funeral home tomorrow and her parents were too emotionally spent to rebuff her.

Kayla called and texted Cam while on her way over to the club, but he had yet to return either method of communication. When Kayla arrived at Cathedral it was well after 10:00 p.m., and the club was still relatively empty. She made a bee line for Cam's office, but he was not there, so she headed towards the VIP lounge.

Kayla pulled on the silver door handle and the heavy door swung open. Kayla was immediately struck by what she saw. When Cam saw Kayla, he shot forward from his reclined position on one of the couches and stood up so fast he bumped into the glass table in front of him. His face was riddled with guilt and nervous surprise. A laughing Delilah was seated by his side while the rest of his friends were scattered throughout the room.

"Kayla, hey! What are you doing here?" Cam sniffed nervously and wiped his nose with the back of his hand. Kayla could tell he had been sniffing something. The cut up white lines of powder on the table confirmed her beliefs.

She attempted to stammer out a response, but nothing came. Cam had thrown a javelin of deceit with the deftness of an Olympic gold medalist straight through Kayla's heart. Kayla stood frozen in time as Delilah stood up next to Cam. Her long, French tipped nails and slender fingers made their way around Cam's torso while she pressed her fake breasts into his back and leaned her face against his shoulder.

Delilah pursed her lips and narrowed her eyes in Kayla's

direction, an evident challenge. A villainous-like smile eerily crept onto her face as if she had just won a game that Kayla didn't even know they were playing.

Kayla's fight or flight response took over and her brain chose flight. She fled as quickly as she could, like the lava flows of Pompeii were on her heels. Cam had taken off after her, calling her name at least three times before she could no longer hear him anymore. She had seen him shrug Delilah off before she bolted, but it made no difference. She saw what she saw.

Kayla wanted to leave the club before anyone could see her; before anyone could notice the film of shame on her face. The club had begun to fill up, so she had to squeeze through the writhing bodies speckled with beads of perspiration, as her tears created roadways down her cheeks.

Kayla held her breath until she was outside in the night air, and she almost fell to her knees in the middle of the street when she finally exhaled again. Steadying herself against a brick building down the street, she let the images of Cam and Delilah wash over her and pollute her mind. Her phone began to ring and she knew it was Cam without even having to look at the display screen, so she powered off her phone—something she never did.

Kayla couldn't believe how stupid she was. She had lost her grandmother, her boyfriend and, considering she could never face Cam again, she had also lost her career—all in the same day. That must have been some kind of world record.

She didn't know what to do next, she just knew that she needed to numb the pain.

twenty

Kayla did not want to go home; the silence in her apartment would eat her alive. She wanted to hide someplace dark and with a bass so loud she wouldn't be able to think clearly even if she tried. Normally, Cathedral would be the perfect place to scratch that itch, but that wouldn't work for obvious reasons. The closest place she could think of was a seedy underground trance club whose name she couldn't even remember. She cried the entire time on her walk over to the club and she must have really looked a fright because the bouncer of the club allowed her entry without so much as a word or a pat-down. She spent an undisclosed number of hours at the club and made questionable decisions, one of which was accepting drugs from a man she met on the way to the bathroom. She knew all too well the consequences that would creep up in six to eight hours if she decided to anesthetize herself with MDMA while in such a state of melancholy, but she didn't care. Kayla spent the night and early morning hours dancing on men, *and* women, of all ages, races and socioeconomic statuses. She kissed three, maybe four strangers. She didn't remember the exact number because she wasn't really keeping count. She made a lot of friends and gave her number away to God knows how many people, but she thought about Cam the entire night.

Eventually, when she felt like her legs could no longer hold her up, she decided to toddle home. Unable to walk a straight line, she took on the gait of a drunken hobo. As she labored down the sidewalk, Kayla wondered why it had not occurred to her to hail a cab. The sun shone blades of gold straight through her eyes, lighting her astigmatism on fire. She held her hand up to shield her eyes until she finally saw her apartment stoop.

She stopped short, her feet froze on the sidewalk and her heart palpitated when she recognized Cam's car parked directly in front of her building. Her eyes zeroed in on the 'CF' imprinted on the license plate, as exhaust fumes from his car ascended in a spiral towards the ozone. She was genuinely surprised to see him there, considering she had turned her phone off hours ago and had no idea what time it was. Judging from the number of people on the street dressed in suits and holding coffees, she deduced that it must have been well into the morning.

She walked past Cam's car, choosing to pretend as if he were not even there. Her anger, which had never really subsided, began to percolate again. She realized that he had spotted her, just as she spotted him because the humming engine of his car died out, along with the radiant red brake lights. The driver's side car door swung open, and Cam emerged while he simultaneously called out Kayla's name. He was the last person that she wanted to see.

"What are you doing here?" she asked rhetorically. "I don't want to see you and I don't want to hear anything that you have to say." She stuffed her ears with invisible cotton, immune to his pleas—regardless of how genuine they may have sounded.

"Kayla, baby, please stop!" He blocked her path, side-stepping with her in unison so she was unable to get past him.

"I've been waiting here all night. I was so worried about you. Where have you been?"

It was then that she noticed the size of his pupils and the monotonous clicking of his jaw. He had continued to imbibe on white powder, either to stay awake or to numb the pain. She could not exactly blame him, as she had partaken in a numbing agent of her own. She had not planned on seeing him, in fact, throughout the night she had gone over scenarios in her head in which she would resign over e-mail, imagining what it would be like never having to show her face at Cathedral again.

The drugs had completely altered her senses and she did not feel like she owed him an explanation, but that did not stop his probing questions.

"You didn't answer me. Where were you? Why did you turn your phone off?" Cam asked, his tone even, but far from relaxed.

"I need to go," was all she managed to say, unable to look him in the face.

"Kayla, please, would you just listen to me for, like, two seconds?" He reached out to hold both of her arms, trying to get her to acknowledge him. "I don't know what you *think* you saw, but nothing was happening. I swear to you."

"Just leave me alone," Kayla croaked out, breaking away from his grip. She was in no mood to have a conversation, let alone an in-depth one.

"Would you please just let me explain?" Cam had gone from calm to exasperated in a mere matter of minutes. "Wait. Wait, look at me. Are you fucked up?" He slouched and ducked his head down to try and get a better look at her face, but she pushed him away before he could.

"It does not matter what I am and there is nothing to explain! I saw her hands all over you and you two were sniffing coke together. I am not stupid or blind," she retorted. "I am angry with myself, not you. I knew something was wrong when you didn't answer my phone call or text. I know now that it was because you were with *her*."

His eyebrows narrowed and a quizzical look formed on his face, but he remained silent.

"It doesn't matter. I'm the idiot," Kayla continued. "I should have listened to you when you said you weren't good at this relationship stuff, because you were right—you're not."

"Kayla, baby, come on," Cam reached out for her again, but his advances forced her feet to step in reverse.

"All I wanted was for you to not sleep around, but oh no no, you just couldn't help yourself, could you?"

"I haven't touched anyone else since I met you. I am not lying, I swear!" Cam seemed manic, as if for the first time in his life he was faced with a decision that would not go his way.

It was damn near impossible to cry with MDMA in your system, but low and behold Kayla had eclipsed that impossibility. She didn't want him to see her crying, but she couldn't keep the tears from pouring out. Fat, ugly tears laden with genuine heartache landed on her cheeks.

She didn't want to be around him anymore, so she pushed past him to access her stoop, but he grabbed her forearm and held on so tightly that she didn't even bother to try and wriggle out of his grip. When he saw that she was subdued, he released her and she rubbed the area where he had grabbed her with her other hand.

"Would you please just listen to me," he pleaded. His hands were steepled together and he was practically begging, which she had never seen before.

Then it hit her. How could she have been so blindly unaware? Without her, Cam would not be able to make connections with DJ's. How could she have forgotten this? He had literally told her that was his plan and then he implied that he would sell Cathedral and move on to the next thing. How had she not realized that she was a pawn in his chess game?

"Why? Why should I listen to you? You used me to make your connections. You never cared about me," Kayla fired back. "You made a fool out of me—in *my* own club!" She had begun to pace back and forth on the sidewalk, and they were catching the attention of people on the sidewalk.

"Please, Kayla. I need you to calm down. Let's talk about this rationally."

"You can't tell me what to do. I'm not your girlfriend anymore." The taunting manner of her words were immature but laced with genuine hurt. Every part of her body, both physical and spiritual, was seething with pain.

"Come on baby, please don't say that." Cam looked like he was about to cry, and it unnerved her.

"Why not? Why shouldn't I say that?"

"Because I fucking love you, that's why!" Cam yelled back at her with fervor, fists clenched tightly in frustration.

"What? What did you say?" Kayla's mind took a minute to register what Cam had just blurted out.

"I think, no I know that I'm in love with you, Kayla," Cam said in a much softer, passive tone.

The ligaments in her knees began to give, barely able to keep her body upright as he continued his confession.

"I'm all messed up when I am not with you. I can never seem to get you out of my head. I feel things for you that I have *never* felt with anyone else." He paused, allowing her a chance to respond, but her tongue was frozen in place, so he

147

proceeded to speak in a hurried cadence, maybe due to the drugs coursing through his system.

"I don't even think about other women, and I haven't been to a strip club in I don't know how long. Shit, I can't even remember the last time I watched porn." He seemed surprised at his own omission, and coming from Cam, his words seemed almost poetic. Kayla watched as his body plopped down onto the concrete stairs of her front stoop. His elbows balanced on his knees, and he rested his forehead in the palms of his hands. He exhaled loudly as if he were completely spent.

"You . . . you love me?" Kayla questioned in disbelief; her face twisted in confusion. After her engagement with Amir had dissolved, the idea of being in love again seemed like an impossible notion.

Cam lifted his head in a controlled manner and studied her. He rose from the stairs and walked over to her, and they both paused before he drew her close to him. She wrapped her arms around his neck and pressed her body up against his; she could hear the grinding of his jaw and the beating of his heart. He smelled faintly like designer cologne and regret, and she probably smelled like a farm.

Cam's bear hug was Spanx tight, but he leaned back slightly and steadied his gaze on her intently. He pressed an index finger to his temple, "you are the *only* person that lives in here."

twenty-one

Once Cam admitted his love for Kayla, she told him that she felt the same way, even though the kind of love that she felt for him was new to her. Couples have explosive fights in the beginning, that was normal. Amir and Kayla had never argued the way she and Cam did, but she reminded herself that it was impossible to compare the two. When she was with Amir, they laughed constantly and she could be silly with him. There was no expectation. With Cam it was different. He offered her a sense of security that she never had before. And maybe that was what true love is really like.

As their relationship bloomed, they did all the things typical New York couples do. They frequented Broadway shows, art and history museums and Chelsea Piers. They walked around the visually stunning Central Park and the lush and colorful Botanical Gardens. They gawked at the animals in The Bronx Zoo and the sea life in the Brooklyn Aquarium. Kayla knew that they toured a vineyard in Long Island, but she became wine-drunk and hardly remembered anything about the trip. They took pottery and cooking classes together and visited the estate sales and farmers markets in Westchester. They did everything together, hand in hand, shoulder to shoulder. They even spent Thanksgiving together in his apartment, just the two of them,

Thanksgiving Eve is also known as Blackout Wednesday, and it is the most popular party night of the year. After years of working at Cathedral, Kayla's parents no longer expected her home for Thanksgiving. She was either too hung over or too tired to attend a family function so she would stop by for leftovers the next day. But for Cam, she was able to cook an entire Thanksgiving meal for the both of them after two measly hours of sleep. Yet, in the past she was unable to ever muster up the energy to make it home to be with her family, even when her dad would offer to pick her up and bring her home.

Thanksgiving turned to Christmas in the blink of an eye. Their waistlines had increased slightly, but Kayla took it as a sign that she and Cam were happy, comfortable, and secure in their relationship.

Cam had agreed, albeit reluctantly, to let Kayla decorate his apartment for Christmas, so naturally she went all out. As she transformed his apartment into a winter wonderland, he acted like it was an annoyance, but the medley of Christmas lights aroused a sense of warmth in their dwelling and she could tell he liked it, even though he didn't say as much. He could no longer hide his budding Christmas spirit when he and Kayla bought her niece and nephew gifts. Kayla could barely keep up with his energetic pace as he circled around the toy aisles, his arms full of presents for the kids. Kayla found it endearing that he wanted to shop for the children, but she was touched and equally taken aback when Cam offered to buy gifts for her parents and sister as well. The touching offer prompted her to invite him to her parents' house for Christmas Eve. They had halted on the parental introductions since the idea fell flat when Kayla brought it up around her grandmother's wake. They had not mentioned meeting her parents to one another much since then. But Kayla's mother knew she was seeing someone and she had been nagging her during their frequent phone calls about when she would meet her daughter's 'friend.' Filled with yuletide spirit, Kayla agreed to bring Cam over for Christmas Eve dinner. Not only would it be the first time that he would be meeting her parents, but it would be the first time he would meet almost every family member within driving distance. Introducing him to her family was the necessary next step and she was ready. As a precursor, they both agreed to tell her family that his money came from his mother, which was mostly true. He could pretend for a day to be a trust fund baby who knew how to play the stock market. It was a better alternative to the truth, anyway.

It was December 23rd, colloquially known as Christmas Eve Eve, and the sun had yet to make its appearance for the day, but Cam was an early riser.

At this point in their relationship, Kayla was aware that Cam often felt most amorous first thing in the morning. Their interactions were routine and devoid of any experimentation. She often awoke to the sensation of fingertips tracing the outlines of her silhouette and that morning was no different. She could feel Cam's chest pressed up against her spine and she welcomed the light kisses that dotted and tickled the back of her neck.

"Good morning," he whispered into her ear. Kayla rolled

onto her back and her eyes caught his, that were intense and smoldering. Cam moved to reposition himself on top of her. His intention was to place his arms on either side of her body, strong and sturdy like a swimmer exiting a pool, but his right hand slipped on the silky top sheet. Kayla felt a sudden pressure on her jugular veins as his palm landed at the base of her throat. His forefinger and thumb splayed out over her neck. As soon as he realized what had happened, he jerked his hand away as if he had touched a hot stove.

"Oh, shit! Are you okay? I'm sorry, baby. I didn't mean to do that, my hand slipped." When she assured him that she was fine, he cursed their Egyptian cotton sheets and moved his hand back to its starting position, eager to refocus his mind on their activity.

"No, come back. I liked it." Her legs locked around his waist and she pulled his wrist back towards her neck, hoping his fingers would latch on.

She had read about sexual asphyxiation in *Cosmopolitan* and heard about it on late-night television talk shows. Truthfully, she wasn't all that sure that she *did* like it, but Cam was not adventurous in the slightest when it came to the bedroom, and she didn't see the harm in spicing things up a bit.

"Baby, stop. I don't like that," he said quietly, wrestling his wrist from her grip. He lowered himself down to kiss her, but she ignored him and asked him to do it again.

"No. Stop it. Come on, you know I don't like that kinky shit." He tried to redirect her, but she persisted. She should have left well enough alone.

"Jesus Christ, Kayla, what the fuck? I said I don't want to do that! Are you fucking deaf?" A deep dark anger grew behind his eyes, black like mold. Cam scrambled out of bed like he saw a spider, knocking the comforter to the floor. He was unable to hide his look of disgust, like a bigot watching an interracial couple kiss.

At the edge of the bed, she clamored to her knees as her anxiety began to boil over. "But why are you so mad? I don't understand." The look of shock that spread across her face displayed the confusion she felt.

"Why am I mad? Really? What in the actual fuck? What is *wrong* with you?" Cam was yelling, spitting mad. She had not seen him like this since Moxie's hand had found her thigh.

"There's nothing wrong with me," Kayla spat back. "We always do *whatever* you want. Why can't we do what I want for a change? I don't see why it is such a big deal."

"Not a big deal? Not a big deal?" His voice was rising steadily. The blackness that began in his eyes quickly consumed his entire being. "You don't think it's a big deal to strangle another human being? Do you have any idea how dangerous that is? And you want to do it to get off? What is wrong with you?"

Kayla's cheeks and chest flushed crimson. He was right, she didn't know why she thought it would be fun. What *was* wrong with her?

"I . . . I don't know. I just saw an article in a magazine," she stammered. "I thought it could be fun . . ." Kayla trailed off, realizing that there was no use in an explanation. She sounded foolish and immature, and he was still glaring at her in disgust. And maybe he was warranted in his feelings, but she was intuitive enough to know that whatever was going on with him was much deeper than face value. She moved to embrace him, but he recoiled.

"Just don't, Kayla. I'm going to take a shower." He threw his hands up in surrender and slammed the door shut behind him, causing her to jump. They never closed doors in the apartment. They even left the door open to talk to one another while on the toilet.

Uninvited, Kayla opened the bathroom door and walked in, but Cam gave no indication that he registered her presence.

She pulled the frosted glass shower door ajar and stepped in behind him. He was washing his face under the stream of water and his hair was spiked with lathered shampoo. Her arms found their way around his torso, and she positioned her toes to his heels and her chest to his back. Her body had become spotted with water, and she raised herself on the tip of her toes so that her chin could nuzzle the space between his neck and shoulder. She whispered into his ear, as a drop of water dripped from his ear lobe. "I'm sorry baby. I shouldn't have argued with you. I'll never try to do that again. I promise."

She was not quite sure what she was apologizing for, as it was his *reaction* that was the problem, but she decided that it was not the time to add fuel to an already blazing fire.

Cam's posture relaxed and his shoulders slumped forward displaying submission. She took his eased stance as a sign to plead, as gently as she could, for him to tell her why he got so upset, but he remained mute. Still behind him, she trailed his left trapezoid with wet kisses. "We don't have to talk about this now, if you don't want to. Do you forgive me, at least?" She hoped the request delivered in a baby voice would further ease the tension. But this happened to be another wrong move and they were still within the 6:00 a.m. hour of the morning. There was no way she could have prepared herself for his response.

"Are you some kind of pervert or something?" His tone was even, dark and sardonic.

"Wha . . . what?" She managed to squeak out, unsure that she heard him correctly.

He whipped around with a quickness that almost knocked her over and she stumbled into the tiled wall. He was sneering, baring teeth like a wild animal.

"I didn't stutter. You heard me. Now tell me the truth. I need to know right now if the woman I let sleep in my bed every night is some kind of freak or sexual deviant or something." His finger pointed at her accusingly.

"No, of course not!" She yelled back. "Why are you acting like this?"

The shower water streamed down in the background but was no match for the tears that fell from her eyes.

She prayed for Cam's domineering stance to lighten. The last time she had a finger pointed in her direction like that was the altercation with Amir's father. Luckily at that time, she could not understand the words he spoke. She wished that were the case now. She would have loved for a language barrier to suddenly appear, to save her from the vile questions her lover spat in her direction.

She must have apologized a dozen times, begging for just an ounce of understanding, but none seemed to be delivered. She tried to hug him again, but he pushed her away and her emotions eclipsed from apologetic to frightened.

Kayla started to back away from him but was only able to make it a few steps. His shower was big, but not *that* big. With nowhere else to go, and Cam positioned in front of the glass door, she slid down the wall onto the tiled floor. Cam stood over her, still pointing, questioning her morals and hovering over her like a vulture feasting on a fresh carcass.

Kayla's hair hung from her head like a sopping wet crown of shame. Cowered down into the white square tiles, she had taken to hugging herself. She sat with knees under her chin, and she secured her arms tightly around herself in a protective,

"X." She was afraid to look up at him, afraid to see the man that she loved seething in anger, filled with revulsion. She started to tremble, and her teeth began to chatter.

"Next time I say 'stop,' you stop. We are not going to have this problem again, okay? Do you understand me? I'm serious, Kayla. Try anything like this again and you and I will be over so quickly, it will make your head spin—and then you really *will* be out of a job. Do *not* test me." He stepped around her in the shower stall and left the glass door open as he exited. He grabbed a mauve colored towel to tie around his waist and stomped back to the bedroom.

Fear had overtaken her, and she felt too scared to leave the bathroom. Unfortunately, the drain was not big enough to swallow her whole and she knew she would eventually have to exit the shower stall of shame to face her scarred king. She took the other matching towel from the rack, wrapped it around her body and took a few slow controlled breaths in front of the foggy mirror. She could hear Cam moving around the bedroom, opening drawers and getting dressed for the day like he did not just threaten to end her livelihood if she ever questioned him again.

Cam re-entered the bathroom fully dressed in a faded black PRPS crewneck sweatshirt and motorcycle jeans. He came up behind her, wrapped his arms around her waist. He leaned his head against hers are we they stared into the medicine cabinet mirror.

"I'm sorry I got so mad. I know your intention was not to upset me," he offered in a way of an apology. Kayla spun around to face him and he pouted jokingly before leaning in to kiss her. She returned his gesture with an obligatory kiss, but she was still rife with unease at the number of questions left unanswered.

"Why don't we go get breakfast? We can go to that French café place you like. You can get a croissant." He said croissant in an exaggerated French accent and laughed to himself. Kayla laughed too even though it wasn't very funny, but she did so because she knew it was the expected response.

Cam and Kayla left his apartment building hand in hand like she was not just cowering in a fetal position in the shower twenty minutes earlier.

At the café, Cam ordered them poached eggs and brioche. He forgot to order her croissant and she didn't bring it to his attention. They kept the conversation light. It was evident that the past incident was not a topic that would be revisited.

They stayed home the rest of the day. The feeling of warmth that Christmas had brought into the apartment had become tepid at best. Cam relaxed in the living room as Christmas movies played in the background and Kayla busied herself in the kitchen preparing dishes to bring to her parents' house for Christmas Eve dinner the next day.

When they turned in for bed and flicked off the lights to go to sleep, she felt his arm wrap protectively around her rib cage. He pulled her into him, and the heat of his body burned against hers.

"You know that I love you, right?" Cam said in a lowered voice that was not quite a whisper. She was certain that that was the closest to an, 'I'm sorry,' that she would receive, so she accepted his apology—in the spirit of Christmas.

She snuggled up against him under the covers and told him that they should get some sleep. The next day they would be braving the holiday traffic to New Jersey, which was always a nightmare. A combination of Cam's steady breathing and her emotional exhaustion lulled her to sleep. They fell asleep with their legs intertwined like puff pastry and Cam's arm slung over Kayla's chest.

twenty-two

When Kayla awoke it was the middle of the night, or very early in the morning, it would depend on how one would look at it. Cam's body was not next to hers and she figured he might have been in the bathroom, but it too was empty—and there was no reason for him to use the hallway bathroom.

After a minute, she whipped the comforter off of her body, sad to leave her den of comfort behind. She sleepily padded towards the bedroom door and paused momentarily when she heard a faint voice coming from the living room.

Quickly she walked down the darkened hallway and peered into the living room to find Cam standing in front of the window. He was on the phone, speaking softly.

"It's going to be okay, sweetheart," he said to the person on the other end of the line. "Lazy should be there any minute, I promise. I really have to go, though. Everything is going to be fine. I'll touch base tomorrow." Cam ended the call just as a creak in the wood floor announced Kayla's presence. He whirled around and clutched his chest in surprise before taking the Lord's name in vain.

"Hey, baby! What are you doing up?" Cam questioned

innocently. He switched on the table lamp, causing them both to squint in reaction to the light.

"Um, who were you just talking to?" Kayla questioned in an accusatory tone; hands placed firmly on her hips to emphasize her displeasure.

Choosing to act as if he had not heard her, Cam lead Kayla by the elbow back to the bedroom, but she jerked herself away and turned to face him.

"Who were you talking to on the phone, Cam? It's the middle of the night. It's *Christmas.*" Kayla crossed her arms over her chest and her jaw instinctively tightened as strands of loose hair fell from her lop-sided ponytail.

"It was just a work emergency thing. Everything is all right now. Let's go back to bed."

"So, you weren't just talking to a woman? On the phone? In the dark? In the middle of the night?" The pointed sarcasm in her voice was undeniable.

"Well, technically yes, but trust me it is not what you think."

"Okay so tell me, Cameron, what were you talking about that was so incredibly important that you needed to discuss it in the middle of the night? And don't tell me it was a business call, because unless you are calling a client in Asia there is no reason why you should be on the phone at this time."

"Okay, if you will calm down long enough for me to explain, I will," he replied cautiously, his hands fanned out like he was trying to tame a wild animal. And maybe he was.

Kayla plopped down onto the couch, crossed her arms and pulled her face into a pout. Her likeness to her niece Anaya was uncanny. "Okay then. I'm listening. Explain."

"One of the girls from Rubies got into an altercation with a client and he got a little too handsy and . . ."

Kayla cut him off and shot up from the couch with a force

and pointed an index finger at him. "Stop right there. *You* said you sold your shares of Rubies! That's what you told me!"

"I did! Well, *most* of them anyway. But it is just not about ownership and shares and stuff like that. I have a history there, I've been involved with Rubies for a long time, and the girls, they depend on me for a lot and even if I was completely out of the picture, they would still probably reach out to me every now and then. And before you get how you get, the answer is 'no', I am not sleeping with any of them."

"How *I* get? Are you serious? If I was whispering to a man on the phone while you were sleeping, I don't think you would have taken too lightly to it."

"You're right. I wouldn't have. But *you* don't have a reason to be speaking to a man in the middle of the night. *I* was on a work call. There is a difference."

"You lied to me and you are trying to justify it. I really can't believe you," she responded incredulously.

"She is a young girl, Kay, and I feel bad for her. She doesn't have anyone. She is from some Podunk town in Pennsylvania. I think her parents kicked her out when she got pregnant or some shit like that. I don't really know but, I was just trying to calm her down. One of my boys went to pick her up and take care of the situation."

"Well boo-fucking-hoo for her! Nobody forced her to be a stripper. Tell her to find a psychologist and not to call you again or she will have a different kind of assault on her hands."

Cam chuckled at her petty response, but she switched off the lights and left him in the dark as she stalked angrily back to the bedroom.

Soon they would be braving holiday traffic driving so that she could introduce Cam to her family. For Christmas Eve. Kayla had been looking forward to her family meeting him, but it had been a wild twenty-four hours.

"Let's just go to sleep," she instructed Cam, who had followed her wordlessly to the bedroom. They laid down in bed and he attempted to spoon his body around hers, hoping they would melt into each other as usual. But Kayla tensed up and eventually he rolled over onto his side of the bed.

twenty-three

Pushing the door open with his foot, Cam walked into the bedroom wearing a fuzzy red and white Santa hat. He held a platter of what looked like an entire package of bacon. He placed the platter on the dresser, held up index finger to indicate that he needed a moment and returned with two coffees. He was evidently proud of himself, like the first time a child ties his own sneakers.

Kayla had just awoken and was still groggy, but smiled at his efforts. It was Christmas Eve and she wanted nothing more than to forget the events of the night before.

"Merry Christmas, baby!" Cam bounced over to her with way too much energy and planted a kiss that she blearily accepted.

"It's Christmas Eve, not Christmas," she corrected him.

"Yeah, but Santa dropped something off for you and plus, I made breakfast." Cam beamed, as he presented Kayla with a snowflake decorated platter of fatty bacon goodness.

"Oh, wow. That you did! A pound of bacon, I see! You are a PETA members' worst nightmare. Thank you, baby." He laughed and kissed her again, having eclipsed from Krampus to a jovial Christmas elf.

Some bacon was burnt, but overall edible, the coffee lacked sugar and had way too much milk, but the effort was appreciated. Maybe it was the Spirit of Christmas, but she believed that they could get back on track.

Cam hopped over to his side of the bed like a bunny and opened his nightstand drawer. His energy level was higher than usual, and Kayla found his child-like excitement to be infectious. The anger from their previous argument had completely dissipated.

"Santa bought you this." Cam presented Kayla a velvet, rectangular navy-blue box. She wanted to tell him that gifts should be exchanged on Christmas morning in front of the tree, but she knew that would kill the mood, so she kept her comment to herself and took the box graciously.

She popped open the top of the box to reveal a six-carat platinum tennis bracelet with diamonds so clear and shiny that they blinded her. Her hand rose to cover her mouth which gaped open like a carp fish.

"Do you like it?" Cam pressed, a knowing smile spreading across his face.

"Like it? Are you serious? I *love* it!" She bounced onto Cam's lap and knocked him, along with his goofy Santa hat, over and covered him in bacon grease kisses.

"I didn't get you anything even close to this. I mean this is just . . . wow." Cam picked up the bracelet and locked the clasp around her wrist. The bracelet fit perfectly and felt cool against her skin. The jewels glinted as they caught the Christmas morning light that shone through the window.

Kayla had wanted to wait until Christmas morning to exchange gifts, but since Cam had broken tradition, she decided that she ought to as well. She made her way over to

THE VOICE WE SQUELCH

the closet to fetch Cam his gift. She sat next to him on the bed and placed a wrapped box in his lap. He seemed interested as he tore through the red and green plaid wrapping paper and his gift was revealed—a DVD copy of the hamster movie they had seen together at the film school. Weeks prior she had called the school to inquire about obtaining a copy. Not surprisingly, the administrator Kayla spoke with was more than happy to fulfill her request. Cam let out a deep, throaty laugh upon unwrapping the gift. She could tell he was as equally surprised as he was touched. Something inside of her made her believe they would have a very Merry Christmas.

As expected, traffic into New Jersey was treacherous. Also, as expected Kayla's family loved Cam as much as her girlfriends had. Cam had a way with people. He could charm a bird out a tree. He also beamed as she showed off her present.

They drove home around 10:00 p.m., even though her mother insisted profusely that they stay over because it was late, dark and cold. Kayla was unsure how time and temperature affected driving conditions, but she figured all mothers saw life differently. She didn't know though; she wasn't there yet.

When they returned to Cam's apartment, Kayla wearily kicked off her shoes and headed to the kitchen to put away the leftovers her mother had sent home with them. They had told her parents that they were planning to visit Cam's mother at the cemetery for Christmas and the leftovers would be welcomed comfort afterwards. Kayla ordered a beautiful poinsettia display and a tiny Christmas tree decorated with little star shaped mirrors to bring to the gravesite. Afterward, they would return to Cam's apartment to pig-out on a banquet feast of leftovers, while they watched classic holiday movies and listened to Christmas music.

She opened the refrigerator, attempting to find room for the numerous red and green Tupperware containers her mother had prepared when Cam came up behind her, took the containers from her hand and tossed them onto the counter.

"What are you doing?" She asked with bemused laughter.

He did not answer her, but instead led her to the living room.

"Sit on the couch. I have something for you. And since it is officially after midnight, I can give it to you now." He slid his arm behind the Christmas tree and plugged it in so that a rainbow array of colors appeared and illuminated the dark living room.

"But you gave me my gift this morning," she protested, genuinely befuddled.

Cam sat down on the couch next to her and covered her legs with a cream colored sherpa throw, another one of her nods to the yuletide spirit.

From underneath the blanket, he produced a small, silver foiled box with a traditional red Christmas bow

"What is this?" Earlier that morning he had gifted her the kind of jewelry that she had only ever witnessed through very thick plated glass—and now this?

She picked up the box and with her thumb and forefinger, she slowly opened the box. Laying atop a white synthetic cotton jewelry pad was a grayish silver key. The curiosity that had graced her face earlier turned to that of confusion, only to be quickly met by a Eureka! moment.

"I know it has only been like six or seven months," Cam

began, "but I can't stand the thought of you living anywhere without me. We are going to break your apartment lease, or let it run out, I don't care which, but I want you to move in with me."

Once her mind registered what was happening, Kayla crawled onto Cam's lap with such an intensity, that the blanket landed on the floor and the key fell into the cushions.

"Of course, I'll move in with you! Oh, my God! Yes, of course! I can't believe this! Wow, you are *full* of surprises today, aren't you?" she said as she shoved him playfully.

There was no possible way for a Christmas to be more perfect.

twenty-four

Before the New Year arrived, Kayla began to box up her stuff in preparation of her move into Cam's apartment. Cam was ready for her to move in immediately, but she had accumulated much more junk over the years than she had realized and deciding what to keep and what to donate was taking longer than expected.

The timing was also not ideal since her girlfriend, Stephanie, was getting married in three weeks and her bachelorette party was a few days away—and it was in Miami. Packing for a vacation in the midst of an apartment move is extremely overwhelming.

To say it was a struggle for Kayla to get Cam to get on board with her attending the trip would be an understatement. It was only a three-day, two-night trip, but Cam was not sold on the idea, not by any means. He held steadfast to the belief that single men target bachelorette parties, which Kayla believed was preposterous. She assured him that their vacay would be very low-key: spa, fancy foods and the beach. They had no intention of staying out all night partying.

Cam reluctantly accepted the fact that she was going to

Miami whether he liked it or not. One of her best friends was getting married and she was in the bridal party. It was a not to be missed event.

Kayla admitted that she would have preferred if she and Cam were going on vacation together, but then he offered to hide in her suitcase. He teasingly instructed her to call when she boarded the plane, when the plane landed, when they checked into the hotel and before they went out *anywhere*. Although these commands were dished out with a comedic intention, she could sense there was an underlying truth to his statements. But it was the twenty-first century in America and he was aware that he could make no such requests without the veneer of jest.

Kayla did not see his desires as overbearing, because it felt good to be wanted. She finally knew what it was like to have another person on this planet actually *need* you. She and Amir had loved each other, but they never needed each other. Kayla enjoyed being immersed in the saccharin-sweet, sit on the same side of the booth in a restaurant, type of love. Their PDA often made sour singles roll their eyes at the sight of them, and deep down inside she kind of loved it

Kayla was truly disheartened about leaving Cam as this would be the longest amount of time they would have spent away from one another. The look on Cam's face when he dropped her off at Stephanie's apartment almost made her want to jump back into the passenger's seat and denounce her eight-year friendship. She found it impossible not to tear up as they said, 'goodbye.' As Cam drove away, and the limo to take the bachelorette group to LaGuardia pulled up, Kayla felt actual pain in her heart.

Vacationing with her girls was incredible, and Kayla did not realize how much she had missed spending time with them. They ate at trendy restaurants and ordered colorful drinks, spent hours at the spa, lounged by the pool and tanned on the beach.

Kayla checked in with Cam often, doing so in private as she did not want her friends commenting on how often she and Cam spoke. The entire vacation had gone on swimmingly and Kayla had an amazing time, but she was ready to fly back home and move into Cam's apartment.

On their last night in Miami, they chose a fancy Cuban restaurant known for their bright blue alcohol served in fishbowls. The girls spent the night talking about the trip and Stephanie's upcoming nuptials.

"Okay, so ladies, since this is the last night, I think we should all go to the pool party, what do you guys think?" Stephanie questioned the group. Everyone agreed, as did Kayla but that same guttural pain she felt when Cam drove away from Stephanie's apartment returned, but it was stronger this time, more persistent.

Kayla chose a neon pink bikini and a black sarong for the pool party. She flat ironed her hair in the bathroom while she spoke to Cam on speakerphone. She was honest and let him know that they were going to a pool party. His tone morphed from loving to agitated upon hearing her plans for the night, but she told him that they were only going for a couple of hours. She joked that they could stay on the phone the whole time if he wanted to. She was slightly alarmed when it took him a minute to answer, 'no,' as if her statement had been serious.

Their group headed downstairs to the lobby level where

the pool was located. Kayla heard her cell phone chime and reached into her purse to retrieve it. Cam had texted saying that he had called the club and paid for them to have a VIP section. She was taken aback by his generosity, as were her girlfriends. She figured it was his way of saying that he trusted her. She called him on speakerphone and they all thanked him, especially Stephanie who made it a point afterwards to mention that her fiancée should have done something like that and that he was going to get an earful when she got home. *Poor guy.*

Everything was going well—until it wasn't. Stephanie called the group in for a huddle and handed each of them a small round pill. Stephanie and two others took their pill immediately, and the rest of the group eyed one another cautiously. One by one, everyone downed their pill until Kayla was the last one left. She did not tell Cam that drugs were part of the deal. She, herself, was not aware that molly was a part of the deal either, but when in Rome . . .

"Oh, shit! I know you!" The drugs had taken full effect and Kayla was yell-talking, dancing and partying like it was her last day on Earth. "I'm Kayla Montero. I'm the GM at Cathedral in New York." She had noticed DJ B-Flat and his entourage in the VIP section next to hers

"Oh, yeah! Hey, girl! What are you doing here?" B-Flat walked over to their VIP and gave Kayla a kiss on the cheek and a hug. Kayla shared with him that she was part of a bache-lorette party. He commented on how great everyone looked and Kayla returned the compliment, because by social protocol that is what one is supposed to do right?

Kayla introduced him to her girlfriends that were standing

next to her and they immediately started fan-girling over him. Members of his entourage began to make their way over to Kayla's VIP section and the two groups began taking photos together. B-Flat made it a point to introduce them to his friend heavyweight boxer Lennon White, whom Kayla had never heard of, but was happy to meet. In her altered state, she was happy to meet anyone and everyone.

She secretly sized up B-Flat. She never really found him attractive before, but for some reason she was now able to see the appeal. He was over six feet tall with mahogany skin, defined features, and a matching chiseled frame. He had no shirt on, so his tattooed chest and arms were on full display. Two gigantic diamond studs hung on his earlobes and a thick platinum chain with a diamond encrusted cross hung from his neck. He caught Kayla staring at him and offered for her group to join his VIP area since it was larger.

Kayla's group of girlfriends happily accepted his invitation and followed him over to his section. They were having an amazing time, taking shots of clear liquor, posing for cell phone photos, and dancing to music about asses, selling drugs and sex.

B-Flat came up behind Kayla and placed his chain around her neck for a few of the photos and she gladly posed with him, not seeing any harm. The heavy, iced out chain made her think about the tennis bracelet that Cam had bought her for Christmas and her heart was suddenly enshrouded in despair. She missed him terribly and wished he wasn't so far away. She unzipped her tiny leather purse to find her cell phone and call him, when *Rack City* by Tyga came on and magically she wasn't sad anymore.

The music took over her body and she began to dance. Her body slithered like a snake being coaxed by a charmer. She was really feeling herself, as her heart rate increased and the bass took over the space between her ears. She should have packed her shit up and gone back to the hotel room. But no. She did not.

Discovering that they were all on the same wavelength, B-Flat handed Kayla and her girlfriends another pill and she believed that everyone took another. As she felt the amphetamines wash over her and turn her into another version of herself, she began to dance with B-Flat and even some of his entourage, but mostly him. Dance is probably the wrong word; grind would be a better description. Kayla had no idea what time it was, but she didn't care. She was having fun and so was everyone around her. That was until she finally did check her phone. She had nineteen missed phone calls, four voicemails and seven texts that got progressively nastier as the hours clicked on. The notifications were from Cam. All of them.

Fuck.

twenty-five

Kayla was too inebriated to read the texts or listen to the messages, so she went to the bathroom to call Cam back and face the music—no pun intended. The phone barely completed a full ring before Cam picked up.

"Kayla? Where the *fuck* are you?" Cam spat out. She could tell his teeth were gritted even through the phone.

"I'm in the club, baby. I'm sorry I missed your calls. I didn't hear the phone ring," she said or slurred rather.

No answer.

"Baby, can you hear me? We took some shots. I'm a bit tipsy, but we are going back to the hotel room soon. Cam?" *Click.* The call ended. Kayla said 'hello," a few more times before she called back.

"Baby, I can't hear you . . . Cam, are you there? Cam? Hello? Hellloooo?" They continued in silence for another minute before he responded.

"You get your ass on the next motherfucking plane or me and you are done!" He screamed so loudly that she had to hold the phone away from her ear. "You know what? Fuck it, don't even bother coming back. You're an embarrassment. I want your shit out of my house," Cam snapped. *Click.* Again.

The pain in her heart returned and she rushed towards the nearest exit. She tried calling him again, but his phone was off. It was after 3:00 a.m., but she panicked, and was severely fucked up, so she called his friend Lazy.

She was surprised that he answered and even more surprised that he knew it was her calling. "Kayla! What the fuck are you doing over there? Are you out of your mind?" Lazy questioned her in a hushed and almost panicked tone.

"I don't know why he is so mad. I didn't do anything," she retorted, sincerely confused.

"Are you serious?" Lazy asked, his voice full of befuddled amazement. "Your photos with B-Flat are all over Instagram. Just look online! He even tagged you *and* the club in the photos. There is even a pic of you hugging Lennon White and wearing his chain. One of our boys showed it to Cam and he lost his shit."

Kayla tried to materialize an excuse, but none came to mind, she just stammered.

"Kayla . . . there is another photo of you dancing with some guy. You know this is *really* bad, right?" Lazy accused.

"Oh, my God. I had no idea. I need to talk to Cam. Can you just give him your phone for a minute, please?" She rattled off, manically.

Lazy told her to calm down, but she could hear Cam's booming voice in the background, and it turned her blood cold.

"Is that her? Is it? She thinks she can make a fool out of me? Tell her not to come back here. She's dead to me. Tell her, Lazy. Tell her that if does, that she will regret it. Hang up the phone!"

The phone call ended and when she called back, it went straight to voicemail.

Kayla called non-stop for fifteen minutes. Cam had turned

his phone back on, but he never answered it. She sent him numerous texts, pouring her heart out with apologies, but to no avail.

The girls had begun to worry, she could tell by their surmounting missed calls and texts asking where she was. In Kayla's state of panic, she began to concoct a lie to tell her friends, but they found her before she found them.

Stephanie called out Kayla's name and Kayla spun around on her heels to face her friend. "Kayla! Where have you been? We have been . . . wait, are you crying? What happened? What's wrong?" Stephanie inquired frantically in a rushed cadence.

Kayla wanted desperately to tell her the truth; that Cam had seen photos of them on Instagram and that she was about to lose the love of her life if she did not do something drastic. But, of course, she couldn't say that. Stephanie would just roll her eyes and say, 'oh well, he will get over it.' But she didn't know Cam and he would *not* just get over it. He was nothing like her fiancée. He was not easy-going. Not at all.

"My . . . my brother-in-law was arrested for DWI, and he is panicking because my sister is going to kill him. I need to fly back home now and get him," Kayla lied. It was a terrible lie, especially since she and her brother-in-law were not particularly close.

"Oh, wow! That is insane! I am so sorry, Kay. Is he hurt? Where is he?" Stephanie had a dozen questions, but they were difficult to answer since Kayla was fabricating the whole thing.

"But, Kay, you can't pick him up. Look at you! Your eyes are as wide as saucers, and you need to chew on a straw just to keep your jaw straight. You can't leave now, it's not safe." Stephanie pulled Kayla in for a hug and then texted the rest of their group to let them know what happened.

Despite Stephanie's protests, Kayla booked the next flight

headed to LaGuardia that left in five hours. The rest of her girl-friends also vehemently disagreed with her decision to fly back, fearing for her safety. Stephanie even offered to fly back with Kayla, but she told her that she would be fine. The group headed back to the hotel room, ready to pass out on the comfy hotel mattresses. Kayla began to pack her things.

twenty-six

Kayla's luggage wheels rolled on the smooth airport floor, as people all around her bustled this way, and that way. She had texted Cam her new flight information after she booked it, telling him that she was coming home early, and naturally she apologized. Again. She had called him too, but he didn't answer, and she wondered where he was and what he was doing. Originally, he was going to pick her up from the airport, but she was not sure if that was still the case.

As she turned airplane mode off on her cell phone, a chime sounded, indicating a message. It was from Cam and her heart skipped a beat.

Lazy will pick you up. That was it. That was all the message said.

Lazy pulled up in a black Escalade and hopped out of the driver's seat to help Kayla with her luggage. She slid into the passenger seat and muttered a, 'hello' and a 'thanks for picking me up." Lazy just nodded and focused his attention on exiting the airport.

They did not speak for several minutes and an awkward silence descended upon them as AM talk radio filled the car. Kayla stared out of her window until Lazy finally spoke.

"Kayla, listen, I like you. I do. I am not sure you realize this, but Cam is not really someone you want to fuck over." Lazy used the upcoming yellow light to slow the vehicle down. He turned to face her as the SUV slowed to a stop. She wasn't entirely sure what he meant, but the intensity that rippled through his face proved to her that he was as serious as a heart attack.

"I wasn't trying to . . ." she trailed off, as any attempt to respond was futile.

"You did see those pictures, right? I mean how are you going to explain that to him?"

She appreciated Lazy's support for his friend, but she did not need the third degree from him too.

The light turned green, and he lifted his foot off of the break, glancing sidelong in her direction every few seconds awaiting a response. But she didn't have one. Not a good one anyway.

"What do you want me to say? I fucked up! Okay?" She hated that she had to defend herself to him, but it didn't matter because Lazy barely registered her answer as an excuse.

"And another thing. Those photos are online. You publicly disrespected him, and it doesn't even seem like you realize how bad this is." Lazy was shaking his head in disbelief, as he recounted the moment.

Overwhelmed and unsure of another response Kayla began to cry. Lazy tossed a thin napkin onto her lap and it felt almost ridiculous to say, 'thank you,' for it, but she did anyway. He was a great friend to Cam, that was apparent. And she was the world's worst girlfriend.

After wiping her eyes, Kayla noticed that they were not headed towards Brooklyn, and she brought it to Lazy's attention. His head dropped and his expression changed from accusatory to sullen. "Cam said to bring you back to *your* apartment."

"That can't be right. We are moving in together like any day now. Maybe you misheard," she offered gently.

"He made it a point to tell me not to bring you to his apartment." Lazy responded half-heartedly. Kayla froze in the passenger seat, coming to terms with what she had just heard. Cam wasn't bluffing. *This can't be.*

Twenty minutes later they were double parked in front of her apartment and Lazy hopped out of the driver's side to fetch her luggage from the trunk.

Before Kayla left, he offered her parting words of advice. "I know Cam can be a bit much sometimes, but he has a good heart. If he is getting *this* upset over you, then you must mean a lot to him. So, just keep quiet and agree with him, okay? That's what the rest of us do."

Kayla called Cam again the moment she was in her apartment, but no answer. Next, she texted him to let him know that she had arrived. He responded two hours later with one word. *Working.*

His terse, brief response triggered an insane response in her. In her state of mania, she grabbed her coat, jogged down the stairs of her building and all the way down the street to a tattoo shop. Once there, she looked around the room at the various designs and artwork, but she did not need to choose one, because she already knew what she wanted hers to say. She laid down on the cracked leather chair, pulled down her leggings and folded over her underwear as the young, muscular tattoo artist permanently inscribed, *Cameron*, in black ink below the right side of her pelvis bone.

Any other day she would have said that getting her first tattoo was the most painful experience she had encountered, but that was not that case. Twelve hours prior Cam had brutally ripped out her heart, so that event trumped any physical pain she had to endure by way of a tattoo needle.

After permanently maiming herself in a hastened attempt to prove her love and devotion, she headed back home with a fresh tube of A&D ointment in her hand. She popped two Aleve's in her mouth and laid down on her living room sofa, unsure of what to do next. Eventually, she drifted off to sleep.

It was the downstairs bell that awoke her from her nap. The bell rang again, this time the buzzing noise sounded longer, and she practically tripped over her own feet to answer the intercom.

Kayla held down the, 'talk' button on the intercom. "Hello?" She asked into the dusty speaker.

"It's me." Cam's voice was flat and without emotion. The pace of her heart quickened, and she pressed the 'open' button until she heard a 'click' noise indicating that he had entered the building. She hastily smoothed down her clothes and fixed her ponytail, as she waited for the front door to open and Cam to enter.

She could smell the cold January air on Cam's coat as he opened the door and stood in the foyer. He was unable to look at her, but she threw her arms around his neck, desperate for the feeling of his body against hers. His arms, as if filled with lead, barely moved to return the embrace.

Nuzzled close into his neck she whispered, "I'm so sorry

baby, I didn't mean to hurt you. I wasn't thinking. I didn't realize how it looked. I love you so much."

Cam sighed and ran a hand through his hair. "What do you want me to say, Kayla?"

Kayla took his hand and led him to the sofa, instructing him to sit because she wanted to show him something. He reluctantly seated himself on the couch, his mouth set in a straight unmoving line. The tension between them hung in the air like a stale smell, but she hoped it would soon dissipate.

She stood in front of him, backed up a couple of feet towards the television and began to lower her black Lycra leggings.

"Look," she ordered.

"I've seen that before," Cam responded dryly.

"No, silly! I want you to see what I did," she chuckled, trying to hide her nervousness. "I did this to prove to you how much I love you."

Her pants crumpled around her ankles as she presented her naked bottom half to him and slowly removed the bandage the tattoo artist had affixed to her body. As the gauze fell away, thick black ink displayed the two-inch tall, six-inch wide cursive, 'Cameron' tattoo.

Cam didn't respond; he barely blinked.

"What do you think? Do you like it?" Kayla prompted. Her eyes pleaded for a positive response.

"Why did you do that?" Cam inquired, stoic and unmoving like a statue.

"To prove to you that I love you and that I am all yours," she responded, hoping a tide would turn sooner rather than later.

"Hmm, that's interesting. And what makes you think that I even want you anymore after what you did?" Cam scoffed. His look of cool indifference had merged into disgust.

She had permanently inked her body with his name, a physical sign of ownership that she gave to him freely and, yet his demeanor was that of pure detachment.

Kayla pulled up her pants, her cheeks red hot from embarrassment and sulked onto the sofa cushion next to him. Their knees touched briefly, but he pulled away from her almost instantaneously.

She had taken a gamble and came out on the losing end. She should have known that he would not go for it; no one in their right mind tattoos a significant other's name on their body without being married. Some people won't even do it then.

What the hell was I thinking? She had officially moved into Psycho Girlfriend Land which, from the looks of it, would very soon be renamed to Psycho *Ex*-Girlfriend Land. And to make matters worse, she began to bawl. But, thankfully, Cam saw her tears and his callous attitude began to soften.

"Honestly Kay, we are not in a good place right now. I really don't see how you can ever recover from this." His head lulled into both of his hands and speech was controlled, but she sensed a change coming. An ashen grey storm impending, and Cam was Zeus sitting atop his Cumulonimbus throne about to pierce Kayla with a razor-sharp lightning bolt.

"Baby, please don't be mad. I never should have taken drugs or hung out with those guys. I swear I didn't even realize how it looked; we were just having fun. I literally talked about you the entire night to everyone!" She hoped that she sounded convincing, but it wasn't looking too good for her.

Pupils like black holes bored into her. "So let me get this straight," he began in an even, yet menacing tone. "You whore yourself around Miami with your slut friends, and I'm just supposed to get over it because you're sorry and got my name inked on your body like a crazy person?" His face was all twisted up in revulsion.

"Cam, please be rational. You know I would never intentionally hurt you. Just listen to me so I can explain. B-Flat has been to Cathedral a few times before, and he was in the VIP next to us. We recognized each other and just took a few photos together, like promotion stuff, ya know?" Kayla explained, but Cam only exhaled and shook his head.

"I swear on your mother, Cam, that I am not lying to you." Mention of his mother, got his attention, and Kayla thought she spied a minuscule spark of hope on the horizon.

He didn't speak, but there was a change in his demeanor, so she took her chance. She leveled her lips to his and kissed him. He didn't return her kiss with much fervor, but he didn't push her away either, so she counted it as a step in the right direction. She pulled her face away from his and he looked as if he were about to cry. Whatever little bit of her heart had been left unbroken, had completely shattered.

"Just tell me that you forgive me," she pleaded. She was near groveling, begging like a mid-century peasant at the feet of a king. "I'll do whatever you want. Tell me how to fix this."

With no other card to play, she began to kiss him again, but this time he offered her his tongue, which provided her with a surge of energy. She faced him and straddled his lap, her legs positioned in a "W" pose. His arms reached around to wrap her in a tight embrace and his still cold hands made their way down the length of her spine. His kiss became hungry and aggressive. An aggressiveness she dismissed as robust passion.

The apology seemed to be heading in the right direction. He shifted his hips forward and she could sense that he wanted to switch positions, so she leaned back into the couch allowing him to lie in the open space between her legs. Between kisses and gasps of air she would repeat how much she loved him. A marble-like hardness formed beneath the fabric of his jeans, leading her to believe that their fight had ceased and they were once again on the same team. A white flag in the form of an erect penis had been waved.

She relished the weight of his body pressed against hers as she ran her fingertips along his rib cage. His lips felt warm against her collarbone, and she bit her lip in anticipation of what was to come.

Then everything changed. Cam stopped suddenly and shot her a look of pure revulsion.

"What? What's wrong?" Kayla questioned, breathless and befuddled.

"Just stop talking," Cam hissed in a voice cloaked in darkness. "I can't do this. You disgust me," Cam backed away from her as if she were tainted. He hastily began to pull up his jeans that had pooled around his ankles. "I can't even look at you. I have to go."

Kayla cried out his name, but he just ignored her and quickened his pace to the front door. With his back still to her and his ears closed off to her pleading, she grabbed his forearm, desperate to pull him back into the living room. But she was really trying to pull him back to her, *back to them*. But it was all for naught, as he aggressively shrugged her off. Her feet stumbled over one another in a drunken two-step, and she bumped into the entryway mirror. Hot, salty tears rained down her face in fat droplets.

"I gave you everything, Kayla! *Everything!*" Cam screamed at the top of his lungs, as he whipped around to glower at her tear-streaked face. The veins in his neck were nearly ready to explode, and she turned away from him as he screamed in her face and spit landed on her cheek bone.

"Fuck!" He screamed as knocked over an empty glass flower vase and various knick—knacks that were displayed on the foyer table. She shielded her face as small, jagged pieces flew towards her.

"This is over, Kayla. I can't do this with you. I feel like I don't even know who you are," Cam looked at her, weary and defeated.

He reached for the doorknob, turned it and her front door opened just as she fell to her knees and begged him, one last time, not to leave her.

The front door slammed shut, ceremoniously concluding their argument.

Then it happened—the rush came as she was flooded with the realization that she was never to be entangled with her love again. Listlessly crawling on all fours back to the living room like a dejected zoo animal, she morphed into a fetal position, ugly crying through mascara clumped eyelashes. Silent screams escaped her body and she felt as if there was not enough oxygen in the room.

The towering fort of packed boxes looked down at her tauntingly. The last few years of her life neatly stacked away into cardboard cubes—homeless now, just like her. Her future dissipated. A tingling began to flow through her hands and feet. She was going numb, one limb at a time and all she wanted to do was vaporize into another world.

Please, come back. I don't know how to be without you.

twenty-seven

Footfalls could be heard outside her front door. Two iridescent gray shadows cast themselves through the inch sized gap at the bottom of the door. Twin feet stood still on the coir mat imprinted with *WELCOME* in upper-case type. The hallway was quiet. Too quiet. Silence lagged on achingly for a few moments before the click of a turned doorknob alerted Kayla to arise from her crumpled position on the floor.

Cam entered the apartment again, dressed in caution and unease. He took a few steps inside until he was standing in front of Kayla, and then slid down against the wall like molasses, finally plopping down on his bottom next to hers.

She wiped her eyes and runny nose with the back of her hand, smearing mascara and foundation all over her face like crude war paint.

"You . . . You came back," she somehow managed to squeak out, albeit almost inaudibly.

"I heard you crying from the hallway—all the way down to the elevator," he said gently. Kayla uncoiled her legs and inched over to Cam until their bodies were faintly touching. Within moments, he wrapped his right arm around her and scooped her close to his body. He held her tightly to his side, and began to speak softly into her hair.

"I'm sorry you saw me get like that, but *you* hurt me so bad. I love you so much. How could you have done those things to me? How?" Cam questioned rhetorically, as he continued to ramble. "Just thinking about you and those men and I just . . . I just," he fists clenched and unclenched, as did his jaw. His skin began to redden, and Kayla could tell that his mood could flare at any minute. She desperately wanted to hang on to the side of Cam that was gentle and loving, so she took his face in her hands and kissed him as passionately as she could. She moved her palms to his chest, gripping his shirt in her fists as if hanging on for dear life.

Realizing that she needed to come up for air, she removed her mouth from Cam's and leaned back to examine his face. She had never seen him misty eyed before, but she could tell he did not want her to see him in a state of vulnerability.

"I'm so sorry, I'll never hurt you again, I promise. I don't want to break up. I will spend every day trying to be better for you, I promise. Whatever you need, I'll do." She buried her face against his neck, which smelled of musk and wood cologne.

Cam shushed her soft sobs, kissed the top of her head, and then began to stroke her hair. "I don't think I can be without you either, so we are going to have to set some ground rules . . . if you want this to work," he continued cautiously, but it was more of a veiled command. Kayla's gut told her to ask what he meant by 'ground rules' but she thought it best not to taunt the tiger, so she straightened up and awaited further explanation.

"I don't want you working at Cathedral anymore." His tone was terse and the way he looked at her when he said it caused her to deflect her gaze in submission.

"What do you mean? I don't understand," she questioned

as gently as possible. He shot an agitated glace in her direction and punctuated it with a deep exhale.

"I'm not trying to fight; I just want to understand." Kayla held up her fanned-out hands in surrender.

"What is there to understand? I am not comfortable with you working at the club anymore. You can work from home. If you want to be with me, I should be your only concern. Nothing else, Kayla," Cam's tone was authoritative, and she was too weak and tried to fight.

She could tell there would be no formal question and answer part to their discussion. Cam rose from the floor. Once standing, he reached his arms down to her to help lift her up and pulled her in for a long embrace. "And you forgot the ''s.'

"I'm sorry, the what?"

"For the tattoo. The apostrophe. You forgot the apostrophe ''s.' You are saying that you belong to me, so it should read Cameron's. Apostrophe 's,' not just Cameron. You are good with grammar; you should have picked up on that." Cameron quipped with a smirk, but she knew that he was serious.

"It is called a possessive proper noun and you are right, I should have thought about that. I'll get fixed soon; I promise. I am happy you like it because afterwards I began to panic that you would think I was crazy," she laughed nervously.

"Yes, to both. Yes, I do like it and yes, I do think you are crazy. Let's go. I want to go home, I'm exhausted," Cam directed as he zipped up his heavy winter coat and Kayla headed off to the bathroom to pee and wash her face.

"Oh, and quick question. Given the location of that tattoo, I am assuming you had a woman do it, correct?" Cam questioned loudly over the flushing of the toilet.

Kayla sucked in a quick breath of panic and with no other choice but to lie, she called out, "yes, of course it was a woman, silly."

"Okay, good because I was gonna say . . ." he trailed off laughing, and then told her to hurry up, as he did not want to hit traffic.

Fifteen minutes into their reconciliation and she was already lying . . . they were off to a great start.

twenty-eight

In the weeks that followed the emotionally charged blowout between Cam and Kayla, they eventually settled into a pattern of normalcy. Well, a degree of normalcy anyway.

The past events still haunted them, but they had agreed to staying together, so she did whatever she could to make their relationship work. Cam ended up being dead serious about Kayla no longer working on-site at Cathedral. And to his credit, the first couple of weeks at home were actually quite fun as they remained entwined in their bubble of love together. But when Cam had meetings, she was left to her own devices in the apartment, and it could get brutally boring.

Cam never discussed exactly what his business work entailed, but she had a general idea and although it gave her anxiety that he could get into legal trouble, he always answered his phone and came home on time, so she never pressed him.

Her first task was to redecorate the apartment which was a ridiculous amount of fun, especially when you are not paying for any of it out of your own pocket. All the while, she ordered every relationship book she could find, and annotated every piece of advice she found pertinent. She also set out to master all of Cam's favorite dishes, even though most had already been perfected, she still set it as a goal. She was even able to watch her favorite chef Estella Marciano every weekday morning at 10:00 a.m. on *PBS*.

A part of her understood what Cam was trying to achieve. He wanted to regain control, and, unfortunately this is how his mind worked, so she played along.

She thought it wise to improve her body and mind simultaneously, so she joined a yoga and sound bath class four blocks away. She had only attended two sessions, when Cam decided to surprise her one afternoon while she was in class—in the midst of a downward dog. He spied three men in attendance, cared not about the fact that they were gay, and had her un-enroll in the class.

"There is a women's only gym a few blocks away, or buy some work-out DVD's," was his rebuttal, when she argued that he was being utterly ridiculous.

One Saturday morning, he woke her with an iced hazelnut coffee and a bakery muffin studded with bursting blueberries and huge grains of sugar. He always awoke earlier than her, claiming he had difficulty sleeping. He said he had planned a surprise shopping trip, but in actuality, it was an overthrow of her wardrobe. To make room, he asked her to donate outdated clothes. He offered to help in his own way by giving any low-cut shirt or too short dress the axe.

Kayla knew it was her foolish actions that caused him to react so irrationally, but his insecurities were getting out of hand, and she was beginning to feel stifled. The suffocation began with the ridiculous work from home order, then canceling the yoga, and then her clothes got the chopping block. She loved Cam, but she needed to love herself too. She took a deep breath and coached herself. It's just an insecure phase he is going through, she reminded herself. It will be over soon, and everything will go back to normal.

Days later a blinding white 7 series BMW was parked outside their apartment and topped with a mammoth pink sparkly bow. Strangers on the street smiled and lingered as Cam presented Kayla with the ostentatious gift, some even congratulated her.

She was shocked and dismayed by the surprise, but cried and jumped into his arms anyway, thanking him profusely and questioning why he bought her such a car in the first place. Then he raised his eyebrows and smiled wide.

"Don't freak out, but there is something in the trunk too." He clicked the trunk button on the key fob, and the trunk lid popped open. A bubblegum pink Kitchen-Aid stand mixer with all ten attachments and an oyster grey Le Creuset cast iron cookware set stared back at her.

Kayla's hand grasped her mouth, covering the permanent 'O' that had formed. Cam stood alongside her and wrapped his arm around her coat covered waist.

"It probably goes without saying that I got you the best sound system upgrade too, right? Only the best for Cathedral's GM," he whispered into her ear, and she didn't have to see his devilish, yet satisfied grin to know that it was there.

Relief washed over her. Cam's temper tantrum was finally subsiding and she was glad that she had not made any rash decisions about their relationship in the interim.

This was Cam's way of saying he was sorry; he wasn't good with words. Everyone was different, she could not hold it against him if he expressed his anger differently than she. He loved her and that was all that mattered. Love is all that ever matters.

Later that night, Kayla awoke in bed alone. Absent was the warmth of Cam's breath against the back of her neck and when she groggily rolled over to touch his side of the bed, it was cool to the touch.

twenty-nine

When Kayla awoke to a partner-less bed, panic soon followed when after a few minutes she could not find Cam in the apartment. During her apartment search, she stopped by the front door as a muffled voice from outside their front door caught her attention. Eyebrows firmly knitted together; Kayla swung open the front door to see Cam clicking 'End' on his phone. He jumped back startled to see her and dropped his phone onto the hallway floor.

"Jesus Christ!" Cam exclaimed, clutching his chest as he shut the door behind him and walked into the apartment. "You almost gave me a heart attack!"

"Who were you . . ." she began to inquire, hand firmly planted on a jutted-out hip, but was cut off.

"Before you get any ideas; it was a work emergency, okay? Nothing else. The conversation got a little heated and I didn't want to wake you up, so I went out into the hall." Cam explained in an even tone.

"What kind of emergency?" she questioned suspiciously.

He rolled his eyes. "Kay, I deal with money; it's a 24/7

thing. Sometimes things happen at night. It is not that big of a deal," he replied calmly.

Satisfied with their conversation, he headed towards the kitchen, and she heard the refrigerator gasket unseal. He called out to her, asking if she wanted something to drink, but she wasn't thirsty.

"What was the problem?" Kayla asked stone-faced.

"You know what? Fine. You want to know. I'll tell you. You may not like to hear this, but in order for us to afford this lifestyle and things like the new car I just bought you, occasionally I have to take calls in the middle of the night and I would appreciate it if the woman that *I* support, supports *me*. Is that too much to ask?" Cam asked, exasperated.

"Well tell me what the problem is. Maybe I can help," Kayla pushed. She was accustomed to putting out fires in Cathedral on a weekly basis, but she could tell that he was keeping something of importance from her, it was written all over his face.

Kayla straightened her back, readying herself for whatever emotional impact was about to blow her way, but to her surprise Cam's shoulders slumped forwards and he agreed with her and recommended that they sit down.

"Before you start, let me just say that you can always tell me anything. And if you are having trouble with money, just know that we don't need it. We do not *need* any of this, Cam," she gestured widely with her arms to all the material possessions around them. "I just need you to tell me the truth."

He didn't look her in the eye, but began to speak. "I still own Rubies. I never sold it. I'm sorry I lied to you, but it belonged to my mother . . . and it meant a lot to her." Cam lifted his head slowly to gauge Kayla's reaction.

"Your mom was a stripper?" Kayla tried to keep the judgment and surprise from her voice, but to no avail—her mother was the second-grade teacher at St. Eugene's Catholic school before she became a stay-at-home mom.

"What?" Cam's face screwed up. "No, no, my mom *owned* Rubies. It was her club. She wasn't a stripper." He chuckled lightly and she apologized for the misunderstanding which he just shrugged off as no big deal, but she was relieved that she was incorrect.

"My mom opened Rubies to help girls that were trying to get away from abusive families or husbands or who just needed a new start. She would help them get back on their feet, or go back to school. It's like a safe haven in a way, Kayla. I can't get rid of it. I know it sounds stupid, but it is like my mom's legacy," Cam turned to her with puppy dog eyes.

"And then she would employ these traumatized girls as exotic dancers?" Kayla asked incredulously.

"Well, yes, but she would connect the girls with counselors, doctors, and day care for their kids. She would get them food, clothes, a place to sleep, whatever they needed. She was a saint really," he concluded, respiring long and deep and releasing the weight of his secret.

Kayla processed his story and she knew she had to choose her words carefully so she would not offend Cam or his deceased mother's *legacy.*

"That is quite a lot to take in. Thank you for sharing that with me, I appreciate you trusting me with that information because I am sure that was not easy to say aloud." Kayla began as eloquently as possible.

"With that being said," Cam interrupted, mocking her voice.

He knew her so well. "Yes, *with that being said,* I understand that Rubies reminds you of your mom, but let's just erect a beautiful mausoleum for her instead and pay our respects that way. I want you to sell the club, Cam. For real this time." She quieted her voice to soften the blow, but she was dead serious.

"Are you making me decide right now?" Cam questioned, surprised.

"Honestly, Cam, I appreciate you telling me about you mom, I really do. But we are supposed to be working on our relationship and you have been keeping a huge secret from me. It is counterproductive; two steps forward and one step back. God knows that I love you with every fiber of my being, but I need you to sell because no matter what you say, I know there is more at play here than meets the eye. Make a choice. Right now, make a choice," she enunciated.

Cam did not respond right away, which is the mistake all men make. The truth never gets held up; it just spews from the mouth like a volcano. Cam's hesitation was the only sign she needed. Kayla walked towards their bedroom and began to root around in the back of the closet for her suitcase.

thirty

Kayla rifled through the closet until she pulled out a maroon canvas overnight bag embroidered with her initials. She tugged at the brown leather handles and fumbled with the zipper until she pried it open and began to stuff random clothing items into it, not thinking clearly or caring much about matching or season appropriate outfits.

"What . . . what are you doing?" Cam asked in utter bemusement. "Are you packing? What is going on?" The look of shock, or maybe it was fear, on his face satisfied her for a mere moment until she refocused her attention to her packing. Cam grabbed the opened bag from the bed and tossed it angrily onto the floor, as if it was the duffle bag's fault that they were in this position, and its contents scattered all over the floor.

"Well, that was mature," Kayla responded dryly as she spied her clothing and underwear strewn around their bedroom floor.

Cam stood in front of her and held her arms down by her sides so that she had no choice but to face him.

"Stop, Kay. Stop moving; just tell me what is going on. What is wrong with you?" Cam glowered.

She did her best to compose herself before she answered, and he loosened his grip upon noticing the change in her demeanor.

"I know deep down you are still upset about the whole Miami thing. I get it, I fucked up and your ego took a titanic blow. I promised you that I would do whatever it took to fix the relationship, and I held up my end of the bargain, but you didn't. I will not be lied to and treated like a fool. I messed up Cam, but I never lied to you," Kayla said, firm in her declaration.

"Okay, Kay, I hear you loud and clear, let me just . . ." Cam began to respond, but she cut him off.

"Nope, that was the wrong answer. You have to choose; it is either me or a strip club and I see where your loyalties lie. Move out of my way. I have to pack," Kayla said as she stepped aside him and bent over to pick up her duffle bag and its strewn about contents.

"You're kidding right? You just moved in. I bought you diamonds. I literally *just* bought you a fucking car," Cam stated, bewilderment still alight his face.

"And if you knew me at all, you would know that I don't care about any of that. That I could be living in a studio apartment in the South Bronx, eating ramen and wearing cubic zirconia and it would be fine as long as we were together, but . . ." She couldn't finish her sentence—it hurt too much.

"Okay, all right! Fine! I'll call the lawyer tomorrow and begin the process. Okay? Just stop and calm down," Cam professed, as he stepped behind her and pulled her body close to his. She could feel his breathing catching pace with hers, as she reluctantly returned his embrace.

"You mean it, Cam? Because I am serious. I am not going to

play second fiddle to anyone or *anything*," she replied, a bit more forcefully than she had planned.

"Shhh, yes, I promise. I would never choose anything over you," Cam responded in a calming tone. "Let me say goodbye to everyone first, and then I will let my lawyer handle the rest." Kayla registered his response, but looked at him leery eyed.

"You can come with me. How about that? But it is going to have to wait. We will go next week—as soon as we get back."

"Okay, but why not tomorrow? Wait, get back? What are you talking about?" She questioned, staring at him inquisitively.

"Well . . . I was going to surprise you tomorrow morning, but since you just went all bat shit crazy and tried to move out, I will tell you now," Cam said sarcastically, as a wide grin set onto his face

Kayla had felt so confident minutes ago, ready to go to war, but she had since had retreated in battle. In his hand he held a white paper envelope that he slipped out from the closet shelf. "I have something for you, something for us," he said.

She suppressed her instinct to smile at the surprise and took the envelope from him. Untucking the back flap of the envelope, she pulled out three stapled sheets of paper folded into thirds. Her eyes took in the photo of a modern style estate and its adjoining amenity information sheet.

"I planned a weekend trip. We leave tomorrow morning. It is a town in Westchester called Bedford, only like an hour away, max. My boy hooked me up with a great spot," Cam beamed, as the beginning stages of his crow's feet exposed themselves around his eyes.

Kayla lowered herself to a seated position on the bed and pulled an errant blanket around her shoulders as she read the papers. A name on one of the folded papers begged to be examined more carefully and out of the corner of her eye, she could see Cam's grin widen.

The printout was e-mail correspondence with the manager of famed old school Italian celebrity chef Estella Marciano. For over twenty years, Kayla and her grandma would watch Estella Marciano on *PBS* together. Up until she passed away, they would watch Estella's cooking program together when she visited—gossiping, and laughing all the while. The rush of memories caused Kayla's eyes to water, blurring her vision and making the papers nearly impossible to read clearly.

"She lives right in Bedford, ten minutes away actually, from the house I rented, so she is going to give you some private lessons. I also told her about you and your grandma. How you two would watch her show together and how your grandma is . . . no longer here," Cam said as he placed his arm protectively around her shoulder. Kayla's lower lashes could no longer hold in her tears as they had welled up with tears of remembrance.

"You *spoke* with her?" She managed to stammer out, as she wiped her face with the back of her hand. Cam nodded 'yes,' and got up from the bed to fetch her the tissue box from her nightstand.

Of course, Cam knew who her favorite chef was, but she never could have imagined he would have thought of something like this. *God, he was good.*

"Wow! I am at a loss for words. I mean, how did you even pull this off?" Kayla asked in utter disbelief. Her previous anger and melancholy had all but dissipated.

Cam took her hands in his and looked at her with genuine care in his face, if not he was an excellent actor.

"I wanted to say I'm sorry for everything, that is why I planned this trip and got you the car and that pot set by that French brand I can't pronounce," Cam said.

"Le Creuset," she offered gently with the correct pronunciation.

"Yes, that's it. I know you probably don't believe me, but I really was going to sell Rubies, I was just dragging my feet and didn't know how to tell you about it. And don't worry, we will be fine with money, I was just being dramatic before."

Kayla perked up, and Cam lifted his head following her lead. "I have an idea," she began. "Hear me out. Why don't we try, like, a reset?"

"A what?" Cam asked.

"A do over if you will. A fresh start," she explained, as her speech sped up. "We both made mistakes, but now everything is out on the table. I forgive you; you forgive me. We both love each other, and now we know the other one's boundaries and what lines not to cross. I don't have any secrets. Is there anything else you want to tell me? Now is the time to get it out and all will be forgiven," she proclaimed.

thirty-one

Cam told Kayla that there was nothing else he wanted or needed to tell her. Everything was on the table and out in the open, he said, and she believed him because what other choice did she have?

The next morning, as promised, they headed to Bedford. The sun shined aggressively that morning, burning through the sky with a Phenix like intensity. Cam had risen a couple of hours earlier than she, as was typical for them and she could hear him in the kitchen talking authoritatively to someone on the phone.

Cam finished his call as she was hopping into a steaming shower, and he sat on the toilet seat and smoked a joint, keeping her company as she got ready for their weekend adventure. Cam was a stickler about timing and lateness. He also hated highway traffic with a passion, so wanting to dissuade any upcoming road rage, she hurriedly dressed in her casual uniform of leggings and a zip up hoodie and tied her damp hair in a knot atop her head.

Their shared suitcase wheels rolled quietly down the tiled hallway floor outside their apartment. Kayla was giddy with anticipation about their trip, but the majority of her excitement stemmed from the fact that she would be meeting culinary genius Estella Marciano the next day.

Their route began on the West Side Highway which moved swimmingly northward toward the Taconic State Parkway. Kayla did not know anything really about the town of Bedford and had only seen a few photos of their weekend rental home that Cam had shown her while scrolling on his phone.

As they cruised up the highway, the elongated sunroof in the car allowed them an unobstructed view of a sandy-brown mother hawk teaching her babies to fly gracefully in the open sky. They managed to catch a glimpse of one of the baby hawks as it plummeted downward from the sky at a swift pace. The mother, without missing a beat, expertly swooped down underneath her baby and guided it back upwards towards the other siblings. Watching them was relaxing, intoxicating.

"Oh, shit."

And just like that, Kayla's relaxation dissipated. It wasn't until after forty-five minutes of driving on the highway, radio playing 90's hip-hop with a crumpled bag of greasy potato chips wedged in her lap did she realize that she had left her birth control pills at home.

That morning, in the excitement that came with preparing for their first weekend trip, she had forgotten to put the flesh-colored compact of pills into her purse.

She voiced her concern to Cam, and he insisted that the 'pull and pray' method would have to suffice, but she did not feel very confident in his solution. She pictured the round pill case laying untouched in the medicine cabinet. Her ovaries would be left unguarded and up to mischief.

The town of Bedford was beautiful—scenic and quaint. The perfect backdrop for those cheesy made for TV holiday movies where there is always a happy ending. Kayla could imagine hopeful, young couples eagerly flocking to a town like this, eager to swallow up real estate. Ready to take root.

Meandering nature trails were set alongside babbling brooks, framed by green moss-covered rocks. The town was busy, peppered with families weaving into and out of farm-to-table restaurants and home décor boutiques.

They drove down the idyllic country roads towards the pine and birch tree lined street of Ravensdale Road. The name of the street forced her mind to conjure up visions of a dark, gothic log cabin, but there was no darkness present. They drove down the winding quarter mile driveway, flanked on either side with naked leafless trees and soon they laid their eyes upon a home that could grace the cover of *Architectural Digest*.

They ascended grey stone steps to a heavy arched door, decorated with a small wrought iron window in the center. Their mouths hung open as they walked inside, their eyes roved up and down and to and fro, as they took in their luxurious surroundings for the weekend. The living room boasted a marble fireplace situated next to a bar. The furniture was overstuffed, plush and cream colored. The house even had its own wine cellar, gym and sauna. The gourmet kitchen featured an oversized range, cabinetry that was, no doubt, imported and a marble kitchen island that took command of the center of the room.

The ample five-bedroom, four-bathroom home was more like a manor, than a house. Every room in the house was more opulent than the next. The master bedroom had its own private balcony, a mixture of luxury and comfort that gave way to the panoramic views of the vista. Kayla imagined what a sunset would look like from that vantage point, seated on the covered terrace in an oversized red Adirondack chair, kept warm by the round firepit.

Standing in the bedroom, Kayla threw her arms around Cam, assaulting him with kisses and thanking him for bringing her to such a beautiful place. "I wish we could stay here forever," she gushed.

Cam nodded in agreement. "Me too, baby. Me too."

As Kayla excitedly awaited Estella Marciano, she could feel her stomach knotting and unknotting itself, as she had no idea what to expect.

Fifteen minutes earlier than expected, the doorbell rang, chiming through the house. Cam and Kayla stood side by side as she opened the front door. Estella stepped inside, smaller than she had expected, but just as grandma-like as she had hoped. Her grey hair was tied into a neat little bun and she wore a long dark purple paisley skirt that stretched around her wide midsection and swept the floor. A small entourage followed her: her sous chef and assistant. Her driver chose to wait outside, although he was offered many times to enter along with everyone else.

After brief introductions and small talk, Estella guided Kayla though her recipes in her heavy Italian accent, moving around at a deft pace as if the kitchen belonged to her. She was a professional indeed and Kayla was honored to be in the presence of a culinary genius, an incomparable master of deliciousness. She was sweet as pie too; her disposition was not just an act for daytime television.

Kayla realized that this had to be the most amazing thing anyone had ever done for her. Cam never told her what the private lesson costs, and she never asked. If he was trying to erase the errors of his past, he was doing a damn good job.

As much as Kayla loved Cam, he wasn't exactly 'Mr. Romantic.' But, for that particular weekend, it felt as if he had studied every early 2000's rom-com in preparation for this weekend. Every morning he would venture into town, returning with armfuls of baked delicacies from bistros in town. Each day it was something new: flaky, butter laced croissants, fluffy, golden colored brioche with thick layers of creamy butter. Onion tarts with crumbly crusts and duck confit hash topped with perfectly poached eggs. Crispy fried pommes frites. A rainbow assortment of macaroons, almond flour and caster sugar married together in the most orgasmic way.

One afternoon, after Kayla awoke from a mimosa infused nap, she followed a trail of rainbow roses, pink, yellow, and orange into the adjacent bathroom. Tchaikovsky's 'Dance of the Sugar Plum Fairy' played placidly in the background. Situated in the center of the bathroom, a deep soaking stand-alone bathtub was lined with flickering votive candles and had been filled with bubbles that mounted over the rim of the tub in fluffy peaks of white. Cam laid with her in the oversized tub, their limbs intertwined like Bavarian pretzels. Kayla felt like she could feel his pulse inside her own body.

There were 7.4 billion people in the world, and she had somehow managed to find her other half.

"Can you make it so that we never leave here?" she asked, hoping to hang onto this fantasy life forever.

"I promise, I'll do my best."

thirty-two

Eventually the weekend came to an end. As much as Kayla wanted to stay, they did in fact *have* to go home and were unable to remain in their suburban dreamland. It was a beautiful fantasy nonetheless, and she tucked away all the romanticized events of the past weekend safely away in her mental memory box.

Their drive back into the city was uneventful, and she fell asleep when they were almost halfway home. As if they had not relaxed enough, they did not do much the next day either, choosing to stay in bed most of the morning and afternoon watching a *Twilight Zone* marathon on the Sci-Fi Channel.

They ordered Chinese food from their usual spot—scallion pancakes, Szechuan dumplings, beef and broccoli and orange chicken, but it gave Kayla stomach cramps. The day had escaped them; ten Twilight Zone episodes, Chinese take-out, and two Pepto Bismol pills later, Cam said he had calls to make and Kayla decided to run herself a bath.

Cam walked into the bathroom as she was soaking and reading an article on her phone about open communication tips for relationships. The article included a check list of ten relationship red flags—she and Cam had ticked off five of them. He squatted on the outside of the tub so that they were eye level and she closed out the article and placed the phone on the floor outside of the tub.

His mouth set in a straight line before he spoke. "I just got off the phone with Lazy and he said that the notary will be at the club in an hour, so that I can sign papers and transfer licenses and certificates, and all that good stuff," Cam proffered as he moved onto the toilet seat to sit. "And I have a few things in my desk there, papers, and stuff like that so I'm gonna head over there in a few. It will only take like an hour, maybe even less. Do you want me to bring back food or anything?"

"I want to go with you," Kayla said, as she stood up from the soapy water, pulled up the drain and asked Cam for a towel, which he cautiously handed her. A mini tornado erupted over the open drain as she stepped onto the steel gray chenille bath rug. He handed her another towel for her hair and she could tell he was thinking of what he could say to contest her statement.

"Don't worry, I won't wear anything that would confuse me with the strippers," Kayla said with a chuckle as she whipped her head forward and towel dried her hair. She straightened up, hung the damp towel over the rack and walked out of the bathroom. Cam had still yet to come up with a response.

Half an hour later, they were seated in Cam's car headed to Rubies, and Kayla was downright giddy with excitement that he would finally be done with the strip club. He proceeded to explain to her what she could and couldn't do at the club while he would be making his rounds and saying goodbye. She agreed just to humor him, as she was barely listening to begin with, but thought she noticed tiny beads of sweat dotting his hairline.

Hand in hand, they walked across the street to Rubies, which was odd on two accounts—one, they never attended a Gentleman's Club together before, and two, they were not big hand holders as Cam claimed that it made his hand sweaty. This time seemed to be the exception, as he made it a point to firmly grasp her hand and interlock their fingers, as they headed towards the entrance.

A bright red sign read *Rubies* in an old school baseball font, and it sat atop the black steel entry doors. The tittle on the 'i' was a replica of a large ruby gemstone, and it was quite fetching. Two groups of men were huddled together outside smoking cigarettes, one cluster conversing more loudly than the other.

Cam approached a bouncer who was dressed head to toe in black and guarding the front doors with his massive frame and inflated muscles. He had a square jaw and a military crew cut that made Kayla feel like at any minute he would yell, "drop and give me fifty!" Cam released his hand from Kayla's, gave the bouncer dap and they proceeded to speak to one another.

Cam introduced her to the bouncer quickly, and without much enthusiasm. They exchanged polite 'hellos,' before the militant bouncer directed his attention back to Cam and they began to converse once again. After a few minutes, the bouncer opened the door for them so that they could enter. Hip-hop music with a thundering bass burst out onto the sidewalk as the front door swung open.

The club was well attended and larger than she had imagined. There were women in various stages of undress floating about, many of them stopping to wave, hug or kiss Cam. Kayla was pleasantly surprised at how many of them seemed delighted to meet her, some even squealing in excitement, and pulling her close for an embrace. She had never heard of any of them, but Cam seemed to have told everyone about her.

He pointed to the far-right corner of the club and whispered in her ear over the booming music that his office was located in the back, its door hidden behind a geometric hill of opaque glass blocks. The entire floor was flanked with tufted leather couches and loveseats, all showing signs of wear. The highly trafficked damask carpet was littered with an occasional crumpled napkin or straw wrapper. They snaked through the high-top tables dotted with frosted amber tealights and he waved to a pretty, full lipped blonde who was laughing with a group of older men with visible liver spots on their hands.

Kayla tried not to think about the number of years Cam had spent in the company of these lithe, attractive, and promiscuous women. She reminded herself that his involvement with that particular lifestyle would be over in a matter of days.

They reached Cam's office, and he released her hand to procure a small, gold key, from the keyring in his jean pocket. He closed the door behind them, and the music muffled.

The room reminded her of a 1950's private investigators office, akin to the ones seen in classic black and white movies. The walls were grey and bare, except for a few framed permits and a calendar turned erroneously to the month of November. His desk was basically empty except for a lined yellow legal sized pad of paper, a few errant blue ball point pens, one with cap, one without, and an empty tape dispenser. A matching green file cabinet stood guard at the far right of the prison cell sized office and none of the drawers were labeled.

Parallel to the unlabeled file cabinet was a silk screen partition, that Kayla was almost afraid to look behind. She pointed towards the partition, and Cam shook his head with a knowing grin and told her to look. When she mustered up the courage, she noticed a toilet with a yellow ringed bowl and two unraveled toilet paper rolls.

"Wow," she responded in equal comedic shock and disgust. "No wonder you used to like to do all of your work at Cathedral. I feel like I am going to need a tetanus shot after we leave here." She laughed, but was only half joking.

"So, what do you think, *of the outside*?" he asked, laughter coating his voice like honey.

"I mean, I haven't really been to many strip clubs, but I guess it looks nice. And from what I saw, the girls we met seemed very sweet, very naked, but very sweet," she joked as she wrapped her arms around his neck. "I am glad you aren't going to be here anymore though; it makes me too jealous," she confessed, as if it wasn't obvious.

A look of utter bemusement, accompanied by a furrowed brow clouded his face. "Jealous? Why? You know that I don't notice anyone else, but you." The sincerity in his response almost made him sound believable.

Three light raps on the door interrupted their conversation and they both turned their heads towards the noise coming from the other side of the door.

A tall, lanky figure with unkempt shaggy brown hair that dusted the tops of his ears appeared in the doorway. He was middle-aged with red and ruddy skin, and he wore a wrinkled, ill fitted button-down shirt.

Cam's eyes brightened, and the two men happily embraced one another with repeated robust pats on the back. After a brief introduction, Cam explained to her that the gentleman to his side, Isaac, was the soon to be full-time owner of Rubies.

In hearing that this was the man that would be taking the club off Cam's hands, Kayla immediately mirrored Cam's enthusiasm and embraced the greasy-haired man with a tight hug of gratefulness and an overstretched grin.

Cam explained to her that he knew Isaac his entire life, as Isaac was a long-time friend and colleague of his mother. She learned that he was a snowbird with a villa in Siesta Key and taught Cam about money management and stock market when he was a teenager.

The introductions were cut short by the ringing of Isaac's cell phone. He reported to Cam that the notary had just parked and was headed inside. The office was small, the three of them having taken up most of the open space, so Kayla offered to wait outside once the notary arrived. Cam seemed to notice the limit in floor space at the same time as she did, and reluctantly agreed.

Placing the rectangular key fob into the center of her palm, Cam offered that it may be better for her to wait in the car until he was finished. She agreed to do so and said her goodbyes to Isaac, but not before courteously inviting both him and his wife for dinner one evening in the future.

Before leaving, she turned to Cam to steal one more kiss before she left. An air of finality hung heavy all around her, and she wanted to bathe in its richness.

She practically floated through the club, unaffected by the shaking of inflated ass cheeks. A craving for a celebratory beverage stirred in her, so she made a beeline for the lit-up bar, only to realize halfway through her walk that the bar was dry —only serving water and soda.

"Yeah, I know. Why do they even have a bar if they don't serve alcohol?" A sultry voice spoke over her shoulder. She spun around to face the voice and was greeted by a smirking Delilah. Kayla's smile straightened into a flat line and her posture became rigid.

Her hair was styled with blunt bangs, a look Kayla knew she could never pull off. Delilah wore an obscenely low-cut crushed velvet cranberry mini dress that knotted around a thick silver ring above her navel and left little to the imagination, but she wore the hell out of it, so the vulgarity was somehow tempered.

Kayla chuckled nervously, suddenly conscious of her homely, purely for comfort outfit of leggings, camel colored Uggs and a hoodie of Cam's. "I'm just waiting for Cam. He is signing some papers, so I just figured I would kill some time, but I forgot about the bar," she laughed, gesturing too much with her hands. They had never really spoken at length to one another before, but since they shared interest in the same person there had always been a budding tension.

"You haven't been to the club in a long time. Cam said that you work from home now—lucky you!" Delilah purred. She pursed her iridescent pink glossed lips, and ran her piano fingers through her long hair extensions, revealing large silver hoop earrings.

Kayla signaled towards the front door with a thumb over her shoulder and mumbled that she would wait for Cam outside in the car.

"It was, um, er, nice seeing you," she said and quickened her step in any direction that Delilah was not. But she was unable to escape, as Delilah reached out to grasp Kayla's elbow as she walked past. Delilah released her grip when she realized she had caught Kayla's attention.

"Wanna go next door with me? They have an *actual* bar—like with alcohol," she persuaded with a snicker.

"Oh, um, I wish I could," Kayla stammered, dipping a

bucket into her well of excuses. "But Cam will be finished with his meeting soon and we have to head out, so I'm just going to wait for him in the car but thank you for the invite though!" Kayla tried to sound appreciative and not panicked, but she was a pitiful actress.

Delilah crouched down behind the illuminated bar, picked up an army green calf-length military coat, and said goodbye to a couple of girls standing nearby.

"Come on, follow me. It is just next door," Delilah countered with an overly dramatic beckoning of her arm. Kayla was unsure as to why she was being so polite to her, let alone even speaking with her. Their past exchanges had been very limited, and thick with competition and envy.

Kayla quickly deduced that if Cam were not part of the equation, in another universe, she and Delilah could possibly be friends. But they were in this universe, and in this universe, that was not an option.

Kayla followed closely behind Delilah as she pushed past the opaque front doors and headed to the adjacent building—an Irish pub that smelled of hops, yeast and shepherd's pie. Delilah strolled into the dimly lit, mahogany encrusted pub like she owned the place. Her saunter and overstated sex appeal drew looks from a few of the male patrons who were slouched over the bar with reddened faces and glazed over eyes. Only one of the bar flies held his gaze to include Kayla as well, the other two casting their eyes downward as she passed; their beers holding more interest than she. Kayla wondered if Delilah was aware of the attention that she drew.

Delilah slid into a wooden booth that resembled a church pew and Kayla did the same, her bottom squeaking as she scooted close to the wall. Faux Tiffany lamps cast muted jewel tone-colored shapes onto the lacquered wood table. Yellowed maps of Ireland and local newspaper articles were affixed to almost every open space on the walls. Portraits and photos of the lush green fields of Ireland's countryside were vivid enough to briefly transfer one to the hills.

A husky, curly haired waitress with a deep brough strolled over to Kayla and Delilah's table, placed a woven basket of complimentary Irish soda bread in between them and inquired as to what they would like to order. Delilah answered before Kayla had a chance to respond and she ordered them two beers and a platter of nachos for them to share. The waitress smiled and nodded, thankful for the easy order. Before she turned to go, Kayla piqued up and asked if she could order a shepherd's pie, fish and chips and soda bread to go.

She looked over at Delilah shyly, who was smirking. "It's for Cam, for later," she explained. Delilah nodded in response, her mouth tight.

"I mean, normally I cook at home for us, but I was being lazy today. That's why I figured might as well order, since I'm here," Kayla rambled on, embarrassed that she could not stop the verbal diarrhea from escaping her mouth.

Delilah raised her hands in surrender, a vintage gold Chanel turn-lock chain bracelet slid down her wrist. "You don't have to explain to me," she replied. "I don't cook at all." She snickered and cocked her head to the side. "You strike me as the real Suzy Homemaker type."

Dumbfounded and unsure of how to respond, Kayla could not gauge whether her comment was a compliment or a thinly veiled insult. Thankfully, she was spared the need to respond as the cheerful waitress deposited two tulip shaped glasses containing their half pints of frothy beer in between them. The ice cold, yellow liquid served as a tension breaker.

The waitress mentioned that she would be back momentarily with their food and scuttled off into the kitchen, disappearing behind the aluminum swing doors. Delilah and Kayla took sips of their beer, and Delilah leaned back into the cracked green leather of the booth. Kayla remained poised and upright after she set her glass gingerly down on the cardboard coasters that the waitress had managed to slip under their drinks.

Kayla was not sure what to do or say next and she could feel a heat rising in her chest.

"I know you are probably wondering why you are sitting here with me right now," Delilah began. She exhaled before continuing and Kayla could see her fake mountainous breasts rise and fall like twin stone melons. "I just . . . I just want you to know that I am just not some jealous bitch. It's not like I have a problem with you personally or anything like that. It's just that . . . well, I have bills to pay. I have a seven-year-old son with asthma to support whose drunk ass daddy never did shit for him. And I'm sure you never even thought about it, and why should you, it's not your problem, but if I came off as rude it's because you fucked that up for me." Delilah's shoulders slumped forward, and she focused her attention on the frothy white bubbles of her beer.

Kayla was stunned by Delilah's omission, but equally impressed by her blatant honesty. "I am not sure how to respond to that," Kayla responded as she waited for Delilah to continue. The waitress appeared as if manifested to ease the mood, but upon realizing she had walked into an awkward conversation, she set the platter of steamy, cheesy nachos down onto the table along with a stack of crisp, white napkins and backed away from Delilah and Kayla without another word.

"I know it's not your fault, but Cam and I had something good going, mutually beneficial, I guess you could say and now I am back to haggling with these cheap a-holes," she chuckled although nothing she said was funny. Kayla pulled a cheesy nacho from its tower and decided to bite the bullet and ask the question she had been wondering about.

"So, I guess I might as well ask . . . is it true you and Cam were never in a relationship? Like boyfriend and girlfriend?"

A small smile crept onto Delilah's face, and she shook her head. "No, not in the way you are thinking." She chose a bunch of nachos and placed them on her plate, selecting the cheesiest one from the group and plunging it into a beige ramakin of sour cream topped with minced chives. Kayla could see the waitress nosily eyeing them from behind the stainless-steel bussing station.

As if being summoned, Kayla's phone rang, and she dug to the bottom of her handbag to retrieve it. She knew it was Cam. No one else really called anymore, a sign of the times with the advent of texting. When she answered, Cam hastily asked where she was. The nervous cadence in his voice relaxed as she explained that she had gone to the pub next door to order them dinner to bring home. He remarked that take-out was a good idea and that the pub had great food. He told her that he would wait for her in the car and even though he ended the call already, Kayla felt the need to add, "Okay, love you too. I'm coming out," before she slipped the phone back into her bag and looked pointedly at Delilah.

"Hubby's looking for ya?" Delilah asked dryly while dipping a nacho in salsa.

"Yeah, I have to go. But, um, thank you for inviting me over here and, um, clearing things up." she added cheerfully, although she was not sure how much *was* cleared up.

Once again, on cue, the waitress appeared with Kayla's to-go orders and placed them on the table. Kayla handed the waitress her debit card and told her to charge the card for everything, even though Delilah balked initially.

The waitress was probably super confused at that point,

poor thing. Kayla slid out of the booth, picked up her plastic bag of food with the pub's green logo printed on it and turned to face Delilah to bid her goodbye.

"Oh, really quick before you leave, I just wanted to say this," Delilah began. "That time you came to the club, and you were upset because you saw Cam and me together . . . well, I didn't know your grandmother had just died. I would not have . . . I would not have acted the way I did; like we were doing something, because we really weren't. Everyone was just sitting around and bullshitting. He was on the other side of the room for most of the night, if I remember correctly."

Delilah grimaced, and Kayla could see the flutter of a lost little girl inside of her. She settled herself back into the booth, texted Cam that the food needed a few more minutes and listened intently to Delilah as her eyebrows knitted together in interest.

"My grandma took care of Dylan, that's my little boy." She reached into her Louis Vuitton purse, which Kayla knew was not purchased on Canal Street and fished out a separate dusty pink Bottega Veneta pouch that held her phone. She scrolled on the glass screen for a few seconds before pulling up a photo of a gangly, tawny skinned little boy with a fade haircut. He was dressed in a matching *Paw Patrol* tank and shorts set, had a wide tooth smile with a missing front tooth and was perched upon a green paint chipped park bench. A melting Mr. Softee vanilla cone with rainbow sprinkles dripped down his right hand, streaming onto an arm that was decorated with faded temporary tattoos. Kayla admired the photo for a minute and told Deliah how adorable her son was. Delilah thanked her and admitted that although he was, 'her whole world,' he could be a smart ass sometimes too. After her blatant honesty and confession, the photo of her son was the heat that finally thawed the barrier of ice that had formed between them.

Delilah decided to speak again as she placed her phone back in its buttery leather sleeping bag and then inserted that bag into her Louie, like a designer Russian nesting doll. "I worked the front desk at the Marriott in Times Square before my grandma died. She would watch Dylan during the day. She was amazing; taught him Spanish too! Well, when she died, I needed money, so I had to, well I had to start doing this," she gestured to Rubies next door. Sadness shrouded her perfectly symmetrical face.

Kayla nodded, unsure of what the proper response should be and she could tell that Delilah could sense her growing uneasiness. She composed herself and quietly apologized before continuing in a dulcet voice. "I guess I just wanted you to know that I am not a bad person, not intentionally anyway," she shrugged. "And Cam, well he is a good guy. He's no saint, that's for sure," she chortled, "but he took care of me. And Dylan. So yeah, I miss the money, but I am glad you two are back together. You're good for him. I can tell."

Kayla ignored the compliment; she was hung up on something Delilah said.

"What do you mean—back together? We never broke up. What are you talking about?" Kayla's face and neck flushed, and she could see panic rise in Delialh's expression as she began to stammer for an answer, an excuse. Anything.

Kayla narrowed her gaze. "What are you talking about?" She asked, her tone menacing.

"Cam said he broke up with you while you were in Miami because of the whole Instagram thing," Delilah responded shakily. She began to rub her neck nervously and shift in the booth.

Kayla took a swig of her beer, allowing the cool liquid to moisten her throat. "Were you and Cam together when I was in Miami?" She asked directly, hoping her heart could not be seen thumping in her chest.

Kayla's phone rang again, a robotic jingle filling the empty space; they both knew who it was. Delilah chewed her lip. Verbal confirmation was no longer needed.

The cheese congealed and glistened on the nachos.

"Just tell me how many times it happened," Kayla said as she stood up, surprised her legs were still able to function. Delilah mirrored her action, rising hastily and knocking her thigh on the edge of the table, causing their beers to slosh in their glasses.

"Just once. It only happened that one night that he saw the photos, but he was a mess, Kayla, he could barely . . ." Kayla didn't let her finish, she stormed away from the table. She didn't need the details.

Kayla could hear Delilah calling after her, but she ignored her pleas for forgiveness. As if speaking of the devil, Cam materialized in front of her, a quizzical look on his face. Kayla pushed past him, thumping her shoulder hard against his.

She felt Cam whiz around on his heels to follow her, but she outpaced him with the long strides she took to the door, steam plumbing from her ears. He called out to her, but she ignored him, hellbent to get outside and as far away from him as possible. Her mind began to whir, but she was too shocked to cry. Too numb to hurt.

Pulling her coat closed around her, she stepped out into the brisk night air, her soul feeling as dark as the sky. She hadn't thought past escaping the pub. She had nowhere to turn, nowhere to go and no time to think as Cam was at her side within seconds.

"What's *wrong* with you?" Cam cried out, breathless. Before Kayla could answer, Delilah joined them outside, equally breathless, and carrying their food in one hand. She rested the take-out on a terracotta planter outside of the pub and her eyes darted between Cam and Kayla, all three of them unsure as to how the situation would play out.

Cam, riddled in confusion, turned to Delilah, "D, what are you doing here?"

Hearing Cam address Delilah so casually as 'D,' was all Kayla needed to witness for every sane cell in her body to violently mutate from Dr. Jekyll to Mr. Hyde.

In an immature fit of rage, she seized the food off the planter and flung it at Cam. Fragrant brown liquid, mushy chunks of potatoes and cubes of carrots covered his torso and dripped down his jeans and onto his sneakers.

Delilah gasped loudly, grasped her clavicle, and tread backwards, seemingly taken aback by Kayla's outburst. Speechless and dismayed, Cam stood arms outstretched like a scarecrow, mouth agape like a cheap blow-up sex doll. Yet, Kayla was the one who felt like she just got fucked.

thirty-three

Kayla only made it three storefronts past Rubies before Cam strong armed her, spun her around, and demanded to know what was going on and what had gotten into her.

"You are a liar!" Kayla roared, her hands involuntarily pushing Cam forcefully in the chest, so that he stumbled backwards. "You fucked her while I was in Miami!" She spat as fire blazed inside her ribcage.

Upon the recognition of her statement, the muscles in Cam's face drooped instantly like he had Bell's palsy. His face registered pure fear. He looked like a child who discovered that the monsters under his bed were real. Cam lowered his shoulders and raised his palms in surrender.

"Baby, listen to me. It is not what you think. Please, calm down and let's talk about this rationally," Cam pleaded as if trying to coax a wild animal or human toddler.

He advanced toward Kayla gingerly like she was a viper that could strike at any moment—and he may have been right. Kayla spied Delilah down the street, waiting apprehensively, but she didn't really care about her anymore. She had a new target in her crosshairs.

Kayla hated him so much. She wanted to punch him in his face and shatter his cheekbone. She wanted to cause him physical pain tantamount to the emotional pain that was roiling inside of her. She wished there was a way for her to harness all her despair into a giant ball and hurl it straight at him.

"How could you?" Kayla cried, tears pricking the corners of her eyes. Her eyes transformed into pooling wells of sadness. "What else are you lying about? Is there more? " Her voice rose steadily until the shrill sounds that her vocal cords emitted were just a remnant of her actual voice. Panic raked Cam's face again as he struggled to find the right words.

He stepped towards her again, reaching out to grasp a hold of her arm, or her waist, or any part of me that he could, but she wriggled and pushed him away again. People on the street were beginning to take notice of the verbal altercation, the bouncers at Rubies keeping a close eye on them the entire time.

"Don't fucking touch me! I have no idea who you are. I'm calling a cab, so get away from me," Kayla yelled as he headed in the direction of the street corner to hail a cab. She prayed that one would magically appear.

"What are you doing, Kayla? Come on, don't be ridiculous. Just get in the car and we will talk about this. There is absolutely nothing going on with me and Delilah. Nothing! I swear!" He had inched his way within arm's length of her and she could smell the food on his clothes. The smell of ground lamb on designer denim was nauseating, and her stomach was turning in response.

"No! I'm never going anywhere with you again! You really are a piece of shit, you know that? You made me feel like I was such a horrible girlfriend and all along you were sleeping with *her*!" She wailed loudly.

A cab approached, but Cam stepped in front of her and waved the driver off. The driver hesitated for a second, but then thought better of getting in the midst of a lover's quarrel and drove off to find a less volatile fare.

The wafting fragrance of lamb had become too much for Kayla's stomach to bear, and she gave way to the billowing vomit that spewed from her mouth onto an unfortunately placed fire hydrant.

Cam jumped back to avoid any more food splatter, digested or undigested, and stood behind her and rubbed her back as she heaved on the street.

When Kayla was finally able to stand upright, she wiped her mouth with the back of her hand and a rocking sensation overtook her body. Her legs and ankles gave out and she slumped into Cam's side, all energy drained from her body. Using her weakened state as a reason to further coerce her into the car with him, she could no longer fight him. She hated him, but she needed a toilet, a shower and then a bed.

Cam led her to the car, one arm firmly holding her up. He spoke softly in a comforting tone as if she were a child, telling her that everything would be okay. He opened the car passenger door with one hand and folded her into the leather seat. Her head lolled to the side, and she could feel more vomit wishing to make an appearance and it did—all over Cam's sneakers. He asked if she was okay, but she could hear him cursing under his breath. He jogged over to the driver's side of the car, and they headed home.

Kayla felt defeated as Cam patted her thigh in a manner that would have normally been comforting. "I know you are sick baby, we will be home soon," he cooed.

Kayla nodded, but all she could think about were his hands roaming over Delilah's poreless skin. The swirls and loops of his fingerprints that Kayla thought were only caressing the contours of her body had recently left their imprint on Delilah.

Tears rolled silently down her cheeks, along her jaw and

pooled on the edge of her chin. A shiny engorged teardrop fell from her chin and landed on Cam's hand that was resting on her thigh. The wetness of the drop caught his attention, and he jerked his head to the side to face her.

"Aw, please don't cry. I'm telling you the truth," he implored. "I have no idea what that hood rat told you, but she and I don't have anything going on. Nada. Zilch. I don't even know why she is trying to start problems," he seethed as he slowed down to a stop at a red light. He held the back of his palm to Kayla's forehead to feel for a fever and remarked that she was clammy but didn't seem to be warm.

"She said you two were together when I was in Miami; after you saw the Instagram pics and lost your shit like a maniac," Kayla stated with barely any emotion injected into her voice. She had wanted to keep the same level of anger and intensity that she had on the street before she emptied out the contents of her stomach onto the sidewalk, but the draining feeling had magnified tenfold and the idea of even lifting her head seemed impalpable.

"That is impossible! I was on the phone fighting with you, and I was with my boys all night. She's full of shit. She's . . ." his voice trailed off and Kayla sensed that he had just registered an unfortunate memory.

Normally a relationship issue this severe would take precedence, but nature was calling. Kayla's stomach gurgled like a witch's brew inside an iron cauldron and all she cared about was getting to a toilet.

Cam rolled down the windows in the car, inviting in fresh air that previously hung in the caliginosity of the night. Kayla let her eyelids fall, allowing the motion of the car to settle her stomach into relaxation until they arrived at the apartment.

thirty-four

Kayla's insides began to bubble as if baking soda had been added to a child's science project, but luckily they arrived at their apartment just before a subtropical gyre formed in the depths of her stomach and swells of vomit rose from the recesses of her irritated gut.

There was no way that a few cheesy pub nachos would do this to her, so she deduced that she must have picked up a stomach bug from somewhere. Vile liquid rushed from her raw throat and points south for the next half hour—sometimes simultaneously.

The smells that were emanating from the recesses of her bowels were unlike anything that she had ever witnessed before. Yet, through the green haze of putrid gases Cam calmly, but firmly held back her hair, knelt supportively by her side during the entire ordeal, and stroked her back in smooth long strokes as if trying to put a baby to sleep.

When she begged for her privacy, he stood at attention outside the bathroom door waiting to be summoned like a dutiful sentry. In any other circumstance, his actions would have been perceived as admirable, a story to tell her girlfriends that they would, '*awww*' about in unison, but the reality of the situation was much different.

Kayla's heart thumped wildly in her chest. Unable to hold up the weight of her own body, she slumped down onto the vomit and shit speckled floor, body lifeless from extreme fatigue. Upon seeing Kayla in such a weakened state, Cam's brave façade began to dissipate. Prompted by terror, Cam pulled Kayla up like he was plucking the string of a guitar and cradled her in his arms like she was a defenseless newborn.

"What is going on? What is happening to you?" Cam's voice cracked, as he cupped her face in his hand. He was searching for an answer, but none came.

He wiped away the sweat matted flyaway hairs that had affixed themselves to her neck and forehead. Fear, thick like syrup, corrupted his voice and his actions.

"I'm going to call someone. You need a doctor." Panic still racked Cam's voice, but he was steadily getting himself under control. Kayla mumbled how she did not want to go to the hospital, unsure if her words could even be heard or if she was even speaking aloud. A topsy-turvy carousel was taking place within her skull and she could not seem to get her footing, unable to dismount the imaginary ride.

Cam stood her up, peeled off her bodily fluid-stained clothes and tossed the soiled garments into the tub. Kayla wanted to brush her teeth but couldn't muster the energy to say as much. Cam picked her up like he was carrying his bride over a threshold and she leaned her temple heavily onto his shoulder. He released her from his arms like precious cargo and laid her tenderly onto their unmade bed so she could rest. Kayla rolled over onto her pillow, pulled the covers over her head and folded her aching body into a fetal position, hoping the constriction would numb the pain of the cramps.

Without missing a beat, he slipped his phone from his

pocket and began to scroll fervently on the screen until he stopped, made a selection and pressed the phone to his ear. Kayla heard him repeat, 'come on, come on' in a rushed cadence as the phone line rang on the other end.

His fingers drummed impatiently on the nightstand until the person on the other end of the line answered.

"It's my girlfriend, there is something wrong with her," Cam spoke hurriedly into the phone, when the person on the other side of the line finally answered. "She keeps throwing up and she has diarrhea too, but it's not like she ate too much Taco Bell, it is something *totally* different. I have no idea . . ." His voice faded as he left the bedroom and walked down the hall.

Kayla could hear an aerosol being sprayed generously in the air. Followed by a plume of manufactured lavender scented air, Cam emerged back at her side, tugging the comforter down to inform her in a soothing tone that she had to put her bathrobe on because a doctor would be coming to check on her soon.

Normally, she would have inquired as to why her boyfriend was able to summon a physician at midnight for a home visit, but the necessity to conserve her energy caused her not to care.

After a spell and another bout of retching, a call from the nighttime concierge to Cam's cell phone indicated that the doctor had arrived. Cam instructed the concierge to send him upstairs and not long after that, a middle-aged man of Indian descent with kind cornsilk blue eyes peered at Kayla behind Alain Mikli glasses. He smiled warmly at her as he set a small duffle bag down on the floor beside the bed and patted her leg.

The doctor's coat hung on his thin frame, he removed it and placed it at the foot of the bed, before setting himself down next to Kayla. Cam stood by the doctor's side like a useless assistant, consternation carved into his face as his thumb and forefinger rubbed his chin methodically. A woven basket of fretful nerves had taken over Cam's sense of confidence.

"Hello, sweetheart, my name is Dr. Pawar and I am a friend of Cameron's," the doctor cooed smoothly, as he flicked on the lamp on her nightstand washing the room with a glowing pyramid of light. He plugged a stethoscope into his ears and smiled down at her, baring his slightly yellowed teeth and causing his crow's feet to deepen.

"I know you are not feeling well, but I am going to ask you to sit up and perform a quick check up on you so we can see what is going on here. Okay?" The doctor smiled warmly and bent down to remove more items from his bag. Cam rushed around to the other side of the bed to help prop Kayla up like a stuffed animal decorating a child's freshly made bed.

Dr. Pawar asked her a series of questions: When did symptoms start? What had she eaten earlier in the day? When was her last menstrual period? Was there a history of gastrointestinal issues in her family? She answered the doctor to the best of her ability while he listened to her chest, looked into her ears and mouth, and took her blood pressure and temperature. Lastly, he asked her to pee in a small plastic cup that resembled a sauce take-out container. He explained to Cam that the sample would be sent to a lab, and he would reach out in a day or two with the results.

"Well, honey, it seems like you may have a bacterial infection called Shigella. It sounds much scarier than it is. It has been going around the city for the past couple of weeks," he said solemnly. "Unfortunately, there aren't any antibiotics I can give you, but I will leave you with these anti—nausea pills, Zofran, to take for the next few days and your symptoms should alleviate in two to three days."

He handed Kayla a flat round white pill and told her to

place it under her tongue. "Just make sure to stay hydrated," he further cautioned before patting her on the shoulder and placing an envelope of pills on her nightstand.

Dr. Pawar rose from Kayla's side of the bed and Cam took the doctor's hand in both of his and shook it gratefully. He told Dr. Pawar to wait for him by the front door and the doctor took his leave before wishing Kayla well once more.

Kayla slinked down under the covers once again and Cam made his way to their closet. He squatted down squarely in front of his safe, twisting and turning until the combination was achieved. From the corner of her teary eye, she spied him removing a thick brick of verdant cash. He leaned over her knotted body, gave her a peck on the top of her head and told her that he would be back after he spoke with Dr. Pawar.

The Zofran calmed the vicious waves within her stomach and her exhaustion finally converted itself into a fitful sleep only made possible by extreme exhaustion and frailty.

Kayla awoke to the sensation of her bladder wanting to empty and leapt out of bed with a start, barely making it to the toilet before urine trickled down her leg. A wonderful sensation of relief briefly overtook her, only to be met with an insurgent wave in her stomach that caused her to spin to the side and hurl in the sink.

The past twelve hours were a blur, practically unrecognizable and then it hit her, like a crushing anvil on a cartoon coyote. Cam had cheated on her. She turned on the faucet and watched her yellow bile spiral down the drain along with the water. She must have stood there for five minutes watching the water from the faucet splash against the sink and then coil down the drain.

Lost within the downward spiral of the water, Kayla realized that Cam was not in bed when she woke. Turning off the faucet, she listened for him, but heard nothing. She stepped gingerly back into the bedroom, reached for the envelope of Zofran that Dr. Pawar had left on her nightstand and popped one under her tongue. Following her weary body's command, she plopped back down into the welcoming mattress and a sheet of paper, a handwritten note on Cam's pillow, caught her eye. In clear and bold black ink, Cam had penned her a note, an apology of sorts she would come to realize.

> Hi Kayla . . . I had to go to work and I didn't want to wake you.
>
> I know you are mad at me, you might even hate me, but I need you to know how sorry I am.
>
> I don't know exactly what Delilah told you last night, but I do know that she is lying. I swear on my mother that I did not sleep with her while you were in Miami. I was very angry at you and got drunk and fucked up, but I didn't have sex with her. I could barely even function.
>
> I love you so much that it hurts. Last night when you got sick and passed out, it was the most scared I have ever been in my life. I thought I was going to lose you and I am not sure I know how to live without you. It's me and you, Kayla . . . forever.

He didn't sign his letter; he didn't need to. Small, rippled circles that crinkled the paper clued her to the fact that he had been crying while he wrote.

Kayla was furious with him, but there was also an indescribable magnetic bond between them that could not shake. She hated to admit it, but she was comforted by the cement that attached them—although it could be porous and prone to cracks. She did not know at the time that trauma can be a bonding agent.

The quiet jury in her head may have been hung, but that still meant that Cam walked away innocent. Her conscience, her gut; the celestial voice that guided her through life spoke ever so faintly that she could barely hear it anymore.

thirty-five

CAMERON

After the grueling night of Kayla expelling rotten liquids from her body, she finally drifted off into sleep in the early hours of the morning. She was in such a terrible state that luckily for me we never discussed what had transpired that evening. I had written her a heartfelt note but was still nervous about what was waiting for me when she regained her strength. I loved her as much as I feared her and I think that is how she maintained power over me.

Needing my own space to reflect, I slunk out of the apartment as soon as the sun peeked in the sky. I had not slept at all the previous night, keeping watch over my ailing patient who spent the night groaning in discomfort. My heart pained for her, but it pained for me as well, and the stupid fucking decisions I had made.

Alone in my car, encased in a luxury metal cocoon, I thought about that terrible night in Miami. The image of an inebriated and overly flirtatious Kayla in a neon pink string bikini buttressed up against athletes and rappers had singed itself into my mind. I punched the steering wheel three times in succession and swore. I still harbored ill feelings about that night, even though Kayla and I had vowed to move past it, but the interaction with Delilah the night prior had reopened a freshly healed wound.

Leaning my head back against the black leather headrest, I recounted the events of that fateful evening.

Upon seeing the online photos that had been posted the night Kayla was in Miami, many of my friends who were with me at the club did their best to keep their distance from me, uncomfortable by the situation that was unfolding.

A few of my friends I was partying with offered words and phrases of support that ranged from, 'fuck that bitch,' to, 'it is probably not what it seems.' But it was Delilah who pounced on the situation like a sly puma, gunning for the kill. I see that now; her ulterior motives should have been obvious, but my fury shaded me from her intentions.

Delilah was a hustler through and through, and that night she saw my vulnerability and seized the chance to sink in her manicured claws.

I have clear visions of her strolling over to me as I sat on one of the leather couches in the VIP. My head was spinning from a bevy of things—the recent news about Kayla, the drugs and the pounding bass of the music.

My friends had been taking full advantage of Cathedrals' VIP area ever since I claimed ownership. Everyone was laughing, drinking, dancing, flirting and having a good time, while I wallowed in my own sadness and hurt.

Lazy had offered to take me home, but I refused. I could see the concern etched on his face when I told him I was staying. He left, but said he would return in a little while.

The moment Lazy left, Delilah chose to break away from her group and seductively perch herself onto my lap. Her arm slinked around my shoulders and her fingers gently caressed the nape of my neck. I didn't initially respond, but her touch felt warm and inviting.

She brought her lips close to my ear and said, "I saw the pictures. I'm so sorry she did you like that." She paused for effect before continuing. "I just can't believe she is out there disrespecting you like that!"

She straightened up so that I could see the disapproving shake of her head that caused her gold hoop earrings to wobble. She pulled her face into an exaggerated pout and pressed her palm hard against my chest.

"You know *I* would never do anything like that to you." She got up to fetch me another drink that I didn't ask for and then sat next to me. She clung to me like cheap cologne, while she rubbed my thigh and went about telling me how I was too good for Kayla.

"She doesn't understand this lifestyle. She's not like us," Delilah explained gently.

I hated to admit it, but she was right. Kayla wasn't like us —she was better. Much, much better. And sadly, she wasn't aware of half of the sins that I had committed. My mind ran on a constant hamster wheel in thinking of ways to impress her. To prove to her, *and myself,* that I was worthy of her presence. But, deep down inside, she and I both knew that I was not her equal and never would be. That was precisely why I was with Delilah at that moment—she felt like my equal. I did not have to put on airs around her. But with Kayla it was different. I loved her more than anything else in the world, but I doubted she would ever accept the real me—especially not after she learned the truth—about *everything.*

After some time, another drink and two more lines of coke later, my half-lidded eyes took notice of a coquettish grin painted on Delilah's perfectly symmetrical face. I got up, unsteadily, and she rose with me, her arm looped through mine just as Lazy was returning.

Lazy gripped my arm and cautioned me that I should let him drive me home. I remember the direct and pleading look on his face as he reminded me that I was not thinking clearly, and that I should not do anything that I would regret later.

I pushed past him *and* my morals, my fingers coiled around a beautiful mistake. I squelched the voice in my head that warned me against the abhorrent error I was about to make, but I forced the voice to shut up and took Delilah with me to my office.

Once we were alone, Delilah locked the door in one swift movement and backed me up against the wall. The wall displayed artwork that Kayla and I had chosen together. It was some stupidly expensive piece that I had bought to impress her, in an attempt to seem worldly and debonair, even though I knew next to nothing about art.

I zeroed in on Delilah and wrapped my hands around her midsection. She wore a skin-tight dress in a brilliant shade of blue, like that of the beauty spot on a mallard's wing. I peeled her dress downwards to reveal two spheres of surgically designed perfection.

"I know you missed this," Delilah purred as she shot me a mischievous smile, lips curling upwards to reveal pearl white veneers.

I rubbed my hand over my eyes a few times—my vision wasn't blurry, but it wasn't exactly clear either. Delilah's body used to arouse me, but not today. Not anymore. What stood before me was plastic, obscure and unappealing.

I reached out to touch her, hoping it would awaken a primal need in me, but it didn't. I dug my fingertips into her skin, but an image Kayla popped into my head. Overwhelmed with sprays of guilt, I felt an emotional punch to my gut which caused me to lose my footing and stumble backwards. A higher power was trying to send me a message, but I was just too daft to realize it.

Believing my reaction was due purely to my alcohol intake, Delilah laughed and guided me to the couch. I landed on the leather cushions with a soft thud and my stomach began to churn. Delilah stood in front of me, shaking her head comically, her hard, grapefruit shaped breasts barely moved as she giggled.

My thoughts wafted over to Kayla again. I thought about how her skin felt against mine. Then I thought about her laugh and the profile of her face. My mind flooded with visions of the tiny brown freckles on her nose that I loved to kiss.

I could feel myself on the verge of tears, and I mumbled to Delilah that I had to go, but she held down my shoulders and cooed into my ear about how she could make me happy.

I drew her arms away from my neck and began to rise from the couch. I thought I had succeeded in exiting the situation, but Delilah was quick, *and sober*. She pushed me back down onto the couch and I knew she was just being playful, but I had had enough.

I could feel her tugging at my pants zipper. I wanted her to stop, I really did, but my throat was sandpaper dry and no words were able to escape.

She pulled out the lifeless appendage from my jeans and stuffed it in her mouth like a wad of gum. She attempted a sucking motion, but the whole ordeal ended up resulting in an action like that of a bird trying to pull a worm out of the earth. A windsock without any wind is a pretty sad sight. If this situation had happened to anyone else, I would have found it hysterical, but it was happening to me, and there was no humor to be found on the horizon.

Sense finally taking over, I steadied my hands on the top of her shoulders, my thumbs pushed flat against her clavicle, and I told her to stop as forcefully as I could manage. She looked up at me with big doe eyes and sheepishly pulled up the top of her dress over her breasts. She sat back on her heels and began to chew her bottom lip, her chin and gaze adverting to the floor. Quietly, she rose from the floor and sat next to me, unsure of what to do next. I mumbled something like, "it's not you, it's me," and "I'm sorry," but it seemed disingenuous.

Awkwardly, I pulled my wallet from my back pocket and plucked out a few hundred dollars. Delilah and I had not been together in forever, and I had forgotten the protocol of our arrangement. I laid the money on her lap and patted her thigh. I excused myself to use the bathroom to pee and when I returned, she had left.

I wanted to call Kayla, but I couldn't bring myself to speak to her or hear her voice, so I did the next best thing, curled up on the couch like a cat and drifted from a drunken stupor to a deep sleep.

When I awoke the next morning, my body ached from the contorted position I slept in on the unforgiving leather cushions. Using my hand as leverage, I propped my body up into a sitting position, knocking over two terry cloth beach towels with Cathedral's logo onto the carpet. The towels had been placed on me as a blanket, and my sneakers had been taken off as well, positioned side-by-side next to the couch.

I scratched my head in mystery and walked stiffly over to the bathroom. I rinsed my mouth with water from the faucet, hoping to wash away the sour taste of my indiscretions from the night before. I splashed water on my face too, hoping the coldness would wake me up, but I wet the collar of my sweat-stained shirt instead.

Walking a bit more fluidly, I headed back to the couch to wipe my face on one of the towel blankets that I was mysteriously gifted last night. As I dried my face, the crushing weight of reality plummeted onto me, as I remembered the events of the night and what Kayla had done to provoke me.

I began to pace my office as I remembered that everyone present in the VIP lounge last night was fully aware of what had occurred. They knew about how Kayla had acted. They saw the photos. My stomach tightened and my blood pressure rose at the thought of my friends and employees thinking of me as weak. She made me look like a fool. In my industry, respect was everything and I would be nothing without it.

In my fit of rage, I demanded that she come home immediately, or our relationship was over. I was speaking out of my ass of course, anger overtaking reason. But if Kayla loved me as much as I loved her, she would have taken the next flight back.

I began to put my sneakers back on and my mind wandered again to who could have come into my office last night while I was asleep. In a quick moment of panic, I checked for my wallet, but it was still there. I relaxed, but that still didn't answer the question. I reasoned with myself that it had to have been Lazy. I pieced together the night and remembered him cautioning me not to go into my office with Delilah.

Delilah. Oh, fuck.

Did I? No, I didn't. That definitely didn't count. It wasn't all together innocent, but no penetration occurred, so technically I was in the clear. Right? *Right?* I did not know who I was arguing with, or what I expected to hear.

As I crossed my office to head out the door, I could hear the maintenance team working diligently and I took a deep breath, praying I wouldn't run into any of them.

From the corner of my eye, three fanned out one-hundred-dollar bills placed on the mahogany counter caught my attention. I stared at them for a second before registering that it was not Lazy who had come to check on me last night. Unable to process Delilah's caring action, I grabbed the cash and thrust it into my front pocket as I made a beeline for the exit.

A chiming noise on my phone interrupted my mental recounting of that night. I looked down at my phone and saw that Kayla had texted me.

I tentatively picked up my phone and viewed the message, hoping it did not display any phrases like, *go fuck yourself*, or *I am moving out*. Instead, Kayla, my perfect human being, simply typed, *I love you*.

I breathed a sigh of relief and started to type back, *I love you too and I'll be home in a couple of hours*, but my thumbs were halted from their tapping by another chime on my phone.

No more secrets and we will be fine. "Oh, baby," I said aloud to no one, "if it was only that easy."

I know how the saying goes—if you love a flower, don't pluck it, let it grow—but I could not allow for the possibility of someone else stealing my flower. Kayla was all mine and I had to do everything in my power to keep it that way.

I knew what to do, I would not pluck the delicate stem but instead would use shears with a surgical precision. A clean slice from the noise and ghosts of my past.

Me and Kayla: upstate, away from the city, surrounded by the woods, water and nature. That is where all the flowers are, anyway, I reasoned with myself. She could be replanted there; she would grow and flourish.

The reoccurring nightmare would be over soon because Kayla was the portal to eternal happiness. She was cloaked in love and innocence and there was no way I was going to let anything get in the way of that.

I shifted my car's gear into reverse and began to back out of my parking spot. I had a destination as I put the car in drive—47th Street, the diamond district.

My metaphorical thinking was interrupted by a ring from my cell phone. It was not Kayla's assigned ringtone. I looked down at my lap to see Dr. Pawar's name emblazoned on the screen. I clicked the green accept button and the car's Bluetooth connected.

"Morning, Doctor." I answered, cheerily.

"Hey, Cameron," he responded in a flat tone. "Do you have a minute?"

"Sure," I responded tentatively. "How are you? Is everything okay?" I pressed, although I could gauge from his initial tone that everything was *not* okay.

"Well, son, yes everything is fine with Kayla. She seems to be a healthy young woman despite this bought of shigella, but she is also pregnant."

thirty-six

Cam arrived home late in the afternoon with two dozen red roses and a lengthy apology in tow. Unless it is Valentine's Day, red roses are the ultimate, 'please forgive me, I screwed up' gift. Kayla accepted the flowers and his excuse—mostly because she still felt nauseous and her fatigue level was through the roof.

She felt depleted, but she knew that Cam would always take care of her. She let him spoon feed her matzo ball soup, bathe her and braid her unruly hair. He was even diligent with keeping her family apprised of her condition without her ever having to prompt him to do so.

They had a pattern—it was far from a pretty paisley, but it was a pattern nonetheless. They loved hard, they would blow up, and then they would forgive each other. Their relationship swirled around a vortex of toxicity, but Kayla had difficulty denying the fact that no one had ever loved her like that before. The passion that she and Cam had for one another burned with ferocity and it drowned out the voice of reason. The thing is, the less you love yourself, the quieter the voice becomes—until one day when the voice is completely squelched.

Kayla rolled over in bed. She wasn't sure if she was waking up from a full night's sleep or a nap. All she ever did anymore was sleep—deep, fitful sleeps. Cam took to mimicking and making fun of her snoring in the hours she actually managed to stay awake. The days and nights were jumbling together. She chalked her messed up circadian rhythm to stress, or the remnants of her virus.

She wiped the sleep from her eyes, and simultaneously swatted at a tickle on her neck. Mid swat, her forefinger hooked onto a long, curly opal colored ribbon. Blinking in confusion, she propped herself up onto her elbows and was greeted by a sea of ribbons, thick as kelp, suspended from the ceiling.

She jolted out of bed with a start, her heart beating at a faster pace than normal. "What that fuck?"

Separating the ribbons like a curtain, she peered upwards towards the bedroom ceiling, which was blanketed with balloons, maybe thirty of them. Large, round globes of latex in pearl shades of pink, white and gold.

She called out to Cam twice, but he kept mum, although she was certain that she heard rustling coming from the living room.

Childlike amazement and wonder flooded her face and a giddiness erupted from deep within. The hall, too, was littered with a rainbow color wheel of latex spheres. Kayla's fingers brushed through the ribbons dragging some balloons along with her as she walked through them.

Hearing her approach, Cam called out to Kayla in a coy voice. "I'm in the living room."

Stepping carefully and filled with anticipation, the trail of balloons began to thin out as she approached the living room.

A grinning Cam stood at the end of a banquet table—oddly placed in the center of their living room. A silk, white table-cloth pooled down onto the floor like a flowing waterfall. Sensory overload barely allowed Kayla to take in all that stood before her.

Cam had set the dining table with an assortment of her favorite pastries, each displayed on tiered silver platters. Tiny, brilliant clear gems were scattered along the length of the table, weaving around the bountiful platters of sugary goodness.

Kayla asked again what was going on, but Cam stood wordless with a knowing smile—forcing her to take in the surroundings in silence. A rainbow pyramid of macarons towered on one side, a croquembouche with an amber sugar spun cage decorated the other end. Flaky and buttery choco-late filled croissants lay next to a tray of almond paste tarts and Swedish butter cookies, thin and crisp, were displayed in two even rows.

Kayla picked up a bite sized barrel of phyllo dough stuffed with goat cheese, honey and thyme and popped it into her mouth. Her eyes rolled back in ecstasy upon the first bite. Wiping away phyllo crumbs from the corner of her mouth, she heard Cam chuckle as her gaze continued to rove over the gourmet platters. Alongside a colorful vegetable frittata, a small stack of papers lay.

Kayla picked up the papers and stole a glance at Cam who had finally advanced towards her. He looped an arm around her hip and pulled her into him, his grin broad and beaming.

"Read it," he instructed, as he motioned with his chin towards the papers that had gone slack in her hand.

"What *is* all this?" She smiled so widely that her cheeks began to feel sore.

Kayla's mind, like a tilt-a-wheel, whirred too quickly to

properly take in the words typed out on the paper in front of her. But, she quickly deduced that it was a legal document. The word DEED, printed in bold, black serif lettering along with Cam's signature, and an address in Bedford burned into her retinas.

"Holy shit. Cameron, did you . . . did you buy us a *house?*" Kayla's heart palpitated as she registered what she had just read.

"Maybe," he replied playfully with a shrug of his shoulders.

"Is this the house where we stayed and met Estella?" Kayla asked, still in a state of shock.

"Hmm, let me see," he responded, peering over at the paper as if he was not aware as to what it said. "Yeah, it looks like it." He slid his eyes towards her without moving his head to gauge her expression.

Kayla's left hand flew to her mouth, as her eyes began to prick with warm tears. Cam uncoiled his arm from around her body and positioned her away from him. With a deliberate stride, he walked over to the corner of the living room and plucked an iridescent pink balloon with a layer of white and silver confetti down from the ceiling.

He picked up a small knife that was on the table, took the house deed from me and placed it absentmindedly next to the croquembouche. He theatrically wrapped her fingers around the handle of the knife.

"Cam, what the hell are you doing?" Kayla laughed, but he shushed her, fighting back a laugh himself, and placed the confetti filled balloon into her free hand.

"Pop it," he directed smoothly as he stepped back from her, eyes glinting and fixated on her every move.

In a rush of excitement she thrust the pointy metal into the fragile latex. *Pop!*

The balloon all but vanished. A silvery and white plume of

confetti erupted. Kayla jumped back, squealing in delight. Aside from the piercing sound of her shrieks of excitement, she heard something that sounded like a marble colliding with their parquet floors. Her eyes followed the sound and found themselves searching the floor in front of her.

Scattered among the paper confetti lay a three-carat canary yellow oval stone diamond ring. Two white trillion cut diamonds framed the canary diamond resulting in a show-stopping triple-stone look.

Kayla had but a moment to process the implication of the brilliant stone that lay at her bare feet. Cam bent at the waist to retrieve the ring, and stood up slowly to face her, the band of the ring poised between his pointer finger and thumb.

"Hmm, it looks like you dropped something," he said with a snicker.

Before she could answer, Cam dropped down on a bended knee. His attention was focused on the platinum beauty clutched between his fingers. He looked down for what felt like an hour, but was probably only a few seconds, and then he stiffened, taking a deep hour before tilting his head upwards to look at Kayla.

Her lips parted and her breathing slowed, while warm tears filled the wells of her eyes.

"Kayla Montero, I love you more than life itself. Will you marry me?"

thirty-seven

Many women want a storybook love. Kayla was no exception. She too, had thrown penny after penny into random water fountains wishing for a handsome, wealthy Prince Charming to ride in on his white horse, swoop her up with a strong, defined arm and shuttle them off to a 3:2 in the suburbs. They would then live Happily Ever After in a good school district, with little Jack and Jill outfitted in vineyard vines and Patagonia fleece. Kayla would awake cheerfully at 6:00 a.m., dutifully apply her makeup and prepare cookie cutter sandwiches for school lunches and schedule PTA meetings in between yoga classes. That life used to be a daydream, a passing fantasy, but it seemed as if it could be reality.

Cam was not the storybook prince that Kayla envisioned. And he certainly did not whisk her off her feet. She was not presented with a valiant prince, but a flawed knight with the confidence of a puissant king. . . and she guessed that she could live with that.

Her initial impression of Cam was that he was an arrogant asshole. Her opinion of him, while now ensconced in love, remained the same. Cam *was* an asshole, and he could be arrogant, but he was financially savvy, a philanthropist and above all, he commanded respect.

A movie reel started in Kayla's head, and began to play a scene of the time Cam screamed at her in the shower for attempting to add a little spice to their otherwise vanilla sex life, immediately followed by the scene of him trashing the trinkets on her foyer table and then claiming his reaction was somehow her fault.

The vivid photoplay continued with Cam demanding that she work from home until he trusted her again, while graphic images of Delilah's hands trailing over his body flooded the peripherals of her mind. And all the while he kept the fact that he still owned Rubies hidden from her.

A tinkling voice like a warning siren rang out to her, but she silenced it as visions of Cam sitting at the dinner table in her parent's house laughing with her family submerged her vision. She saw him crouched down at eye level with Anaya inquiring as to which overpriced toy she wanted, while rocking Joseph in the car seat carrier when he began to fuss.

She remembered when she watched his posture droop, and his shoulders hunch as he teared up at his mother's grave on Christmas. She could feel the warmth of his body all around her as she was reminded of the countless hours they had spent lying in each other's arms surrounded by the plush security of their bed. And lastly, she thought about the way his face softened whenever he said, "I love you."

Cam was scarred and emotionally disfigured, there was no doubt about that, but maybe she could look past his imperfections.

So, when he asked her to marry him, she said "yes."

thirty-eight

After Kayla said "yes," they imbibed themselves on the artfully curated spread of sugary and salty treats. Lucky for Kayla, her stomach had finally settled, so she could properly enjoy her feast.

They selected their first bites from the buffet, placed them on two white scalloped plastic plates and retreated to the couch. Kayla pummeled him with a barrage of rapid-fire questions about how he managed to pull off such a romantic stunt while she slept. His answers were simple. Wide-eyed, Kayla listened as he explained his master plan.

Kayla had left her Pinterest boards open one night on her iPad and he saw some ideas that she had pinned when she was engaged to Amir. They were ideas bloomed from pure fantasy that she was certain would never come true. But she liked the photos, so she saved them anyway.

It had been so long since she had even looked at her engagement/wedding board that she had completely forgotten that she wanted a room brimming with confetti filled balloons or a gourmet spread out on a banquet table like a charcuterie board for a giant. She had even forgotten about the snapshot of the giant canary yellow engagement ring, belonging to some famous Hollywood actress. She had pinned the photos of the ring with the caption, "I WISH!"

Kayla lauded his cunning investigative skills and told him how impressed she was. Cam took the plate from her lap, placed it on the coffee table in front of them and lovingly hooked his arm around her neck and pulled her into his chest, "I hope you are happy," he whispered into her ear, even though there was no one around to hear them.

She chose to kiss him in lieu of a verbal response, finding that expression to be more fitting—they both tasted of butter and salt. The glint of the diamond caught Kayla's eye and she smiled appreciatively at him, still in awe.

Cam grasped her fingers and kissed her knuckles twice before he flipped Kayla onto her back, and a giddy shriek escaped her lips. Her head landed on the soft jacquard chenille couch pillow, and he planted soft kisses on her neck dotting down towards her collarbone. Try as she might to focus on her fiancée as he trailed wet kisses down her stomach, she could not help but wonder how long it would take him to finish so that she could go to the nail salon and get a French tip manicure.

Over the next two days, the ceremonial engagement ring finger photos were posted to social media. Announcement texts to friends and family were sent with an embedded picture of the glistening rock.

Kayla made it a point to call Ben and share the news with him, unsure of how to go about telling him since she never informed him that she and Cam were dating. Caring for his wife was a full-time job for Ben and they had yet to see each other since his retirement. Ben didn't answer, so she left a voicemail and texted him a photo of the ring.

Excited to tell her parents and sister about the proposal, she was surprised to find out that they already knew. Cam had invited her father out for a round of golf and informed him of his intentions, and her father gave his blessing.

Amid their post engagement bliss, Kayla was still plagued with occasional vomiting and fatigue that just would not quit. She was thankful for her surprise sugary feast, but unfortunately, it seemed as if the heavy foods restarted some of her stomach issues. She didn't tell Cam, as she did not want him to feel bad. It wasn't his fault that she caught a bug that was still holding fast to the caverns of her body.

The thick fog of fantasy that came along with the proposal had cleared. Reality, in its massive and unapologetic form, quickly revealed itself.

"How about we take a ride upstate to see *your* new house tomorrow morning, Mrs. Fiorletti," Cam asked coyly one Sunday afternoon, as she chopped onions for chicken noodle soup.

"Yeah, sure. I would love that!" Kayla responded with an added air of excitement sprinkled in for show. She wished she could have been more enthusiastic, but she was a hair overwhelmed by the recent, unexpected events.

Cam had come to calling her Mrs. Fiorletti, even though she was still very much a Montero, but she thought it was cute, so she left it alone. He had also mentioned in passing that he found it disrespectful for married women to hyphenate their names, so she already knew that issue would be an uphill battle. She decided not to broach the subject for a while and let sleeping dogs lie.

"How excited are you for your new kitchen?" Cam questioned excitedly as he leaned up against the kitchen counter as Kayla switched out the onion on the cutting board for some fresh and fragrant cilantro. The question must have been rhetorical because he just continued.

"I bet your kitchen puts Estella's to shame! I saw the way she was looking around and eyeing everything," he joked. She laughed as well, deciding his jovial mood would allow her to bring up her pressing concerns—albeit delicately. She didn't want to lose her last name, but that was superficial and only the tip of the iceberg.

"Um, baby, you know I am kind of worried about you diving from the city to Bedford all the time. I was just wondering, um, how do you think that is going to work out?" She tried to inject as much smoothness into her voice as possible, hoping it would mask her film of concern. Kayla peeled and quartered the potatoes, revealing their yellow Yukon gold flesh, as she awaited Cam's response.

"Well, it's not going to be a forever thing. I mean I'll keep Cathedral for now, but I'll probably sell it soon, six months or so," he shrugged nonchalantly. "I have much more viable investments in my portfolio. I don't want you to worry."

"*Sell* Cathedral? When did you decide that?" Kayla asked, hoping her voice didn't reflect the panic she felt.

Cathedral was her baby. She wasn't ready to let it go. Not yet.

Cam wedged his arm around her rib cage and she placed the chef's knife down on the cutting board, allowing him to turn her body towards his. She smelled like onions and told him so, but he didn't seem to care.

He smiled faintly and titled his head slightly, seemingly to examine her closely. "I hope you see now that I just want to make you happy. I knew how much you loved that house and that *kitchen*. I listened when you said that you wished we could stay there forever. It was what you wanted, so I made it come true."

Kayla silently screamed, "*Fuck!*" as she kissed him to mask her true emotions. She *had* said that, but she never actually expected him to *buy* the house. Like, who does that?

She viewed the Bedford house as a retreat, an oasis, not an everyday dwelling. The house was perfect, but it was too far away from their life in the city. She knew that her reaction was unfounded. She should have been over the moon from the proposal, and the purchase of the house, and the promise of a secure future, but she couldn't ignore the fact that something did not feel right. She felt conflicted, ambivalent about her own feelings.

Kayla zeroed in on her multi-faceted ring and took a deep breath as Cam walked away to take a work call. She cut rainbow carrots into rounds and imagined her life in suburbia as the aromatics of chicken stock filled their Brooklyn apartment.

thirty-nine

The drive up to the new house was rescheduled as Kayla got car sick ten minutes away from the apartment. She had only ever gotten motion sickness from a boat, never a car, but there was a first time for everything she supposed. By the time she felt better, it was too late to make the drive, so they decided to watch *HGTV* shows in bed to get décor ideas for the house.

"Look at that! I like that! It would be so cool to have a pond with fish. And that rock fountain thing, I like that too," Cam exclaimed, as he pointed at the TV. He sat up straighter in bed, as the contractor on the show explained to the owners of the home about the issues that come with pond installation.

Cam began to tap furiously into his phone, taking notes on what the television contractor was saying while he mumbled things to himself. Kayla rolled onto her side and glanced over to see that he had created a 'to do' checklist for the house. She was proud of his organizational skills and determination, but equally struck by pangs of jealousy as she wished she could share in his enthusiasm. She vowed to herself to try harder.

"I like that pond a lot too!" Kayla added, purely for show. "That *would* be a really nice addition. I'm going to Google local pet or fish stores. Maybe they can give us some direction about a good pond contractor."

The look of happiness on Cam's face at her response could have brought her to tears. She had not realized that her lack of excitement about that house had been conveyed outwardly.

"Oh, yeah, that is a smart idea. Good thinking!" Cam started to say something else, but then thought better of it and gave her a quick peck on the lips before returning to his phone.

"What is it? You were gonna say something else and then stopped." Kayla inquired.

"No, it's nothing," he smiled dimly, only meeting her gaze for a moment.

She placed her hand, with its glinting rock, on his phone and blocked his fingers from tapping on the screen.

"Tell me. We are getting married. We said no secrets, remember?" She reminded him.

Cam exhaled and glanced at her side long before stiffening his back and pivoting to face her. "It's not really a secret per say,' he began. "It's just that, I don't know. I am happy to see you finally excited about the house. You hadn't really said much about it, and I was beginning to think I did something wrong." He got quiet and she intercepted the silence.

"No! I don't want you to think that I am ungrateful. It's just that, honestly, I was shocked. I didn't even know the house was for sale." She chuckled nervously, but continued. "I'm not going to lie; I am nervous about moving far away and leaving the city. And I just had so many ideas for the club—for the club's future."

Kayla could see the agitation rising in Cam's face—at any moment he could switch from calm, cool and collected to Mount Vesuvius circa 79 A.D.

"Kayla, baby," he began in what she surmised was a patronizing tone. "We are getting married. You are about to be a *wife*. Don't you think it's time to start focusing on other aspects of your life? You have been tethered to Cathedral for how many years now? Ten, eleven? It's time to let that part of your life go. There is *so* much else out there for you." Cam gestured grandly like a ringmaster at the beginning of the circus and her face fell.

"I'm sorry. I am not trying to be mean and don't take this the wrong way, but you haven't been to the club in a while now, and everything is running just fine. You do your emails and planning and stuff right here, right in bed." He patted the bed for emphasis.

She began to protest, but he held his hand up indicating that he wasn't finished speaking, so she bit her tongue.

"I'm just going to say it, Kay—you working at the club is bad for our relationship, our *marriage*. It's. . . well, it's just not appropriate anymore."

"Appropriate? Are you fucking kidding me?" Kayla sat up from her reclined position and sat cross legged in front of him on the bed. They needed to be face-to face for this conversation.

"I am not trying to argue right now, Kay, I'm really not but I hate the idea of you hanging around inebriated men *and* DJ's, *and* celebrities, *and* athletes as a career choice." His cadence drawled on sarcastically as if he was exhausted listing the various genres of men with whom she apparently interacted.

"I don't make it a career to hang out with men! Have you completely lost your mind? What are you even talking about? I have never given you a reason to be jealous."

Cam shot her a look and she retracted her last statement and corrected herself. "Okay, I messed up once. One time!" She held up her pointer finger to emphasize her point. "How many times have *you* fucked up? Huh?"

"Are you kidding me, Kayla? You made me *sell* Rubies! I

bought you a house, a forty-thousand-dollar ring and a car that you barely drive—but heaven forbid I ask my soon to be wife to stop working at a nightclub."

He was no longer lounging on the bed, but standing on the floor looking down at her, his voice levitating with every word.

"Do you even hear yourself when you talk, Kayla? Do you?"

Cam had taken to pacing the room and running a tattooed hand through his hair. A sure sign that he was stressed. Kayla's shoulders slumped down along with the rest of her body. Cam had a point. Try as she might to argue with him, he was right. She had been tethered to Cathedral for ten years. It *was* her comfort zone. And who was she kidding? It's not like she would ever own the club, no matter how badly she wanted it to be hers. Nightclub ownership was a pipe dream—an impossibility.

She would never admit it out loud, but she stayed at Cathedral because she knew that she could never cut it in the corporate world. Her girlfriends who still worked had administrative jobs, and two of them were RN's. She was the only one who had an atypical career. She was the one with the 'cool job.' No one knew the reality, though. She was too chicken shit to try anything else. And up until that moment, no one but Cam had called her out on her bullshit.

"You're right," she squeaked out with the force of a church mouse.

"What?" Cam questioned cautiously, as if he had misheard her.

"You're right," she repeated a bit louder this time. Cam walked over to her side of the bed and plopped down next to her, his expression softened.

"I got too comfortable. And you're right . . . there are other opportunities out there."

Cam moved closer to her, listening intently as she continued. "I've always wanted to open a little café where I make pastries and stuff like that. Maybe, I could do something like that."

She *really* wanted to own a nightclub, but maybe making cupcakes in suburbia could satiate her urges.

"Exactly, baby! Just like that! That's my girl! Now you're getting it!" Cam gave her a one-armed hug. "We can lease you a place in the town whenever you are ready. It will be the best food for miles around—that will be a given." Cam burst upwards with an air of showmanship, and it caused her to giggle.

She hated how his mood could go from glacial to jubilant within a matter of seconds, but she could not dispute that this time he happened to be correct.

"How about this? I have an idea. We'll keep your apartment until I sell the club and we can stay there one weekend a month so you can check in on everything and hang out with all your DJ friends and you can dance around like a whirling dervish. How does that sound?" Cam questioned with a smile, as he interlocked his fingers in between hers. He was trying to meet her half way and she appreciated his efforts.

"I think that is a good compromise," she answered, replicating his smile. "You are acting like the perfect husband already."

She leaned back down onto the bed with a coquettish smirk and pulled Cam towards her. She squealed with laughter as he pinned her wrists down above her head and whispered into her neck, "and you're going to be the perfect wife."

She closed her eyes and nodded faintly in agreement until she realized what she had forgotten.

"Oh, wait. Hold on." She propped herself back up on her elbows, forcing Cam up with her.

"What? What is it?" he asked.

"My birth control pill. I forgot to take it this morning. Stay right there, give me a second." She pulled herself into a sitting position and slid her legs off the edge of the bed so that she could root through the drawer of her nightstand to look for the beige pill compact.

"Just forget it. Come back." Cam tugged her forearm forcing her to return to her previous position. She laughed at his vigor and smacked his hand away playfully before she plucked the compact from the drawer. She snapped the lid open, but Cam gently removed it from her grasp.

"I'm just saying . . . maybe you don't need those anymore, ya know," Cam said. His voice was smooth and convincing as his face searched hers for a glimmer of acquiescence. When she produced no verbal retort, he tossed the pill compact onto the nightstand and flashed her a devilish, yet undeniably sexy smile.

"Baby, you can't be serious," she said. "I'm not trying to squeeze a pregnant belly into wedding couture." She laughed out loud, hoping it conveyed the ridiculousness of the matter. But Cam's attention had strayed elsewhere.

"I would love to see your tummy swell up," Cam murmured as his fingers ran across the expanse of her flat-*ish* stomach. She chuckled again at the ridiculousness of it all and swatted his caressing hand away.

"Shhh," Cam hissed quietly in her ear. She bit her bottom lip as he shushed her and she dug the tips of her fingers into the soft flesh of his backside, and they moved together in familiarity.

They were just caught up in the moment, Kayla thought. She would just have to remember to take her pill in a couple of hours. No big deal.

forty

Kayla was awoken by an early morning phone call from her mother. Cam stirred as well at the chiming of the phone, but rolled back onto his side when he heard Kayla groan in exasperation.

"Ugh, it's my mother," she said aloud groggily. Early morning phone calls were no stranger to her mother. She had no concept of time. She rose at 4:30 a.m. every morning, a time that Kayla would usually come home from the club.

Kayla answered the phone. "Mom. It is so fucking early."

"Kayla Mariella Montero, watch your language! I never!"

"Jesus Christ, Mom. What do you want?" Kayla groaned, rolling her eyes.

"And don't take the Lord's name in vain either. I swear, it is like I taught you nothing!" She continued to scold Kayla, but it was too early for a parental verbal chastising.

"Mom!" She exclaimed to interrupt her.

"Don't yell in my ear, Kayla," her mom continued, "I am at the bagel store and am calling to see what kind of bagels Cameron likes."

It had slipped Kayla's mind that they had agreed to brunch

with her parents that day. Brunch was her mother's favorite meal. Once she perfected her mimosa, one would think that she invented the cocktail herself.

"Sesame, Mom. He likes sesame," Kayla repeated loudly hoping it would end the conversation, but she could only be so lucky. Cam pulled the comforter over his head to drown out their conversation. Kayla felt bad as Cam never slept in, and the one morning he did, her mother called and woke them.

"I know you like poppy seed, Kayla, even though I don't know why. The seeds always get caught in your teeth. And you never carry floss with you! No matter how many times I tell you! Oh, and I want to get rainbow bagels for the kids, but your sister is all crazy about food coloring and additives or whatever. I don't even know what she is talking about half the time, with all this organic non-GMO stuff. I always tell her, 'I fed you and your sister those things and you two turned out just fine.' Your father likes everything bagels and I usually get those too, but I read an article about the bialy the other day and . . ."

Kayla held the phone away from her ear and let out an exasperated sigh as she saw no end in sight to the phone call. A minute later she placed the phone against her cheek and floated back into the conversation.

"But I'm not going to buy the cream cheese here because it is just *too* expensive. I'll stop off at the supermarket anyway before coming home. I need to buy milk for Anaya. Only get one percent your sister says even though I'm certain she should be drinking whole. Organic, of course! But I only buy the half gallons because you know your father and I won't drink it . . ."

Kayla heard the cashier at the bagel store yell, "Next!" in the background.

"Sesame bagel, Mom. Cam likes sesame bagels. I gotta go. I'll see you guys in a few hours." Kayla ended the call before she could rattle off anything else. Her mother was a force to be reckoned with. She possessed the ability to command any room and conversation for that matter. Celeste also retained this special ability when she wasn't harried because of her children. And although not connected by blood, Cam too was blessed with this skill.

Kayla felt like she stood in the shadows on a daily basis. Only within the comfort of darkness and the noise pollution of Cathedral did she feel authoritative. It was one of the only places that she truly felt alive.

"We have to go to my parent's house for brunch today," Kayla said to a half-asleep Cam. He grunted a response, which she took as an affirmation that he had heard her.

She let her phone slide between their pillows and slipped back underneath the covers, draping her arm over Cam's torso.

They stayed at Kayla's parents' house longer than they had expected, but that was a commonplace occurrence, so she wasn't exactly surprised. Celeste arrived to brunch toting one sleep deprived child and one that was over stimulated. She immediately handed off Joseph to their mother and told Anaya to go see Auntie Kay. Celeste's hair was tied in a messy bun atop her head, her t-shirt had a set-in spit up stain and her eyebrows were not penciled in evenly.

Kayla was reminded of Cam's antics of the night prior and shot him a look that she was not sure he was able to decipher. He may have thought he liked the idea of pregnancy, but he was a man and therefore simple minded. He only cared about the fact that her boobs and butt would get bigger. The thought of his wife barefoot and pregnant awaiting his arrival was but a fantasy. Reality stood in front of them in the form of Kayla's sister. Once young and vibrant, she had transformed into a grumpy 30-something version of herself, laden in dry shampoo with offspring glued to her hip.

Kayla set a reminder in her phone to refill her birth control at the pharmacy.

Tired and in a zombie-like state, Celeste was still able to curate a bevy of wedding magazines for them to pour through together with their mother. They flipped through the glossy pages, taking in photos of rail thin models swathed in varying shades of white satin and silk. The women looked unhappy and on the verge of starvation, but their dresses were master-pieces—sheer perfection. Cam and Kayla's father had no interest in wedding talk and snuck away to peruse new golf clubs at the strip mall down the street.

Hours later, Cam and Kayla were finally able to break free from her parents' living room. Cam navigated the roads and street signs while he drove them home and they laughed about the funny occurrences that had taken place while they were at her parents' house.

Kayla's tummy began to rumble, and she had a sudden urge for roasted peanuts. Before Cam came into her life and finances were *always* constrained, she could have existed on hot dogs, oversized pretzels and NUTS4NUTS alone. Her stomach rumbled again, and she began to plead in her baby voice if they could stop off in the city first for peanuts.

"Ugh, baby really?" Cam whined. "Is there any place by the apartment that you'd rather go to instead?" he asked hopefully.

"No, I want NUTS4NUTS! I don't know why, but it's like I can taste them already. It's like *have* to have them," she begged. Kayla could feel the crunchy texture as it crushed against her teeth, her tongue running over the ridges of sweet clumped up sugar. She needed some damn peanuts, and *now*.

Cam straightened up, and with a sudden change of heart and endearing smile he agreed.

"Yeah, sure why not. Whatever you want." He took her hand that had been resting on his thigh and kissed it gently before setting it back down on his lap. Kayla squeezed his thigh and hooked his neck towards her for a kiss as he slowed down at a red light.

She began to talk excitedly about some of the ideas she had seen with her mother and sister in the wedding magazines. Cam mostly nodded, interjecting a few times with questions and ideas of his own. Their idea train came to a halt when they were interrupted by the chiming of Cam's phone. He retrieved it from his back pocket and scanned the message on the screen.

"Oh, perfect timing," he said to himself as he dropped his phone into the cup holder between them. "Lazy left some papers for me at Cathedral. Would you want to stop by there quickly?"

"Of course! I would love to stop by. I know it's early, but maybe some of the maintenance staff will be there and I can see them." Kayla agreed happily. "And then I can go home and cuddle in bed with my handsome hubby," she purred. Cam turned in his seat to smile at her and then focused his eyes back on the road as he calculated the change in route.

Even though Kayla was aware of the daily happenings at the club, since she took care of much of it on the back end, she hadn't been inside of the club in a long time. None of the employees at Cathedral knew the true story behind why she really stopped coming in. The majority of Cathedral staff assumed that because she was dating the boss now, she chose to stay home and live the spoiled girlfriend life. Of course, that could not have been further from the truth.

Cam's idea of relationship therapy, although extreme, had in fact worked, but it still plagued Kayla to her core that she had lied to some of her closest friends. Friends who were with her at her darkest and brightest times. Friends who attended her grandmother's wake and sat teary eyed by her side when her boyfriend, albeit *new* boyfriend, but boyfriend all the same chose not to be present. He had been forgiven for that infraction, but it still hurt when it came to mind.

Nostalgia washed over Kayla as she and Cam walked down the street to the club. In about five to six hours there would be a long line of patrons waiting impatiently inside the black vinyl retractable stanchions.

Cam pushed open the heavy doors of the club, the air significantly warmer once they passed through the threshold. They passed by a couple of maintenance personnel as they were mopping the acrylic overlay of the main floor. They ceased their stride to say, 'hello" to two of Kayla's favorite staff members, Helga and Marissa. Both women were warm and loving matronly types in their late sixties who reminded Kayla of her grandmother. She flashed them her ring, as she was not sure they were aware of her and Cam's engagement. The women embraced Cam and Kayla and began to offer their blessings in Spanish.

Cam took the opportunity to excuse himself so he could retrieve the papers from his office. He hugged Helga and Marissa one last time, this being the most interaction he had ever had with them and ascended the staircase. Kayla chatted with the women and inquired about their families, particularly their grandchildren. Once they had sufficiently caught up, Kayla departed and headed up the stairs, and Helga and Marissa headed home, having completed their work.

Kayla could hear Cam and Lazy speaking to one another as

she ascended the stairs to Cam's office. She could hear them exiting the office, so she stopped mid-way on the staircase to wait for them.

As soon as Lazy saw Kayla, he hugged her tightly and congratulated her on the engagement, and she showed him the ring even though he didn't ask to see it. The three of them continued to exchange pleasantries as they headed towards the exit.

Lazy pulled open the door for Kayla, allowing her to exit first. She said, "thank you," and stepped onto the sidewalk. Her cell phone pinged, and she ceased walking to retrieve it from the bottom of her purse. Cam and Lazy continued walking and laughing, outpacing her by a few steps as she checked her phone. Celeste had texted Kayla a few photos of the kids from that afternoon at their parent's house. A photo of Cam coloring with Anaya caused Kayla to smile from ear to ear. Her eyes were still glued to the phone screen when she heard her name being called.

The voice was familiar—easily recognizable. Kayla's body froze in position and her heart thumped against her rib cage. Kayla's head felt heavy like it was made of lead, but she lifted her gaze slowly until her eyes met the voice who called out to her.

The air left Kayla's lungs as Amir stared back at her.

forty-one

Cam registered Kayla's name being called at the same moment that she did. As if in slow-motion he spun on his heels and stormed towards Kayla and Amir.

"What are you doing here?" Kayla squeaked out. With Cam and Lazy in her peripheral vision, her voice seemed to be caught in her throat, unable to reach full volume.

"Kay, I know you hate me, but I just want to explain to you what happened that day," Amir cautioned in a rushed cadence.

Shock seared itself into Kayla's face. She could not believe Amir was standing in front of her. She had not seen him since his family removed him from their apartment by force.

"What's going on here?" Cam asked irritably. The question was directed at both Amir and Kayla, but Cam quickly zeroed in on Amir. "And who are you?"

"This is Amir," Kayla said, answering for him. "He's my ex. We used to live together." She explained flatly, pretty sure that Cam had pieced everything together by that point.

"Ah yes, I remember," Cam patronized. "Aren't you the one who had a wife in another country and then left Kayla alone with an apartment she could barely afford?"

Amir opened his mouth to answer the rhetorical question, but Kayla stopped him.

"What are you doing here, Amir?" She asked, her tone coated in annoyance as she remembered the agony she felt for months after Amir left her high and dry. She had not realized that she was still mad at him, but seeing him standing in front of her brought back a flood of painful memories.

"I just wanted to talk to you, Kayla. I want to explain myself. Please."

As expected, Cam answered for her. "Sorry bro, but that's not going to happen. So, do me a favor—stay away from my fiancée and go back home to *your* wife."

Kayla hooked her arm through Cam's, and he gave Amir a cocky smirk.

Amir shot Kayla a pleading look. "Kayla, please. It will only take a minute."

At this, Lazy interjected and placed a hand assertively on Amir's shoulder. "I think it would be best for everyone if you turn around and start walking the other way."

Amir tried to push past Lazy, but it only made the situation worse and tempers began to flare all around. Kayla held out her arms like an armadillo in a t-pose to separate the men from coming to blows on the street.

Unsure of how the situation would pan out, Kayla begged Cam to calm down. Catching the pleading look in her eyes, Cam took a deep breath and a step backward. He cocked his head to the side and warned Lazy to, "be easy." Kayla could see the gears turning in Cam's mind as he figured out how to rectify the situation.

"I think we all need to get on the same page. But, we're not gonna do it here on the sidewalk. Let's go inside the club and discuss this like adults." Cam directed.

"I'm not going anywhere with you." Amir spat back at Cam

before he turned to Kayla and implored. "Kay, please, you need to get away from him. He isn't who you think he is."

Cam's face fell and Lazy's eyes grew wide.

"What are you talking about? You sound crazy, Amir," Kayla accused. "Cam is my fiancée, and unlike you, he actually stuck around!" She flashed him her ostentatious ring to drive the point home.

"Kayla, I'm so sorry about all of that. I really am, but he's dangerous!"

"Dangerous?" Kayla responded with a mock laugh. Lazy remained stoned faced, but Cam made a snort of derision.

"It's true!" Amir shrieked.

"Okay, Amir, calm down. Maybe Cam is right. Let's just go inside for a minute and talk about this." Kayla fanned her hands out in front of her and turned around, walking the few feet back to the club's front doors.

Amir and Lazy followed closely behind Cam and Kayla. She typed the passcode into the keypad and the door clicked open. Kayla glanced over her shoulder and the four of them walked into the club together. Kayla turned on the lights with a flick of the switch and the group of them stood awkwardly in silence for a minute.

Not exactly known for his patience, Cam broke the silence. "Okay, buddy, why don't you tell us what you are really doing here and why you need to talk to my fiancée so badly," Cam said to Amir, a smug look on his face.

Amir's eyes bore into Kayla and she could tell that he was trying to send her some kind of subliminal message. It was a look that a year ago would have caused her to stop dead in her tracks and follow him blindly. But those days were over. Amir ignored Cam's questions and chose to reach out for Kayla instead.

A slight gasp escaped her lips before she could fully process what was happening in front of her. Cam backed Amir up against the wall and Amir stumbled backwards at the force of being pushed. Lazy was at Cam's side in a flash awaiting direction.

"You don't seem to get it, do you?" Cam sneered, his face inches away from Amir's. Amir attempted to push Cam away, but to no avail.

"No, I get it. I understand *everything*. Kayla is the one who is in the dark," Amir shot back at Cam, his finger pointed in Kayla's direction. "I bet she has no idea about the drugs and the fake passports and IDs."

Cam's face hardened and his chest rose and fell methodically. Amir looked at Kayla, gauging her reaction to the information. She remained stoic, although the news of IDs and passports was new to her. She knew about the drugs, obviously, she just chose not to ask too many questions.

"Yes, Amir," Kayla said. "I know what my fiancée does. He and I don't keep secrets from one another like you and I did! And where are you even getting this information from?" She questioned with furrowed eyebrows and a defensive hand on her hip.

Amir didn't need to know that she and Cam had raging trust issues. Cam would most definitely have to explain the whole passport and ID thing later. She just thought it was best to show a united front.

"I hired an investigator," Amir admitted. "Did you know about the strip club he owns? And those poor women he exploits—do you know the kinds of things that they have to do?" Amir yelled at Kayla, practically breathless until Cam's fist connected with his jaw. Kayla sucked in a breath as she heard a bone crack. And then Cam punched him again in the eye socket. And then again in the cheekbone. And then again in the jaw. Lazy stood at Cam's side, arms folded over his chest.

Kayla was horrified at the scene unfolding before her eyes, but she was powerless to stop it. When Amir had succumbed to a fetal position on the lobby floor, Cam finally backed away and shook the throbbing sensation away from his hand.

"Stand him up," Cam instructed Lazy. Lazy lifted Amir up like a rag doll and blood mixed with saliva dripped from Amir's mouth and down his shirt.

"Jesus, Cam! What the fuck!" Kayla yelled. She knew he was agitated, but this seemed excessive.

"I don't want you here. Go home," Cam directed and handed her the car keys from his pocket.

Kayla began to protest, but he jerked his head in her direction and she could see the flaming red anger behind his eyes and that alone cautioned her to bite her tongue.

She walked towards the door to leave as instructed, glancing over her shoulder every few steps. She heard a loud thud that made her jump and Amir let out a long wail. She turned toward the sounds of fists and feet pounding on soft flesh and brittle bones, but Cam yelled for her to leave again, so she did.

Still jittery from the scene she had just witnessed, Kayla slid into the driver's side of Cam's car and slammed the door shut.

She drove past a NUTS4NUTS cart, but didn't stop for any peanuts.

forty-two

Five hours had passed since she drove home on autopilot from the club. Cam was still not home. She called him after two hours had gone by, but he didn't answer. She texted him as a follow up telling him she wanted to check in, but still no answer.

Kayla's thoughts swirled around like liquid in a blender. What was Amir doing back in New York? Why was he saying that Cam was dangerous? And why did he feel the need to hire an investigator? How insane can one be? There was no way to make sense of any of it. A pulsing in her temple alerted her that a migraine was imminent. She squeezed her big toes to relieve the pressure in her head, but it didn't work, the throbbing persisted.

The longer Cam was gone, the more harried with worry she became. After throwing in a load of laundry, running the dishwasher and cleaning up the living room, nervousness transformed into nausea and nausea into vomiting. She threw up twice before she curled up on the couch with a wedding magazine.

Sometime later the clattering of a buffet lamp colliding

with the floor startled Kayla and she shot up from the couch as the wedding magazine and a pillow tumbled onto the floor.

"Cam?"

"Mmhmm, yeah it's me," Cam answered. His words, as well as his gait, were unsteady as he picked up the lamp from the floor, returned it to the foyer table and straightened the lampshade which had shifted to one side.

Concerned, she walked over to him, her arms firmly crossed in front of her chest. "Are you . . . are you *drunk*? Where have you been? What happened with Amir?"

She could tell from his state that he could not possibly answer all three questions at once. His eyes were bloodshot, and his knuckles were bruised and stained with flecks of dried blood. Normally impeccably dressed, his clothes were wrinkled, and he had a cigarette or joint burn on the hem of his t-shirt. Using the wall as support, Cam pushed past her and headed towards the bathroom.

She followed close behind him, hands still on her hips, awaiting some sort of explanation. He steadied himself against the wall with his shoulder and the side of his head as he attempted to undo his zipper to pee. It took him over a minute. In an unsuccessful attempt to pull his jeans back up from around his ankles, he accidentally knocked over a slew of her cosmetics and lotions that she had left on the sink counter.

"You're a fucking mess, Cameron! What the hell is going on with you right now?"

He mumbled something incomprehensible and then dropped all his weight onto her in a drunken bear hug. His girth took her by surprise, and she stumbled backwards into the bathroom door, stepping on and crushing a bronzer palette in the process. She swore under her breath as it was brand new. She patted Cam's back in a comforting, 'there, there,' motion, although her annoyance was building.

She swatted at the toilet seat cover to bring it down, and slowly eased Cam onto the toilet. He landed with a thud. She bent down onto the cool bathroom tile and started to untie his sneakers, slipped them off his heels, rolled down and removed his sweaty crew socks and pulled off his jeans, tossing them off to the side. Cam leaned forward, held his head in his hands and began to whimper. The whimper turned into a soft sob and his breathing began to hitch.

"I don't deserve you. Oh, my God, I am such a terrible fucking person. What have I done? What have I done? Oh, my God. I love you so much. I am so sorry." Cam began to sob uncontrollably, he sniffled and mucous dripped from his nose and landed onto his knees.

Kayla pulled a few pieces of toilet paper from the roll and wiped his nose before she rested her forehead against his. "Talk to me, baby. Tell me what's going on."

His response was to cry even harder. His shoulders quaked as his chest heaved. She hoisted him up, positioning her shoulders underneath his arm and she wrapped her arm around his torso, lifting him up with her. She led him down the hall to their bedroom. Cam's hysterical bawling had relaxed a bit, but he was still sniffling, and his mouth was downturned dramatically like a sad clown.

As soon as they approached their bedroom, and they had made it close enough to the bed for Kayla to drop Cam onto it, she did. Breathing out hard, she slowly approached the bed and sat down, glancing sidelong at Cam who was slowly rising to a sitting position. His head fell forward into his hands again and the hysterics ensured once more. Growing somewhat tired of his overly emotional antics, Kayla placed a firm hand on his shoulder and leaned into him.

"I want to help you, but I need you to talk to me."

"No!" Cam yelled like a toddler. "You'll hate me. You'll leave me," he blubbered.

"Did you hurt Amir? Like *really* hurt him?" She asked incredulously.

"What? No, of course not. He just got fucked up for running his mouth. And he said some things that triggered me."

"Cameron, what did you do? Is this about Delilah?" She stammered and her heartbeat quickened. Her jaw dropped in astonishment that they were even having this conversation, yet again.

"No, it is *so* much worse than that," Cam choked out, wiping his cheeks with the back of his hand.

Kayla relaxed a bit at hearing this because what could possibly be worse than your fiancée sleeping with another woman? Not a damn thing, as far as she was concerned.

Until she heard what he said next.

"She's dead, Kayla! She's dead 'cause of me."

forty-three

Kayla didn't realize she had been holding her breath since Cam's drunken confession. She had to remind herself to exhale. Certain she had misheard him, she asked him to repeat himself.

"I killed her, Kayla . . . It was my fault. She trusted me. How could I have let this happen?" Cam lamented.

"Baby, you're drunk. You don't know what you are saying," Kayla coaxed him. "You didn't kill anyone. Just slow down and explain to me why you are so upset," she said, but made sure to lower her voice when she said the word, 'kill.'

Cam shot up with an energy he did not possess five minutes ago. "You're right!" he slurred. It was Ben! It's all his fault. He put me in this situation!" And then he dropped to his knees and renewed his sobbing spree.

"Did you say, Ben? Like *Ben*, Ben?"

Exasperated and tired, Kayla rolled her eyes and ran a hand through her hair. She helped Cam up from his knees, guided him back to the bed and placed her hands on his shoulders to steady him.

"Okay, baby, I don't know what you are talking about, or

what you are on, but you sound fucking nuts. I need you to listen to me. No one is dead and Ben, who is currently taking care of his dying wife, is certainly not going around killing anyone. You are mad because Amir showed up out of the blue, that is all. So, I am going to make you a cup of black Bustelo to help sober you up. We are going to turn on a tv show and you are going to sleep whatever the fuck this is, off. Got it?" Kayla directed as authoritatively as possible. She patted his leg affectionately, not really wanting to scold him. She headed towards the bedroom door to leave so she could brew him a pot of coffee in the kitchen.

"It's how I got the club, Kayla," Cam said, barely louder than a whisper.

She stopped in her racks and glared at him. "What did you say?"

The pillows on the bed made it difficult for Cam to sit up straight and when he did his chin lulled forward.

"Please don't leave me. Please, Kayla," he begged.

She lowered herself onto the edge of the bed and Cam clasped her hands in his. She couldn't decipher the pleading look in his eyes and it unnerved her and the hair on her forearms stood on end.

"I'm not going to leave you, Cam, but I do need you to try to compose yourself and explain to me exactly what is going on."

Cam took a deep breath and raised his eyes to meet hers, his face pulled into a grimace, and she prayed that he wouldn't start crying again.

"Kayla, baby, I love you, but I need to um . . . I need to tell you something and um, it's real bad."

"Okay," she responded cautiously as she removed her hands from Cam's sweaty grasp. Kayla sat up straight, readying herself for the blow.

Cam slipped a little clear plastic baggie from his pocket and poured out a bump of cocaine onto the base of his thumb, raised his hand to his nose and sniffed aggressively. He rarely snorted coke, so his need to level out his mood before he spoke to me further piqued her worry. He wiped the powdered residue from his nostrils and bit his bottom lip.

"I wasn't, um, fully truthful about Rubies, Kay," Cam paused to gauge her facial expression, but she remained stone faced.

"Go on," she prompted.

"There is a certain group of clients at Rubies that we offer additional services too. Really *special* services. . . and Ben was one of our hard hitters. That is how I met him."

"What kind of special services?" Kayla asked, eager to hear the answer. Even though the idea of Ben getting a lap dance grossed her out to no end, it suddenly dawned on Kayla that she had never really pressed Cam, or Ben for that matter, on how they had met one another.

"Like private dates, stuff like that," Cam explained.

"Cam . . . are you saying what I think you are saying?"

He nodded slowly. "But that is not the worst part, Kay. Ben, he um . . ." Cam choked up and stopped speaking. He stared off into space and Kayla feared that he would zone out, so she shook his thigh to bring him back to reality. He began to shake his head slowly, as if hoping to make an awful thought disappear.

"Kay, baby, Ben isn't who you think he is. He's into some fucked up shit," Cam said with a shudder that seemed to chill him to the bone.

"What do you mean by that? I don't understand." Kayla questioned, bewildered. Deep lines of worry burned into her forehead.

"Cam, these women, are they like escorts? Are you, a . . ." She trailed off, unable to bring herself to say the words.

Cam held his hand up for her to stop talking. "Just let me get this out. Please."

She swallowed hard and braced for impact.

"Ben was into some kinky shit and a lot of the girls didn't like going out with him, but I kept working with him because . . . well because I could charge him a much higher price because of what he wanted.

"What kind of things did he want, Cam?" she asked, preparing herself for the worst.

"He liked it rough, but not like how normal guys like it rough. Apparently, he was on like a whole other level and the girls started to complain about him. A couple of them even came to me with bruises, so I spoke to him about and told him he had to chill the fuck out, ya know?"

Kayla nodded slowly; certain she was having an out of body experience as she processed the information. Cam poured out another little white bump onto the base of his thumb, dipped his head back, pinched his nose and sniffed hard. He wiped his nose and continued his confession.

"A few months before I met you, a new girl started working at Rubies. Her name was Julianne or Julianna—I don't know, it was one of those. Anyway, she was some naïve, ninety-pound chick from middle America who came to the city to be an actress or some shit. Honestly, I didn't even want to hire her at the club because she was flat like a board on both sides, but she said she really needed the money, so I told her about Ben." Cam dropped his head and sniffled. She could tell that he was gaining the courage he needed for what he was about to say next.

"I know that I shouldn't have set her up with Ben, but I explained what he wanted. I even told her to look up some videos online just so she knew what she was getting herself into. But it was good money and she needed money."

"How much money is *good* money?" Kayla asked.

"A grand per date. I remember her eyes got really wide and bugged out when I told her how much she would get. She said she would just take a painkiller and deal with it. And it was going good for a while, really good actually. Ben was booking like twice as many dates. But, then . . ."

"But, then what, Cam? What happened between this girl and Ben?" The pace of Kayla's words quickened even though she wasn't the one who was coked up.

Cam took a deep breath and began to rub his knees repeatedly in a nervous tick. "Ben liked to tie the girls up in these fancy knot things. And he liked to um, he liked to choke them, too. But, it got out of hand one night and . . ."

"And what, Cam?" Kayla whispered.

"He fucking killed her, that's what! He choked her to death with his meaty fucking hands and then he called me!" He started to pace the floor frantically, pointing to his chest repeatedly. "Me, Kay! Me! I had to clean up his fucking mess. And I had to go over there and see her limp fucking body, all tied up in red rope!" Cam screamed before he dropped to his hands and knees on the floor and vomited.

Twenty minutes ago, she *thought* she was having an out of body experience. But as she watched the man she viewed as her security, her protection—heave, wretch and sob on all fours at the foot of their soon to be marriage bed, she was certain this time that she truly was having an out of body experience.

"This can't be happening," Kayla stage whispered into the air, up to the heavens. She felt like a plastic ballerina in a mirrored music box, circling 'round and 'round and 'round with no end in sight.

The idea of Ben engaged in the type of sexual practices in which Cam spoke about made her shudder. It also dawned on her why Cam freaked out so badly when she asked him to replicate the *Cosmopolitan* article. It all made so much sense now.

Cam wiped his mouth but stayed on the floor. "And that is how I got Cathedral, Kay. Ben signed the club over to me as collateral for cleaning up his mess and *that* is why he retired and basically left the country."

How much negative information could one person receive before their head literally explodes? Kayla surmised that she would be the guinea pig for such an experiment.

When she snapped back to reality, Cam had fallen onto his side and was lying on the floor curled up next to his pool of frothy yellowed bile and vomit. Kayla crouched down next to him, accidently got throw up on her knee and wiped away the sweat that had accrued at his temples. His breathing was labored, and silent tears ran down his cheek.

Kayla had an urge to hold him, but at the same time she was completely and utterly terrified from his omission. How could she hug him and run at the same time? It is impossible to stay and go at the same time, but that is what she wanted to do. She had thought the betrayal from hanging out with Delilah was bad enough, but this? *This?* This was some other worldly shit, and she was in no way prepared to deal with any of it.

Entranced, she walked slowly down the hall so she could fetch some cleaning products and clean Cam's throw up. Her ankle gave out and she leaned her weight against the hallway wall, her hand further supporting her. She caught a glimpse of her stunning engagement ring and her heart dropped into her stomach like a rock into a well.

She had no time to think as Cam began to call out to her from the bedroom.

"Where are you going? Kayla? Kaylaaa!" Cam's voice filled with panic as he shouted her name like Stanley calling for Stella in *A Streetcar named Desire*.

Cam came rushing out of the bedroom and they both stood facing each other in the hallway, the recessed lighting beating down on them. "I was getting stuff to clean," she answered, feeling uncertain.

"Baby, listen . . ." Cam approached her slowly, his hand outstretched towards her.

Her brain told her legs to step backwards, and so they did. She took two calculated steps backwards while she kept her eyes trained on Cam. Prey often keeps an eye on the predator from a distance.

"Baby?" Dread and worry draped over Cam's face as he watched her step away from him.

"I love you, Kayla. I'm so sorry that I kept this from you, but you would have . . . you would have left me," Cam pleaded as he continued to advance towards her. She froze in place as her legs and brain ceased all communication. Cam wrapped his arms tightly around her back and she felt like he was trying to pull her into his soul. He smelled foul, like sweat, liquor, weed and vomit.

She used her palms as a wedge between them and gently pushed him a few inches away from her. He had been resting his chin on her shoulder, and he lifted his head up slowly like it was made of stone and wiped tears from his eyes.

"Cam," she began slowly, "I need to know what you did with the . . . the body." She was barely able to get out the word.

Cam looked down and shook his head slowly, "I have someone who takes care of things like that." He spoke quietly, but she heard him loud and clear.

"You've . . . you've had to do this before?" She cried; a yelping noise emitted from her throat.

"No! No! I swear!" he retorted as he braced his hands on her shoulders.

"So then how do you have *a guy,* Cameron? Like what the fuck?" Kayla shot back, her temper flaring. He backed her up against the wall, planted his hands on either side of her, so that she would listen to him and not storm away.

"I work with people that will scare someone if they owe me money or whatever, but *those guys* . . . they know people that handle more serious problems—like the Ben one."

Kayla dropped down to her knees and hugged them. Cam slumped down next to her and kept his gaze locked on her every move.

"Cam, are you telling me that you are like a pimp?" Kayla questioned suspiciously.

"What? No!" Cam snickered, and it enraged her. She stood up with a fervor and stared down at him practically spitting.

"You think this is funny? What is wrong with you?" she yelled.

Cam rose slowly, his hands up in defense. "No, it's just that no one uses that word anymore, it's not the 70's, baby. I'm sorry I don't mean to laugh."

Kayla's mouth was tight, but her mind was racing. She needed air, she had to get away.

"I know you don't know much about this lifestyle, and that is one of the reasons why I love you so much, but almost all strip club owners do this on the side."

Kayla knew he was just explaining the situation, but it felt as if he was trying to defend his actions as commonplace—and that sent a shockwave of anger down her spine.

"Cameron . . . you're a pimp," she said slowly as she backed down the hallway once more. "You exploit people and you are a liar. You betrayed me, yet again."

"Kay, please," he began.

"No!" She held up her hand. "You have been talking all night. It is my turn now. You helped cover up something horrendous committed by a man that I've looked up to for almost ten years."

Cam didn't respond, but his mouth drooped, and his puppy dog eyes welled up with tears again.

She clasped her chest as she put two and two together.

"This is about what Amir said! He found out about what it is you do with those girls, and he was going to tell me! You only told me because you were going to get caught! That is why you beat the shit out of him . . . you didn't want him to say anything else around me." She was screaming at the top of her lungs. Their neighbors were probably not amused.

Cam blinked a few times and his chest rose and fell before he nodded in agreement. Silence fell thick in the air like a humid August afternoon.

"I don't know what to say, or do, or think . . . I gotta get out of here, I feel like I am suffocating," Kayla said after some time had passed and the silence between them had become too much to bear.

"I'll come with you," Cam offered eagerly.

"No, I um, need to be alone for a while," she answered, unable to look him in the eye. She headed towards the front door and grabbed her purse and keys from the brown armchair in the foyer.

"Why are you taking your bag and keys? I thought you were just going out for air?" Cam questioned, his voice shrill and panicked.

"Cameron!" Kayla screamed. "You literally just told me that Ben strangled a prostitute to death in a kink scene gone horribly wrong and you, my fiancée, are for lack of a better word a glorified pimp. Is that right? So please, excuse the fuck out of me if I need to get some goddamn air by myself for a minute! Is that okay with you? Or do I have to clock in and out like one of your whores?"

Cam didn't answer and she couldn't let the silence settle again, so she reached for the front door, but Cam reached out for her forearm and pulled her back.

"Cameron, what the fuck? Let go of me!" Kayla spat as she wretched her arm away from him.

"Okay, Kayla, okay!" Cam stepped back and stared at her like he was being cornered by a wild animal.

"Take a walk, take a drive, whatever you need just please don't leave me, I'll make this right I promise," he begged as his voice dropped an octave.

"I don't know, Cam. I have no idea how to digest this information." She walked away from the front door and lowered her voice. "A girl is dead, and you are involved. Do you have any idea what that could mean for you? For Ben?"

"I know, baby, but it has been taken care of. I don't want you to worry about that. It is all over now," he said in a calming voice. "I just needed to tell you; it has been killing me."

"*Killing you*? Are you serious right now? A girl is dead, but it is killing *you*?"

Kayla's bewilderment was at an all-time high and she rushed towards the front door, pushing past Cam.

"Cam, I can't do this. I'm sorry, but this is just too fucking much."

Kayla went to remove her ring and Cam's eyes grew wide like full moons as she pulled the platinum band up over her knuckle.

"No! Kayla, no, please! You can't leave!"

Kayla could see the hamster wheel in his head turning wildly, searching for a trump card.

"And why the fuck not?" She yelled back angrily, her fingers firmly grasping the doorknob as fire lit behind her eyes.

"Because you're pregnant!" Cam cried out exasperated.

forty-four

Cam's words pierced Kayla's eardrums. As much as she wanted to bound out of the apartment and onto the street, she needed him to clarify.

"What the hell are you talking about?"

"Dr. Pawar said so," Cam began, as her posture began to take the form of limp spaghetti. "When you peed in that cup the night you were sick, he called me afterwards and told me that you were pregnant."

"I'm what? Is this some kind of sick joke?" She searched around the room frantically as if looking for an answer.

"Just come sit on the couch with me and we can talk about this," Cam coaxed. He wiped his nose with his fingers, and she could tell he was going to go for another bump.

"I didn't know how to bring it up because I knew you would be mad that I found out before you."

Kayla had never been hit with a stun gun, but she was told by her fiancée that she was pregnant, and she was quite certain that the feeling was similar. She felt like she was going to pass out. Cam suddenly felt like a stranger, and she needed to create a distance between them. Kayla needed a safe space and Cam no longer offered that.

"I, like, don't even know who you are. Who have I been sharing my life with? My bed with? You are like a stranger to me!"

"It's me, Kay. I am still the same person."

Kayla shook her head in disbelief and rose steadily from the couch.

Cam stood up to block her next movement, but he was still unsteady from the drugs, liquor and emotional trauma so she took the opportunity to bolt past him. She grabbed her keys from the table by the front door, decided to forgo her purse, wallet and phone, yanked open the front door and made a hard left to the emergency exit stairwell.

She could hear Cam calling her name from inside the apartment as she pulled open the heavy metal stairway door. She ran down the stairs, desperate to feel the asphalt on her fuzzy socked feet. She had reached the downstairs landing when she heard the stairwell door open from our floor.

"Kayla!" Cam called down to her, his voice echoed and reverberated against the reinforced walls.

She craned her neck upwards towards his voice and in doing so, her right foot missed the next step. She tumbled forward in slow motion, tried to put her hands in front of her to brace her fall, but it didn't work. Her knuckles came crashing down onto the grey painted concrete steps like she was punching them. Her body continued to roll down the stairs like a tumbleweed blowing through town during a Wild West gun fight. Kayla's spine connected hard with the flight of stairs on her way down, as did her butt, and her thigh, and her elbow, and her ear, and her forehead.

She could hear Cam's erratic voice and footsteps simultaneously rushing down the stairs to her. Her body looked like a pile of molded clay lying on the landing, barely moving but groaning in pain. A spark in her brain went off and Kayla intuitively cradled her stomach and pulled her legs up into a fetal position, further protecting her belly.

Everything hurt, from her scalp to the tips of her toes. Cam hunched over her protectively and gathered her up in his arms like a pile of dirty laundry. He was speaking rapidly, asking if she was okay and if she hit her stomach on the way down. He cursed and with a tear-streaked face cried out to God for forgiveness. She wished that his eyes would stop crying and that his mouth would stop talking.

She wanted him to go away. Leave her be. Leave her in *peace*. How could she have attached herself to such a corroded man? How could she have been so mentally weak as to allow such a relationship to continue? Besides financial security, what else did he bring to the table?

What made her think that could love another when she could barely love herself?

forty-five

The harrowing confessions and events of the night had pummeled Cam into a state of semi-sobriety and the effects of the cocaine and liquor finally dulled. Kayla could feel bruises starting to bloom. Roses of purple, blue and maroon soon to appear clear as day on her fair skin.

After she tumbled down the stairs like a slinky, Cam had hoisted her up like Mary held Jesus' body in the Pietà and proceeded with a delicate gait up the stairs to their apartment.

Kayla felt trapped, like they were characters in the spin-off: Beauty and The Beast from Brooklyn.

Cam placed her gingerly on the bed and lifted her t-shirt to check her stomach again, like he had done five times before in the stairwell. The sudden acknowledgment of this new life brewing inside her was just one more mind-fuck to add to the very long list that Cam had procured for her this evening.

Kayla rubbed her stomach rhythmically in utter disbelief. The news of Ben and his deadly sex practices, along with the fact that her soon-to-be husband facilitated and profited off the sexual services vulnerable women provided to beta males caused a black hole of disgust to form in her gut. The same gut that held her baby. *Their* baby—the one she and Cam created together.

"Baby," Cam began as he kneeled like an armored knight on the floor next to her side of the bed. "I think we need to see a doctor. You're banged up pretty bad. And I don't know if you hit your stomach, but you were holding it, so I am not sure if you damaged anything."

"A doctor? *You?* You think I would let one of you fucking doctors see me now? Does he even have a medical degree? Yeah, no thanks. I'll take care of my own healthcare from now on, thank you," she replied smugly.

Cam seemed only mildly defeated. "Okay, let's go to the ER then."

"I don't feel like sitting there alone for three hours," she countered, full of aggravation, stress and pain.

"Alone? Why, alone? I'll be there with you," he retorted, as he clutched both her hands in his.

She looked over dramatically at his bruised knuckles and then tilted her head back to exchange glances with him.

"Well, Cameron," she enunciated like she was speaking to a child, "because they will take one look at *your* hand and then all of *my* bruises and because they are medical professionals, and not blind, they will naturally assume that you beat the ever-loving shit out of me, that's why," she explained, her words heavy with sarcasm.

His mouth became tight as he rose up from bended knee and perched himself carefully on her side of the bed, as if he did not want the mattress to make a single sound or creak.

She exhaled deeply and turned onto her side away from Cam.

"Why didn't you tell me Cam? *Why?* It's *my* body. I should be seeing a doctor," she reasoned as she winced in discomfort.

"I wanted to. I really, really did, but the whole Delilah thing happened, and I knew how pissed you would be that I knew about the baby before you. Of course, I knew how messed up it was that I found out first."

"So, you just lied to me instead? Is that why you didn't want me to take my pills the other night? So, you could just pretend I got pregnant then? You know what—don't even answer that. I already know."

Kayla stared off into space. Her line of sight focused in on her framed Electric Daisy Carnival poster she had affixed onto the wall. The acronym 'edc,' was emblazoned across the center of the poster, every inch of the glossy paper chock full of colored flowers and speakers, with the setlist in bold white typeface aligned in the center.

She daydreamed about the last time she went to a music festival or danced, saw her friends or spoke to someone of the opposite sex without getting questioned suspiciously.

She thought about the last time she physically went into work. A hot tear stung her eye, and rolled down her soon to be purple cheekbone.

She missed the club. She missed the music, the people, and the camaraderie. Cam was correct when he said that she used the club as a crutch, an excuse not to mature, but being with Cam made her grow in a negative way. She grew from trauma. Was it possible that she bloomed in the darkness? Is that even possible?

Cam was still at her side, stroking her hair and back, doing his best to bring comfort to the situation he created.

"Do you want some pain killers at least?" Cam offered gently. He had a host of pharmaceuticals in his safe that she tried not to think about.

"Yes, nothing too strong though. And then go to Walgreens and buy me some pregnancy tests," she instructed, keeping her gaze affixed to the wall.

"Okay, yeah, sure! Of course! Whatever you need. Do you need anything else?" Cam asked, eager and ready to please.

She told him, "No," and he hurried out the door to retrieve her items. He must have sped to Walgreens because he returned in record time. He shot through the bedroom door with the white plastic bag containing three different brands of pregnancy tests.

Kayla rose from the bed, feeling groggy and Cam rushed over to assist her. Her tailbone ached as did her shoulder, the side of her face and her right wrist.

She shrugged off his help, assuring him that she was fine, even though she was far from it, and took the bag from his open palm.

She didn't have to pee on three tests, to confirm that she was pregnant. One test was all she needed. Two tests displayed twin pink lines instantaneously and the last displayed the word, Pregnant. Obviously, she knew the doctor was correct, but she still needed to see it for herself.

Cam knocked gently on the bathroom door, "Are you okay? Do you need anything?"

She wanted to be petty and immature and shoot back, "Yeah, a new fiancée." But she chose the high road and just *thought* it instead.

"No. I'm fine," she answered as she flushed the toilet and exited the bathroom. Cam leaned up against the door frame and she handed him the positive test. She walked past him and heaved her pain laden body onto the bed.

He dropped onto the bed next to her and mouthed the word, "wow," under his breath as he inspected the tests. Kayla deduced that just like her, he too was taken aback by the visual confirmation. It was one thing to hear it, but it was quite another to *see* it.

"What now?" he asked Kayla, as if she was the one with all the answers.

"Nothing. I'm tired. We go to sleep."

forty-six

The melody of birdsong informed Kayla that it was morning-time. From the window in their kitchen, the sun resembled a large egg yolk freshly cracked, eager to welcome the day.

Kayla was hoping that last night's events had not occurred, but it was no nightmare, nor had she stepped into a parallel dimension. Her bruises from the stairwell fall were delicate to the touch and exposed themselves in a kaleidoscope of colors. The painful marks prostrated themselves all over her body. Even a light graze caused her to retract in pain.

Kayla brewed herself a cup of decaf tea, since she knew from her many conversations with Celeste that caffeine was a no-no, even though she was desperately craving a mocha cappuccino. She googled what time her gynecologist's office opened so she could make the first available appointment.

She rehearsed the bullet points in her head of what she would tell Cam when he awoke.

He had set 'ground rules,' in a rogue relationship therapy treatment attempt to fix their problems and she played along, but the tables had turned and now she would be the one making the demands.

Cam awoke almost two hours later. He was groggy and his face was covered in lines from the pillow or blanket or both. He yawned, his mouth stretching open wide like a lion and leaned down to kiss Kayla on the top of her head.

"Is there any left," he asked in a voice hoarse from sleep, referring to the coffee mug in her hand.

"It's decaf tea. No caffeine for me in my delicate state," she said dryly, and Cam nodded slowly as if he was just piecing together the previous night's timeline.

"Make your coffee and then sit down. I want to talk to you," Kayla instructed.

Cam's eyes shifted back and forth, and he said he would forgo the coffee and just wanted to listen. He looked scared and she hated to admit it, but it gave her a surge of energy.

"We cannot go on this way, Cam—you and I. It is not healthy, and you have a lot of demons. I understand that you can't get professional help due to the *nature* of your problems, but you need to go on some kind of self-therapy journey if this is ever going to work. And that is a big, 'if.'"

"Sure, of course! I have no problem doing that. I'll do whatever you want," Cam pleaded with an uptick of energy. He took her hands in his from across the table and kissed them. He liked the way things were going. As far as he was concerned, all he had to do was read a few self-help books and he would be golden. But his bubble was about to burst.

"That's not all. There are a few more things," she continued.

"Yeah? What else? Anything you want," he further appeased, as a smile spread across his face.

"I want you to sign Cathedral over to me. Today. We are

going to the bank this afternoon. And I am going back to work —as the owner."

Cam's smile dropped and he let go of her hands. "What? I don't understand."

"And I don't want to move to Bedford, either. The house is beautiful, but it is too big and it is too far away. I am not ready to move to the suburbs, not yet anyway."

Cam opened his mouth to speak, itching to rebuff what she said, but she held up her hand to stop him and he swallowed hard. What could he say, really? She had him by the balls.

As she laid her demands on the table, she struggled to remember the last time she felt that good.

forty-seven

The proper paperwork was filed, and Kayla became the new owner of Cathedral Nightclub in New York City. It did not matter how she attained it, she got it, and it was *all hers*. In theory, Cathedral had always belonged to her, but now it was official.

Neither Cam nor Kayla mentioned Cam's confessions again, skirting the topic at all costs. They even switched off *Law and Order* one evening, both feigning fatigue when an episode about a murdered stripper aired.

A heavy cloud of guilt and omission hung menacingly over their heads, forever threatening a Category 5 storm, yet they did their best to slip into normalcy. And it worked. For a little while at least.

Kayla hoped that their hot and cold merry-go-round would finally stop circling and she could get off the ride soon. She was dizzy. But Kayla jumped right off the paint chipped horse on the merry-go-round, and slid right into a seat on the tilt-a-whirl—because one week later Cam was arrested.

Cam was booked on drug trafficking/distribution of

MDMA, marijuana and cocaine, with intent to supply. He believed it was Amir who had something to do with his arrest, although there was no way to prove it.

Cam's lawyer was a hook-nosed lanky man with flecks of dandruff. The lawyer's office was all mahogany and smelled of Pine-Sol. His desk was neat and orderly with a slew of silver framed photos of his family. Kayla wondered if she would ever display such photos on her office desk.

If convicted, prison time would be imminent—the lawyer estimated around three years, less with good behavior probably. If such occurred, the lawyer said he would petition to delay sentencing so Cam could be present for their wedding and the birth of their baby.

He shared this information with them like he was handing them a brightly wrapped Christmas present, and Cam thanked him earnestly. The lawyer promised to do everything he could, and that Cam shouldn't worry too much, but he would collect his abundant retainer either way, so it didn't affect him all that much.

Kayla stayed silent during the meeting with the lawyer— she had nothing to add. Her stomach was doing back-flips and she likened the cramping to anxiety due to the nature of the meeting.

Minutes later, they exited the lawyer's office and walked to the car together like they had not just received another bout of soul-crushing news. Cam reached for her hand to hold it and she let him.

She thought about how their once bright future was now dull and cloudy, like looking through a plastic bag. Could it even be considered a marriage if one of the individuals might possibly be gone for years? And he was only being charged with intent to sell. What if his other malfeasances were discovered later on? What then? Kayla's head was in the clouds and she felt dizzy.

A young mother with ripped jeans, exposed brown roots and imitation camel colored Uggs ran past them on the sidewalk. She grabbed the jacket of a toddling preschooler who was leaning dangerously close to the street. She was on her phone, distracted, talking to someone about not having any time to date and that babysitters were too expensive. Kayla spied her left hand, and it was ringless. She was all alone, a single mom. Kayla wondered if a higher force was holding up a mirror to her future.

Cam and Kayla continued to walk hand in hand to the parking lot. The lawyer's office was one among many in a large office building in Riverdale. Cam walked over to the parking attendant booth and gave the man sitting inside our ticket.

The attendant had been typing on his phone and put it down when we approached. He greeted them and Kayla noticed that he was quite attractive—tanned with a strong jawline and thick black eyelashes and eyebrows to match. The attendant examined the number on their ticket and punched the numerals into his computer. He squinted at the result on the screen and then swiveled in his stool to retrieve the fob from a wall of hanging metal car keys tacked up alongside his desk. He left the small booth and went to retrieve Cam's car.

Cam and Kayla patiently waited side-by-side for him to return. She clutched her stomach as a cramp rang through her abdomen like a lightning bolt. A brief look of agony must have washed over her face because Cam furrowed his brows in concern and inquired if she was okay.

"Just a little tummy cramp," she replied, and smiled weakly as he squeezed her hand and said they would be home shortly so she could rest.

They exchanged a couple of shy smiles between them, both of them too anxious to discuss what the lawyer had said and how their life together could possibly be stalled for years. If one could even call that having a life together.

A minute later they heard the screech of Pirelli tires driving up the ramp, as Cam's oil slick black Ashton Martin appeared. The good-looking attendant hopped out, complimented Cam on his car, as most young men do, and rushed over to open Kayla's door.

The attendant flashed Kayla a smile that could have been considered flirtatious. She returned a similar expression before casting her gaze downwards, heat briefly blushing her chest. Cam stared hard at the both of them for a second, but he was unable to discern the situation clearly or maybe he was just too emotionally drained, and he ducked down like a gopher into the driver seat of the car.

When they were both situated in the car, Cam exited the lot and turned onto the street, carefully navigating pedestrians. Kayla's stomach cramped again and she shifted uncomfortably in the passenger's seat.

They drove past a bar that had an aluminum and glass paned awning erected onto its facade. Kayla had been interested in installing a similar awning for Cathedral on the side of the building where the patrons waited on line for entry. When the weather was inclement, it pained her watching club goers enter the dance floor soaked to the bone.

She brought up the idea to Cam as she rolled down the window and pointed her arm outwards towards the awning. He agreed it was a good idea and with a squeeze on her thigh he said that *all* her ideas were good ideas. She leaned her head up against the buttery soft headrest and smiled to herself.

Cam was right. She did have *a lot* of good ideas. And she no longer needed anyone's approval to enact them. Cathedral *belonged* to her. She flipped down the sun visor and slid open the mirror. She looked at her reflection in the small, enlightened rectangle—Kayla Montero, owner of the hottest dance club in New York City.

Another cramp ripped through her stomach, this time causing a low moan to escape her lips. Kayla could feel a slimy warmth spread through her underwear. She lifted up her blue shift dress over her stomach, scootched forward and slipped her hand into her leggings and down into her underwear.

"What's happening? What are you doing?" Cam asked, puzzled as he shifted his gaze from her to the road, back to her again.

A warm mucous flooded her fingertips and nailbeds. Kayla yanked her hand out from her underwear and inspected the tips of her fingers that were covered in brownish-red blood.

Cam's face dropped down like Van Gogh's *The Scream*.

Kayla should have panicked, maybe even screamed. But all she managed to choke out was a slight gasp. She had already seen her gynecologist earlier in the week and the doctor had informed Kayla and Cam that the baby was growing according to schedule.

The doctor had said the baby was fine, but what was this? Even worse, Kayla wondered why she was not nervous or frightened.

She wanted her baby, but she also wanted what was best for it—and that meant a secure home life. She wanted him or her to have the best life possible and she did not know if she and Cam could sustain a healthy life together.

But for the first time in her life, Kayla felt free.

She owned Cathedral and no longer needed to be tied to anyone.

Her future was crystal clear, and it emitted the brightest prism of colors.

THE END

epilogue

An adept lawyer and a magician are often one in the same. Unsurprisingly, Cam was leniently sentenced to nine months. Kayla did not feel like it was just coincidence, as nine months would have been the same amount of time it would have taken to fully form their baby. A baby they would never hold. A life that would never be. Cam was distraught, but Kayla not so much. She feigned sadness only because she knew melancholy was the correct response.

The strings of codependency slowing dissolved and Cam could feel Kayla pulling away. A hollow emptiness settled between them and, emotionally, Kayla and Cam were light years away. Cam prayed to God and any other spiritual being that would listen. He begged for forgiveness and swore that he would change for the better. Change for Kayla. Change for *himself.* His affirmations did not, however, dissuade his fears about Kayla leaving him. Doused in apprehension, Cam would take a deep breath every time he inserted his key into the front door, nervous that that apartment would be empty. He lived in an ever-present state of anxiety. He would constantly ruminate over how their already fragile relationship would fare in his absence.

Cam suggested couples therapy, not because he actually wanted to go, but he figured mentioning the idea would show that he was making an effort. Kayla saw through his act as if it had been freshly coated in Windex. She agreed to therapy under the condition that she could choose the therapist. Kayla did not need a psychological run-down of what had occurred in their relationship. She was aware of the reasons as to why their ship was sinking. She had no interest in relationship strengthening tips. She only wanted a safe space to speak her peace.

During their second appointment, while perched at the edge of the gray tufted loveseat in their therapist's office, Kayla stated firmly that she wished to see Amir again. In order to grow and move on, she required closure about their ill-fated relationship. The closure was not a want, but more of a need. Kayla knew her relationship with Amir had deeply affected who she was. In retrospect, Kayla realized that had she given herself the proper time to heal after Amir left, she would have never tolerated Cam's lying and secrets.

Upon hearing Kayla's assertion of her needs, Cam's jaw tightened and his knuckles whitened as he gripped the armrest of the loveseat. To his credit, most men wouldn't exactly be jumping for joy at the sound of their partner wishing to interact with a past love. But Kayla did not care about how he was feeling. He was an adult and needed to figure out how to manage his emotions effectively. Kayla no longer wished to be his crutch. She was tired. But, not so fatigued that she was unable to see the light at the end of the tunnel. Kayla knew she would not return to a relationship with Amir. They had experienced something that was akin to love, but ultimately he was weak and a coward and she would certainly never be in that place in her life again.

Kayla anticipated that with rehabilitation and self-reflection Cam could be the person that she originally fell in love with—the person that she knows he is deep, deep down inside. She had wanted to walk through life with Cam by her side, and a small kindling of desire still hoped that could still be the case, but for the first time in her life she was perfectly fine walking alone.

acknowledgments

I was a sophomore in a new high school when my English teacher returned the classes' first creative writing assignment. She placed the stapled papers on my desk, emblazoned with a perfect score, and tapped on them lightly. She then asked, "you like to write, don't you?" I nodded my head, surprised by her comment. She then responded, "I can tell. It shows." She could have never known the profound impact that one comment would have on me. I have been writing every day since. Immense gratitude goes to my tenth grade English teacher, and every other teacher that has paved the way for young minds.

A gigantic thank you to Stephanie Larkin and her outstanding team at Red Penguin Books. I deeply appreciated all of your guidance and feedback throughout the entire process. The Red Penguin team truly turned my dream of writing a novel into a reality! Fred, THE publicist extraordinaire, thank you for the fifteen plus years of laughs, mentorship and support. You have been an amazing boss to me, but an even better friend.

Chrissy, my first reader, I am beyond grateful for the time and effort you spent reading my manuscript and taking notes. Your support of me during this process will never be forgotten. Vanessa, my Day 1. Many people do not have the luxury of having the same best friend for a quarter of a century, but I guess you and I are just lucky.

Thank you a million times to my family for putting up with me! Dad, I am beyond fortunate for all that you do for me and the boys, and we would be lost without you! Mom, I will always look up to you as the strongest woman I know. William, my twin and my actual heart, and Grayson, my little artist and cuddle bug—Mommy loves you both. Thank you to my husband, Victor, for affording me the ability to stay home with our boys, and read and write every day until my heart is content. I love you, like, a lot.

Lastly, an adoring thanks to Charlotte Brontë for penning *Jane Eyre* all those years ago and fostering my love of literature.

about the author

Jillian Ibelli is a public relations specialist and a business owner. When she is not reading, she enjoys cooking for her family, *Lifetime* movie marathons and staring at the ocean. She resides in Westchester County, New York with her husband, two sons and their maltipoo, Beauregard. The Voice We Squelch is her debut novel. You can connect with her on Instagram @jillian.ibelli.

   (Photographer, Enid Alvarez)

www.ingramcontent.com/pod-product-compliance
Lightning Source LLC
Chambersburg PA
CBHW050136120726
47903CB00002B/384